# Open Sesame...

After graduating from college, Kateri Kovach thought her biggest worries were finding a job in a bad economy and figuring out how to break up with her college boyfriend, swordfighting gamer Alex O'Donnell.

But when she travels to Virginia to meet the O'Donnell family, she discovers that's just the start of her problems when a mysterious website discovered by Alex's dad leads to unexpected wealth, and then murder.

Kateri realizes that in dating Alex O'Donnell, she got way more than she bargained for ... and maybe that's not such a bad thing.

# Alex O'Donnell and the 40 CyberThieves

## by Regina Doman

Other Books by Regina Doman

*The Fairy Tale Novels*

The Shadow of the Bear: A Fairy Tale Retold
Black as Night: A Fairy Tale Retold
Waking Rose: A Fairy Tale Retold
The Midnight Dancers: A Fairy Tale Retold
Alex O'Donnell and the 40 CyberThieves

*For children:*

Angel in the Waters

Edited by Regina Doman for Sophia Institute Press:

*For teens:*

Catholic, Reluctantly: John Paul 2 High Book One
Trespasses Against us: John Paul 2 High Book Two
both by Christian M. Frank
Awakening: A Crossroads in Time Book by Claudia
Cangilla McAdams

*For adults:*
Bleeder: a Mystery by John Desjarlais
Rachel's Contrition by Michelle Buckman

… and more to come!

# Alex O'Donnell and the 40 CyberThieves

a fairy tale
retold

by regina doman

CHESTERTON PRESS
FRONT ROYAL, VIRGINIA

2010 cover design and interior by Regina Doman
Photographs by Craig Spiering

Chesterton Press
P.O. Box 949
Front Royal, Virginia
www.fairytalenovels.com
www.reginadoman.com

Summary: When his computer hacker dad discovers a secret website, Alex O'Donnell and his girlfriend Kateri become embroiled in a mystery that leads to sudden wealth and murder. A modern retelling of the classic Arabian Nights tale "Ali Baba and the Forty Thieves."

ISBN: 978-0-9827677-0-2

Printed in the United States of America

To my parents, who taught me
by their example,
what it takes to make a marriage work.
And with grateful appreciation to
## G.K. Chesterton.

# Once upon a time...

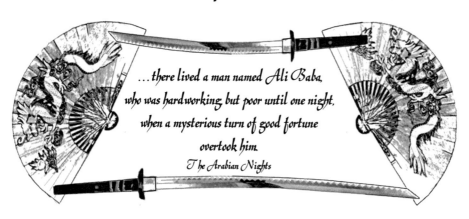

...there lived a man named Ali Baba,
who was hardworking but poor until one night,
when a mysterious turn of good fortune
overtook him.
*The Arabian Nights*

Nighttime.

The crickets were louder than the sound of the neighbor's air conditioner, the television across the street, or the incessant shushing flow of traffic. But the man ignored them as he sat down at his desk by the window, opened his laptop and eagerly touched the ON button.

As the cheery tinny jingle of startup music began, he reached into a desk drawer and pulled out the USB drive: the battered one with a cat-face sticker grinning up at him and plugged it easily into the laptop port. He couldn't wait to take the MouseCatcher for a ride.

Sure enough, the walking cat icon began pacing back and forth at the bottom of the screen, wavering slightly as the program booted up. The man grinned at the cat as he drummed his fingers on the keyboard bank, and thought to himself that he should add some music to this long opening sequence. Maybe the Looney Tunes theme song. *Next upgrade.*

At last the computer cat arched its back and stretched its claws, and the program began. The man opened a computer browser window. *Okay, MouseCatcher: where do we go tonight?*

It was a complicated computer interface that had started as an implant on browser code but now allowed a multi-faceted access to the main hub of the internet. The servers read the MouseCatcher as a view-only admin which was fine with him. He didn't want to affect data changes or capture viewer input. He only wanted to watch.

"Thirty-three percent software engineer, thirty three percent computer hacker, and thirty three percent damned curious guy," he murmured his mantra to himself as he fiddled with the browser window. He had gone to Amazon.com, and his eyes fixed on his own little white cursor on the screen, as he changed the preferences on MouseCatcher. *Show one user.* Select *Show ten users.* Select *Show one hundred users.* Select *Show All Users.* He hit the enter button.

Instantly his screen was crowded with thousands of white arrow cursors flicking in and out of the screen like so many electronic flies. Maybe millions of them. People all over the world going in and out of the website, and he could see them.

But more importantly, he could follow them wherever they went.

His own cursor had changed into the shape of a cat, and he moved around the mass of darting arrows, musing. So many, so many: which one would he choose?

A random capture was always the most fun. He snagged one, and the cat emitted a red superhero cape. He removed his hands from the keyboard and sat back to watch. The ride was beginning.

The pages began to change as the user being followed clicked on icons, leapt from page to page to page. First he clicked on the bestseller of the week icon, where he lingered, either reading or comparing prices. New browser window, but the MouseCatcher nimbly leapt along with him. Search engine: maybe a title + cheapest price input? Yes, because the search results included lots of deep discount prices. *Wonder who I'm following tonight?* The man right-clicked to see if he could get any information: the cookie indicated a Kansas user with the IM name of jerry2002dknight.

Bargainbasementcloseoutbooks.com—at last the user selected one, went to the bestselling titles page, then the shopping cart—there the mouse lingered. Suddenly it flicked back and forth, as though sensing the Cat whose claws were tracking its movement.

*Relax, Jerry. I don't want your credit card number; I just want to watch what you do.* But he scribbled some notes on the paper, wondering if the MouseCatcher was producing a slow response time on the other user's end. *Not good.*

At last jerry2002dknight's cursor shifted through the payment screens and the "Thank You for Your Purchase" screen blinked on. The user's mouse hovered, dragged, suddenly highlighted the link at the bottom that led to a .sex site and clicked.

Abruptly the man darted to the keyboard and disengaged MouseCatcher and the flying cat became a sitting one. Curious or not, he wasn't following anyone into a porn site. *Hope you're not married, Jerry.*

Now he fiddled with the cat cursor, which strolled around the screen. Finally he retreated a step back to the homepage at the discount book site and selected *Show All Users.* As he guessed, there weren't too many cursors flitting around this site. He wondered what this site actually was. *Probably some fly-by-night site operating out of someone's basement. A slick graphic interface with inventory access to a competitor's database and a subtle redirect. A scam operation.*

He considered the thirty-some cursors flitting around the screen, some sluggish, some purposeful, and selected an odd one. *MouseCatcher, spring!* The cat leaped and its red cape flew out behind it as it cruised after the user, who halted and remained on the page an absurdly long time. Perhaps the user had gone to get a cup of coffee? The man's own stomach grumbled, but he sat, waiting, stroking his graying beard. This was part of the game.

While waiting, he right-clicked on the user, to find out who he was following. Nothing. No name, no info. With a few clicks, he tried to override the anonymous browser. Nope. The user's personal identity remained encrypted.

At long last, the cursor moved slowly up to the bar on the browser and began to add some letters to the address in the browser.

```
/admin
```

The browser clicked a login page. "Welcome to Bargain Basement Closeout Books' Employee Area." The man whistled. *How random is that? I'm following a site employee.*

The MouseCatcher had no problem reading non-encrypted passwords, so he followed the user into the administrative area of the site. He watched while the user scrolled down through lists of menus and clicked a tab that said, "SSH." A new tab opened with a black screen and white font face, a blinking green box indicating the cursor.

*Ah. Wonder if he's doing a backup or something?*

But instead, the user began to type something unusual:

```
>open hitechhelpdesk.com
>Trying 127.63.228.10...
>Connected to hitechhelpdesk.com.
```

The man tensed, recognizing the process. *No, wait. This isn't a site employee. This is a hacker. He's using this server to hack into someone else's website.*

He switched the MouseCatcher into keylogger mode so that the Cat would keep a record of everything the user did, and watched intently. *If I don't capture his passwords, I won't be able to follow him,* he justified his actions to himself. *Plus, I don't mind sneaking after someone who's already doing something illegal...*

The user had arrived at the server of the next site: a tech site with the label www.hitechhelpdesk.com. Quickly the user went to a directory and typed a command to "show hidden files." A new file suddenly appeared:

```
underground_access
```

*Ah. That's why he came here. He's been hiding an invisible folder on someone else's site for safekeeping. Wonder what it is?*

A command appeared on the black screen.

```
Underground_access>find file:sesame
Underground_access>open sesame
```

Data flickered rapidly across the screen. Suddenly, the MouseCatcher flickered and lost his cape. The digital cat paced mournfully around the screen, and the man realized what had happened.

The user had vanished.

Bewildered, the man stared at the screen. *Where did he go? Did he log off the Internet? Or has he gone someplace where the MouseCatcher can't follow?*

Puzzled, the man checked the keylogger data the MouseCatcher had collected and scrolled through it. It took him a few minutes to understand it. The final lines read:

```
Determining remote address...
Checking http://microblogger-cool.com/ssessamme
Found current post: MTI3LAuMC4Mjc
ADDRESS: http://127.0.0.1/combination_unique
```

*The Sesame program jumped to a website, grabbed data, decrypted it, and...generated a link to a web address.*

*That's where the user went.*

The man's fingers hovered over the keys.

*...What's to stop me from going to that website too?*

It was too tantalizing. Before he could help himself, he gave the command and hit the enter key.

```
>open sesame
```

*Where am I?*

A page had loaded swiftly: deep, utter blackness.

Purple letters began to appear on the page.

## Who are you?

A security question. The man floundered, but then suddenly, the MouseCatcher, which had been sitting sedately at the bottom of his screen, began to flash, and its cape fluttered.

*So the guy I was following is still here,* the man realized. *And the MouseCatcher's hooked right onto him again. Good cat!*

An answer appeared below the question.

*Hasherking, master of trees.*

An image of a blowfish appeared. And the words hovered before him in long script.

*What is this?*

And the user the man was following typed his answer.

*We are Samurai. The Keyboard Cowboys.*

The black page faded into gray that became white, gleaming white. Then something came into focus. A cave with gleaming walls, in high definition sharpness.

The man whistled at the graphic interface. You couldn't see a pixel anywhere. *Nice! Must be one of these new gaming sites. This is what that guy was trying to get into.*

Suddenly a ninja in black stepped onto the screen. The ninja's movements were a bit more nuanced than those of the typical online avatar, and the man marveled at the computer engineering that had created it.

*So this is what the user looks like in this environment. Wow. I can see why he wanted to get in here!*

The ninja turned so that his back was to the man, and began to stride purposefully down the cave tunnel. He didn't seem to notice that the MouseCatcher, now looking pathetically pixilated in this hi-res environment, was following him.

The shining bronze walls of the cave moved around him, the scene changing like a camera following over the assassin's shoulder.

The man watched, fascinated. *Okay, a gaming site sure isn't what I expected to find. Well, I'm hooked onto this guy, going where he goes...*

They began to pass niches in the walls of the cave that looked like passages. One passage had gold coins in bags lying spilled on the floor. Another passageway had ropes of pearls and gleaming jewels cascading out of chests. A third niche was scattered with what looked like credit cards in bright colors. Another gave a glimpse into what looked like an art gallery of paintings. The ninja ignored all of these, passing them more quickly than the man trailing him would have liked.

*Oh well. But I'm just here to watch.*

The ninja abruptly turned left and entered a room full of windows: each one looking out onto a different scene. One was the skyline of Chicago: another looked out on a Caribbean island: another on the ski slopes of Switzerland. The ninja paused before a window that showed the rooftops of Vienna, Austria. And nothing happened: the scene froze.

The man waited. The ninja continued to stand still. Nothing on the screen was moving. The man watched and waited, but nothing seemed to be happening. Tentatively he clicked, but there was no response to his cursor.

*I bet there's a floating menu I can't see,* the man guessed. *He must be giving some sort of input.*

He seemed to have guessed correctly because the ninja abruptly turned and strode out of the room. He was back in the passageway again before the man realized what had happened.

*This game is pretty fascinating. Wish I knew what was going on. Wonder how you join?*

The ninja looked at his feet and the room tilted downwards as he did. With one finger, he touched a puddle on the ground and backed up.

Out of the water, a large column of brick came with a sloping board on it, with faint surface variations that resembled a text box.

*Maybe I'll get to see what happens here.*

All of a sudden, grooves appeared on the rock, forming into random shapes. A string of numbers appeared, grew sharper for a moment, and then slowly sank back into the surface.

*Cool,* the man thought.

Then more numbers, then letters appeared, in random patterns, which sharpened and then sank down before the man could read them. He glanced at the keylogger. It hadn't captured any input this time.

Having subsumed the input, grooves appeared in the stone again which shifted and formed into a message:

## ALL INPUT HAS BEEN PROCESSED AND ERASED

It sank into the blank square of the rock.

The man was watching the numbers flicker away when the ninja abruptly touched a round black stone embedded in the cave wall. And vanished.

The MouseCatcher flickered, wilted, and lost his cape again.

*The guy must have logged out, and in the process, detached the MouseCatcher. That's the second time that happened. Weird.*

*Um—now how do I leave?*

The man was tempted to just close his browser, but he strongly suspected that he'd better log out properly if he wanted to cover his tracks. Tentatively he clicked on the black rock, but in response, the square blank block in front of him glowed. The man hit an arrow key to turn around, but each time he did something, the stone merely flashed a white glow.

*Ah. It's a menu, but I can't see all of it. Still, I need to close it, or give it input before I can do anything else. What does it want me to do?*

He typed an "A" but the stone surface hiccupped and the A vanished.

*No letters then. Number input?*

Pausing for a moment, he quickly typed

## 123456789

The stone seemed to approve. The numbers grew sharper, then slowly sank into nothingness.

But then the stone smoothed itself out again, wanting more from him.

Trying to remember what he had just seen the ninja do, it suddenly dawned on the man what the string of numbers and letters had been.

*It wants a street address.*

Now the man was a bit nervous. He'd never given any personal input when he'd used the MouseCatcher before. *I'd better just shut down and go,* he told himself. But the black rock remained un-pressable. And the square rock screen glowed insistently.

*Wait: it said that all data would be processed and erased. Maybe that means, if I give an address, it'll erase it.*

*Maybe it'll just mail more clues to the game to that address. I could find out what this place is I've stumbled onto.*

It was a tempting possibility.

Almost before he realized what he was doing, the man entered the number of a post office box in his town.

The address sharpened for a brief moment, then sank down before the man could change his mind.

But the same comforting message appeared:

## ALL INPUT HAS BEEN PROCESSED AND ERASED

Feeling a bit reckless, the man hit "enter" and now the large stone sank back into the pool of water and vanished. And conveniently, the round black rock on the wall flickered, as though to indicate that it could now be pushed.

Gratefully, the man pushed it.

The cave rushed by him, faded to black, then all that was left was the plain black screen with white font, with the last string of letters.

```
>open sesame
```

The man realized what he needed to do next. He typed

```
>close sesame
```

The screen responded:

```
>cleanly logging out
>you're safe - bye.
```

The black box closed, and the session ended.

He had left the cave.

*If that was a game, it was the oddest one I've ever seen.*

*If it was a game.*

Feeling a sense of worry, he re-saved his session log so he would have a record of everything he had just done, and then closed the MouseCatcher down. Then he pulled up some menus, enhanced his security, erased his browser history, made sure his firewall was in place. He closed down the browser, background programs, and the laptop. As an extra precaution, he even unplugged it from the wall.

Back in the real world, he checked the locks on the house door and closed the deadbolt before he turned into bed beside his sleeping wife.

Outside, the crickets continued cheeping, as though none of this had happened.

# Chapter One

*He had chosen to marry a poor but good
woman, and lived with her and their three sons
in a small village outside the mountains.*
The Arabian Nights

usic blared from the speakers of the beat-up red Toyota as it flew down the highway, windows open, speakers cranked up. The air conditioning was broken, but at least the stereo system worked.

The young driver, steering easily with one hand, was on the shorter side, stocky, long-haired, tattooed, one ear pierced, wearing black sunglasses. He was driving just over the speed limit, fast enough to pass other vehicles, slow enough not to catch the attention of any policemen. Behind and around him, the car was crammed with stuff: books, clothes, duffle bags, a large picture of the Sacred Heart, and an odd array of boxes and cabinets and cases. One item hadn't fit into any of the cases, and lay on the seat beside him—a long Japanese sword, gleaming silver.

Alex O'Donnell was on his way home from college.

He whistled along with the music as he sped down the miles of cracked asphalt on the Pennsylvania turnpike, dexterously avoiding the potholes. He breathed in relief when he hit the turnoff for 80 East. A few more hours or so and he'd be back in Virginia, Fairfax County, the suburb of DC where he lived.

It had been a good year at Mercy College. It should have been his graduation year, but he had a few more courses to take, due to some costly prevarication his freshman year, where he'd changed majors three times before settling on his final choice, political science. He had a couple more credits to earn: no biggie. One last semester, and he'd be free. Most of his friends had already graduated, and he figured that was just as well: he'd have more time to study and less time for the goofy adventures they'd always seemed to get sidetracked by.

He shook his head, thinking of some of those adventures, which had involved near escapes, brushes with the law, even danger of death. Yes, it had been interesting, but he couldn't expect the rest of his life to be quite as adventurous. At some point, he was going to have to settle down, get serious about life, maybe even cut his hair.

Naaah.

He checked his cell phone, wondering if Kateri was nearly home by now. (She refused to talk on a cell phone while driving, even if it was legal in New Jersey, so he knew better than to try and call now.) They'd said goodbye only an hour ago, at dawn at a rest stop where the highway forked into north and east branches just outside of Harrisburg. She was headed north: he was going east and south: their paths had split. He missed her already.

He had promised to be a good boyfriend, send her presents, call a lot. She thanked him and wondered aloud if that meant she'd have to be a good girlfriend, and what did that mean?

"It means you love me, no matter what," he had said, grinning.

She had only rolled her eyes and kissed him.

Then she had gotten into her own beat-up car, an old farm truck, gathered her long, wild black hair into a ponytail, waved a final goodbye, and driven off. As he had watched her go, he felt the same wistful longing that he always regarded her with, but it was magnified by the circumstances. Kateri was cool, almost too cool for him. She was a slight, sturdy girl with a blockbuster personality. She always wore ripped jeans and wrapped thin braids in her hair with colored thread like a Native American: lots of people thought she was Cherokee. But she was Asian—well, half Vietnamese.

And to Alex, she had about her the mystique of the Far East, even though her father was Polish-American. She had that aloofness, those dark, inscrutable eyes—and that hair! Long, black, wavy, tumbling down her back like a waterfall. And she was—well, *put together* nicely. Since Alex himself was on the shorter side, he liked that she was so petite. For a long time he hadn't been able to figure out if he just had a massive crush on her, or if this was true love, but now he decided he was willing to gamble that it was the real thing.

Back a few years ago when they had met at Mercy College, it had been a moment of no significance for either of them. Neither of them had cared much for the other. They ran in different circles, had different interests. Ironically, they only met when Alex had developed a slight crush on Kateri's roommate. Even after being formally introduced, they had spent most of their time arguing with each other. But in the course of several very colorful and fairly epic adventures, somehow he had swept Kateri off her feet—literally at one point—and, he admitted, she had knocked him off his high horse as well.

So for the past year or so, they hadn't been able to get enough of one another, and now, driving home, he was starting to wonder if that had ramifications for both of their futures.

For a person as organized and goal-oriented as she was, Kateri was fairly cagey on that point. He strongly suspected that her future plans had never included taking up with a sword-wielding martial artist from the suburbs like himself. She had just graduated—the Kovach family wasn't rich, and she'd gotten her mental health degree as quickly and cheaply as possible. Last summer she and Alex had gone to the missions in South America together, which had been another set of adventures, but this summer she had indicated the time had come for serious plans.

Alex agreed, but he wasn't entirely sure she was ready for the serious plans he was starting to think about now.

The problem was, he didn't want to be in the position of proposing marriage to a girl who was going to say no. And Kateri just might say no to him, whether she liked him or not.

He sighed as the song shuffle came to an end, and briefly clicked his mp3 player to shift to a mix of adventure movie themes. He was coming into the suburbs of DC: home. A whole different adventure. His mom's health was better these days—she had muscular sclerosis, but was surviving. Even though she could no longer walk, she had managed to keep going strong, even on crutches. His kid brothers were always in trouble, between sports, karate, and computer club. And he wondered what his dad had been up to. Most likely, Dad had figured out a new way to hack into the government computer database and reprogram their coffee makers. Or create software that would change every traffic light from yellow to purple, or something. Alex had better get home and find out.

In another hour, Alex turned off the highway and into one of the hundreds of neighborhoods that sprawled out from the DC beltway. He drove past green spaces and gated communities and gateless communities, condos and apartment buildings, tiny rows of little shops, boutique strip malls, and gargantuan big box stores separated by landscaped slabs of banked earth and color-coordinated flower beds.

He turned right, and took a highway that shunted him through several miles of woods and towering concrete sound barriers and slid off an exit into another older town of assorted stores that stood like islands on half-acres of concrete, past trees huddled like lost tourists in groups around drainage ditches, past overgrown woodland developments, and developments built hurriedly on old farmland, vinyl split-levels and ranches with strings of spindly bushes and privacy fences dividing the lots. He pulled over to check out a neighborhood yard sale.

Then he took a bypass to avoid the shattered remnant of an old main street with one or two blocks of old-time buildings, which had survived just to sell postcards and antiques to Civil War pilgrims. He turned right into an even older development of small brick Cape Cods separated by lines of chain-link fences that were mostly hidden beneath piles of vines and embedded in hedges. This development had trees stuck at random in yards and sidewalks, some trees so old that their roots buckled the cement sidewalks and their branches spitefully dropped limbs during every storm.

Last year's hurricane season had seen the demise of the two octogenarians who hemmed in Alex's parents' house. During the tornado in the wake of Hurricane Zeno, the two trees had fallen upon each other viciously, as though motivated by a long-held grudge, and toppled into the yard, narrowly missing the roof but destroying the front porch and the chain-linked fence. Insurance and the town had paid for a new fence (green chain link) and sidewalk, and Alex's mom said she had never liked the front porch anyway, which was too small to even put a lawn chair on. The facade of the house now had slightly pinker lines of bricks flanking the front door where the posts for the porch had been, and the ragged yard had a growing fishnet of crabgrass spreading over the eight-foot circles of clay that marked the trees' graves.

Alex parked his car, levering himself into the five-foot curb space between a minivan and a compact with one practiced maneuver, and got out, grabbing several bags and his sword. With a karate yell, he leapt over the fence into the yard, instigating cries of "Alex is back!" Seconds later, the front screen door banged open to let loose two sandy-haired boys who immediately threw themselves upon Alex with yells of their own. Alex thrust the sword into the turf, dropped his bags, and tackled his first assailant, dropping him to the ground. He flipped the ten-year-old over his back, and roared in dismay, "You guys haven't been practicing!"

His brothers ignored him and went for his luggage instead. "Hey, did you get Drive Maniac III?" David said by way of greeting.

"No, I did not!" Alex swiped his backpack back from David. "Hey, leave that alone!" he said to Sam, who was swinging the sword around, decapitating tiger lilies. He yanked the weapon away and turning, grabbed a metal throwing star from David's hand. "Barbarians!"

"Did you bring me a present? Are you home now for good? What did you bring home?"

"No, yes, wait and see." Alex said, stepping inside and sliding the sword easily into the hooks by the door that marked its place. The staircase wall was filled with weapons both Eastern and Western, and Alex's sword was positioned just between his dad's Spanish rapier and David's gladiator dagger. The messy room was decorated with bamboo scrolls and glass Japanese fishing weights that dangled in nets from the ceiling, souvenirs of his dad's army years overseas. With careful aim, Alex tossed the throwing star, and it made a new jag in the trim over the mantelpiece, which had been its home ever since it had accidentally landed there many years before, making a gash which grew bigger by the years, and to which his mother had resigned herself.

He strode through the tiny living room past the blaring video game console with the cracked screen to the bedroom next to the kitchen, meeting his mom who had struggled to her crutches to greet him. Her blond hair was cut short, and she was wearing an oversized shirt in a cheerful pink print and jeans.

He kissed her. "Hi Mom! I'm back!"

Mom accepted his hug affectionately. "Did you have a good trip home?"

"Oh, yeah. I would have made it in three hours if I hadn't stopped. Hey dad!"

Dad was home from work—that was unusual. Maybe Mom had had a bad day? He was also intent on the bedroom computer—not unusual at all. Finishing a keystroke sequence, his dad tore his eyes from the screen and set them on his oldest son. "Alex! Glad to have you home!" His dad's black beard and sideburns had a bit more gray in them, but the eyes behind his glasses twinkled and the laugh-lines were firmly fixed in place. Mom must not be doing too bad.

As if answering his thought, Mom said, "I had a doctor's appointment today, so Alan stayed home to take me."

"Everything okay?"

"All clear."

Alex kissed his mom and dad. "Good! Hey, I'm going to run to the post office. Anyone need anything while I'm out?"

"Diet Coke," his mom said. "And green tea for your dad. Can you go by the grocery and see what's on sale in the meat section? I haven't planned dinner for tonight yet."

"How about I pick up Chinese? My treat."

Mom grinned. She always looked cute when she smiled. "Sure! I'll take you up on that."

His dad had swiveled his chair inexorably back towards the computer, but dug into his pocket. "You said you were going to the post office? Here. Check the P.O. boxes for me." He flipped the keys over his shoulder and started on the keyboard again.

Alex caught them with one hand. "No prob, Dad."

Whistling, he went out to his car. His brothers were bringing in his luggage and belongings from the car and piling them on the front room carpet. "Hey, bring that stuff upstairs!" He snatched up something wrapped in a brown paper bag, grabbed the Sacred Heart picture and propped it on top of an overstocked bookshelf near the rosary prayer table.

"Are you going out? Can we go with you?"

"Only if you behave!"

Without answering, the younger boys jumped into the car with him and settled themselves comfortably in the back and front seats. David grabbed the mp3 player and cranked up the loudest song.

"Turn that thing down," Alex said, checking his mirrors while he reversed out of his parking spot. "So what's been going on?"

"David's grounded *again* from computer games but he's still watching me."

"Shut up!" David said. "Dad's working on new tracking software."

"How's the MouseCatcher coming?"

"Dunno. He used to talk about it all the time, but he's been quiet lately. Bet he's working on something. So how's the hot babe?"

Alex groaned. "David, let's get this straight. Women and girls are *ladies*. Not chicks, not babes, not anything else. Okay? Show some respect, or Kateri's going to slam you upside a wall when you're least expecting it."

"Is she coming down? Do we get to meet her?" Sam, the ten-year-old, cut in.

"I don't know. All depends on whether she can afford it. Life's hard when you're a poor college graduate. I might go up and see her sometime."

"Can you take us?"

"Yes. I'll enslave you to Kateri's younger siblings and you can work on the farm and learn some manners."

"Pig manners." That was David.

"You start acting like a pig, I'll let them send you to the slaughterhouse. Okay, stay here!" They had reached the Post Office. Alex grabbed the brown paper parcel and got out.

"What's that?"

"Present for Kateri. Got to mail it."

"What is it?"

"Something I found at a yard sale. Stay in the car, don't fight. At least not to the death." He strode through the glass doors to the lobby and joined the line. While he was waiting, he picked out a box and two rolls of colored bubble wrap, and packaged the present. It was going to be expensive to send, but he couldn't resist. He mailed the package, and recollecting himself, stopped by the line of boxes to check the mail for his dad.

His dad had a string of post office boxes, the result of several failed online business ventures, maintained now primarily for collecting junk mail and catalogs. After the hunt and peck of locating and emptying the boxes, Alex had an armful of junk mail. He figured he had better sort through it. No use bringing even more stuff into their crowded home.

Catalog, catalog, catalog. He kept one of each and threw out the duplicates. Mom loved catalogs, and who knows what she was into these days? Restaurant supplies, gardening, skiing? Maybe the last catalog was David's. Next he sifted out the credit card offers and tossed them. The fundraising solicitations were a bit harder to detect, but he trashed all the ones he could find. Now he had about fifteen envelopes left. Slipping into his typical role as Dad's unofficial secretary, he started opening letters and checking them out.

Ah. Several of the "serious" letters were actually money-begging letters from political PACs. He tossed those and opened the remaining handful. That's how he found the check.

It was printed, like a payroll check, from the Sundance Fun Foundation, but the memo said "Winnings." Paid to "Cash" in the amount of $1,234,567.89.

"This isn't real," Alex said. He flipped to the back of the check, expecting to see "This is a sample" inscribed in red on the back. Nothing. "This isn't real," he said, looking for background printing, any sign that this was just a scam. "Nah. This isn't real."

But the typed amount said *one million, two hundred and thirty four thousand, five hundred and sixty seven dollars and 89/100.*

Finally, not knowing what else to do, he folded the check, stuck it in his pocket, grabbed the rest of the remaining mail, and went to the car.

As he could have predicted, his brothers were fighting, but fortunately blood had not yet been shed.

"Where are we going now?" Sam demanded between yells and accusations of David.

"Bank."

"What for?"

"Just going to try something. I'm curious."

"CKTC!" David shouted.

"Hm?" Alex was turning on the motor.

"'Curiosity killed the cat.' Mom's taken to using the acronym with Dad. That's how often she says it these days."

"Interesting," Alex murmured.

In the lobby of their family bank, Alex handed over the check to the teller, folded his arms, and leaned forward on the ledge. "Can you tell me if this is a real check?"

The teller did the same thing he had done: looked it over, flipped it to the back, scanned it again. "Looks okay to me. Why?"

"I got it in one of those junk mail letters."

She nodded with a knowing smile. "Want me to try to deposit it?"

"Sure, might as well."

"With that kind of amount, they'll probably put a hold on it. Maybe two to eleven business days."

"That's fine. No rush."

It couldn't hurt to try.

# Chapter Two

*And though he often wished he could make his fortune, yet not for all the gold in the moneyhouse would he have changed his wife and fine sons.*

*The Arabian Nights*

The girl sloshed through the muddy field in her barn boots and paused, looking out over the rooting animals to the hilly landscape and the silver clouds beyond. Part of her hoped that she didn't get any response from the stack of resumes she had just sent out. Working in an office just wasn't going to compare with farm work. Even farm work with smelly pigs.

Absently she poked a stick at two of the younger hogs, who were squabbling over the same banana peel. "C'mon, settle down," she said equitably.

Her attention was caught by the roar of a truck, and she looked over at the rundown little farmhouse where the remainder of her ten brothers and sisters lived with her parents. A white mail truck was cautiously backing up their winding gravel driveway.

Curious, she dumped the rest of the compost onto the grunting pigs, grabbed the bucket and the hose, and walked back towards the house, coiling up the hose as she went. Between the wet and the mud, the hose was dirty, which meant that by the time she reached the house, her hands and overalls were muddy as well. She deposited the coil of hose in its place by the cellar steps, stacked the compost bucket with the other empty plastic ones by the porch door, and walked to the truck, fully aware that she was a mess.

Wiping her hands on the wet grass helped a little. "Sorry," she said to the driver as she took the stack of mail and bulky package. Walking back to the house, she glanced at the address on the box. It was from Alex. Kateri rolled her eyes and went inside to wash up.

Inside, the farmhouse was the usual jumble of large-family detritus and farming implements. The fragrant smell of stir-fried pork with fish sauce came from the stove, where her mother, a short Vietnamese woman in a long blue apron, was cooking dinner. Kateri set the package on the kitchen table, and began to open it. *What had Alex sent now?*

She groaned as she pulled off the last round of bubble wrap from the bulky object inside. It was an Oriental statue, super-gilded and beflowered with purple magnolias—the Chinese good-luck cat with raised paw.

"Pretty," her mom said. "Chinese."

Kateri sighed. "Oriental." Alex was like most Westerners, lobbing together Chinese, Japanese, Korean, Filipino, and Vietnamese culture into one thing: Oriental culture. She'd tried to explain to him that Vietnamese culture was very different from Japanese and Chinese culture but he couldn't seem to grasp the distinction. Nor did he get that she preferred plain American to Chinese kitsch.

She read the card he had scribbled. *Miss you. Hope you can come and visit soon.* She didn't know how to answer that. If she found a job, she couldn't visit. But until she found a job, spending money on pleasure trips didn't seem wise.

"What does the card say?"

"He wants me to come and visit him."

"You should." Mom tested the pork.

"But I'm still job hunting."

"If you find a job, you won't be able to go. So go now."

"Mom!" Kateri exclaimed. "You're so—impractical sometimes. Like Alex."

Her mom chuckled. "Aren't you and Alex still dating?"

"Yes. Sort of," Kateri set the cat on the table and raised an eyebrow at it. *What exactly am I supposed to do with this thing?*

"You keep saying that," her mom wagged a bamboo spoon at her. "'Sort of' dating never got anyone anywhere. Either choose or not choose. Court, or don't court."

Kateri laughed. "You sound like Yoda."

The problem was, she liked Alex. A lot. And that was illogical. He was a suburban guy. White collar. Wouldn't—couldn't farm, didn't have a job, couldn't do anything practical, an expert in nothing except video games, martial arts and swordfighting.

Well, she admitted, *sometimes* those last two items were practical. Those skills had already come in handy a few times in their friendship.

She had to confess it was fun to be with Alex. They connected on a very basic level. But was that really enough?

*I'm like that peasant girl in the Hiroshi Inagaki film and he's like the samurai. Except they were Japanese. But it didn't work out between them either.*

"What is wrong?" her mother prodded.

Kateri exhaled. "When it comes to Alex, I just have too many questions about whether or not he's right for me."

"That is fine!" her mother said with a shrug. "Courtship is the time for asking questions! Too many people only start to ask questions after the wedding is over!"

Kateri pushed back her hair. "So what do you do if you still have questions after the wedding is over?"

"Ignore them," her mother said tranquilly. "After you have leapt off the cliff, it is too late to wonder how high the mountain was."

She handed her daughter a small bowl of *pho* soup, and Kateri drank it and pondered, giving occasional glances at the smiling ceramic cat. Her mother went outside to yell at Kateri's brothers, who were supposed to be weeding the strawberry crop.

What she had to do, Kateri resolved, one of these days, was sit down with Alex and have a serious talk about their relationship. What were they going to do now, practically speaking? *I'm graduated, I'm going to get a job, and you're going to do what? Play at college for another year, and then do what? While I wait for you?* It might be better for them both just to work, study, and go on with life. Neither of their families were wealthy: it would be more practical to focus on making a living. And if after two years, he was ready to get married and she wasn't dating anyone else—then maybe…

The problem was, she really did like Alex.

Emitting a cry of frustration, she finished the soup, snatched up the cat, and stalked to her room.

She had shared the large bedroom with four sisters, but now they had all moved out. Only Faustina was still single, and she was living in New York and working as a secretary: Teresa and Marietta and Philomena were married. But the remnants of their tastes and souvenirs of their pasts were still scattered about on the walls: posters, photos, scrapbooks, stuffed animals. Polish flags and Vietnamese art. A large poster of an unborn baby in the womb, pro-life bumper stickers, collages from protests and slogan signs. Though the variations on themes were unique, the décor was the typical mishmash of teenage life. Kateri didn't have the heart to take everything down and start over, even though no one else slept in the double bed with her any longer, and the daybed really was just a couch these days.

*Maybe I'll be leaving this room soon too.*

The thought depressed her, even though her job search was not going well. It seemed the market was flooded with mental health majors: what had seemed like a shoe-in was proving to be scarce. No one was even offering internships. With years of pro-life experience and sidewalk counseling under her belt, she had counted on one of the crisis pregnancy centers she'd worked with being able to hire her, but it seemed like everyone was under a budget squeeze. She'd have to move to New York, most likely, to find any kind of entry-level job. And she hated the city.

Given that her life was in such flux, her instinct was to take a step back from her relationship until she figured out where she could find a job, and what God wanted her to do with her life. It might be easier on Alex too: she knew he still didn't have a job. But how could she tell this to Alex?

Out of habit, she started cleaning the room, the best way to improve her mood. After straightening up her dresser and folding her clothes, she cast about for a space to stash the oversized cat statue. After a few minutes searching, she moved a stack of hats—random straw farm hats and soft felt hats—off the green dresser and slid the cat on its surface. Now the hats didn't fit. She was about to toss them on the floor to deal with later, when something made her put the stack on the cat's head. They fitted perfectly: the cat's head was just the size of the bottom hat. And her baseball cap could dangle from the cat's upraised paw. It looked almost as though she and some decorating maven had gone out to purchase a unique hat stand and come back with the cat. A perfect fit.

Her cell phone rang with a familiar tune: the theme from *Karate Kid*. Alex was calling.

Was this the time for her to break it off with him?

She stared at the singing phone and glanced back half-heartedly at the smiling cat. Alex would ask her about her job search, she would confess her failure and inadequacy, and he would reassure her. He would brainstorm for new strategies, new ways to get a job. He was probably praying for her. No, she didn't have the heart to break up with a guy friend who was supporting her during this uncertain time. But would it be any kinder to do it later?

Growling again, she picked up the phone and answered. She'd thank him for the statue, maybe agree to come down and visit for a weekend. No time like the present. Pun resented.

So it was that one week later, Kateri was on the bus to DC. She was taking the bus because her brothers Mark and Tobias needed her old truck for their job, and the other spare car had a bad fuel pump and had stopped shifting. Alex had agreed to split the bus ticket with her, since it saved him the trouble of driving to pick her up. Even though she hated to leave the farm work and the job hunt, she probably did need a break: she fell asleep as soon as she got on the bus, and slept until they had nearly reached the beltway.

When she opened her eyes, she stared out the window at the passing scenery in some incredulity. Obviously this had all once been farmland. But now it had become a monotonous pattern of strip mall—housing block—strip mall—housing block. Sometimes the developers had left the trees in. Other times they seemed to have sheared them all down. Either way, a completely artificial carpet of civilization had been dropped over what was once arable land: she could even spot an occasional barn marooned between lots. She felt nauseous. Or maybe that was just the fumes from the hundred thousand shiny compact cars that darted everywhere like oversized bugs.

By the time they reached the bus stop in Northern Virginia, she had counted six Home Depots and ten Bed, Bath and Beyonds, and countless supermarkets and clothing stores. So this was where Alex lived. She was ready to leave.

But there in the massive bus station was Alex, waiting for her as she stumped off the bus with her luggage. As usual, he was dressed in black—black t-shirt and trench coat, jeans, and boots. Black sunglasses, too. He was smiling at her, and holding a huge bunch of long-stemmed red roses.

She sighed: even jobless and short of cash, Alex could be so generous. And so impulsive. Too impulsive. She kissed him, took the roses, and only then noticed that he was still grinning.

"What?" she said suspiciously.

He took her arms and pulled her close.

"We're rich."

"Yes, in God, family, and one another. But that doesn't—"

"No, my family. Is rich."

She stared at him.

"We've come into money. C'mon. I'll tell you how it happened."

Incredulously, she glanced down at the roses.

Alex said significantly, "They were *not* on sale."

Once she had gotten into the car, he told her about the money. How he had gotten the check. How he'd deposited it, on a lark. How it had actually cleared.

"So now?"

"We have over one million dollars in the bank. And we're still not sure how it happened."

Kateri frowned. "But if it's a check—you must know who sent it."

"The Sundance Fun Foundation. And here's something weird: it closed its doors two days after our transaction went through. It's listed as a place that holds contests, but none of us remember entering any sweepstakes. The only thing Mom can think of is that it might have been one of those things where you're automatically entered into a drawing when you sign up for a service."

Kateri was still trying to take this in, and a feeling was growing inside her. "I don't like this," she murmured. "You're right: it's weird. You should—"

Alex shot her a look. "I know what you're thinking, Kat. I'd like to do some research, find out more, but the odd thing is, Dad doesn't want me to. Plus he doesn't want us to tell anyone about the money until he can figure out where it came from. I had to promise him up and down that you were one of those inscrutable Asian types who would never breathe a word to anyone."

Asian types. Kateri sighed again. "And of course, your dad agreed."

"You know I've told you how much he loves anything from the Far East. I know he'll love you, too."

She shifted a bit nervously, having remembered again that she was meeting Alex's family for the first time. A significant relationship moment. A sign that things were 'serious.' Again, she felt she was in the wrong place at the wrong time. "I hope I'm going to be more than just your trophy Asian girlfriend."

"Oh, absolutely, you are." Alex said. "But I've always liked trophies. They tell me that I've won big." He pulled to a stop at a red light, leaned over, and kissed her.

Why did his corny romance always give her goose bumps? "Nowadays everyone gets trophies, even if they didn't do a thing."

"The analogy holds," he murmured. "I didn't do a thing to deserve you, did I?"

Groaning, she pulled away from him. "The light's green."

He obligingly turned his attention to driving but kept talking. "Obviously, Dad doesn't want us to spend the money. Unfortunately my brothers were with me when I went to deposit the check, and we've had to threaten them with Chinese water torture to keep them from talking. But that hasn't stopped them from begging us to upgrade our video game systems, get new computers, cool cars—"

"Probably good not to rush into anything."

"Exactly. Though I can't help looking at the new Nissan Civics." He heaved a sigh. "Mom's been trying to persuade him to use some of the money, but he doesn't want us to touch a cent."

"What is he waiting for?"

"Federal agents to show up on our doorstep? The IRS? Who knows? Anyhow," he glanced over at Kateri. "I'm so glad you're here. You couldn't have picked a better time to visit. It's very interesting at home just now."

"Kateri," Mrs. O'Donnell leaned forward on her crutches and took Kateri's hands. "I'm so glad to finally meet you face to face."

"Thanks. Same here, Mrs. O'Donnell," Kateri said, suddenly feeling a bit shy.

"Call me Kitty. That's what Alan calls me." Mrs. O'Donnell was in her fifties, Irish-faced and freckled cheeks. Kateri, who had already seen enough of coiffed and manicured Northern Virginians, liked that Alex's mom's short blond hair was streaked with gray. Although her legs were frail, Mrs. O'Donnell's shoulders and arms were tough, showing that even on crutches, she kept herself active. The wooden crutches were decorated with shiny painted flowers, with plaid fabric covering the tops.

"The wheelchair doesn't fit well in this small house," Kitty said. "So I use my wooden legs, as I call them. Couldn't get around without them. And they keep me upright and off my duff, which is a good thing. My two younger boys are helping out at our parish's summer festival, but they'll be back later." She glanced out the door. "And here's my husband Alan. He must have beaten the traffic today."

Mr. O'Donnell had just driven up in a battered car that resembled Alex's red one, except that it was green. Kateri watched as a heavyset bearded man got out of the car and came slowly up the walk. Even though he was smiling, she could sense that he was burdened by some secret.

*He knows*, she thought. *He knows where that money came from. Did he—steal it?* She knew from Alex that Mr. O'Donnell was a computer genius who could hack into almost any computer. But would he have stolen money?

This thought certainly cast an odd aura over the "meeting the parents" moment, as Kateri shook hands with him and exchanged pleasantries. He seemed pleased to meet her, but preoccupied. *Guilty?*

"So, Kateri," Mr. O'Donnell said heartily. "Does anyone ever call you Kat?"

"Sometimes," she said, shooting a glance at Alex, the usual culprit.

He put his head to one side. "I call my wife Kitty, so that's just too funny. Driving home, it occurred to me that while you're here, we'll have a Kitty and a Kat in the house."

The men hooted with laughter, but Mrs. O'Donnell only rolled her eyes in a gesture that Kateri found comfortingly familiar. "See what I have to put up with? How about I show you the house?"

It wasn't much of a house to show. Two bedrooms, a living room, a kitchen. But it was probably all that the O'Donnells could afford. Kateri guessed that this part of Virginia was as overpriced as New Jersey. And the house was cluttered with a jumble of necessities and knickknacks, both Western and Eastern, which made it seem more crowded. Mr. O'Donnell followed them around, pointing out curiosities in the rooms.

"We got those nunchucks on a trip to Korea," he said, indicating two black tubes dangling from a chain looped around a bedroom door. "They're pretty hard to use: unless you know what you're doing, you usually end up just hitting yourself in the face with them."

"And this is the bathroom," Mrs. O'Donnell pushed open a white door to reveal a narrow room in lavender tile hung with lots of mobiles and paintings. "Isn't the color hideous? It was like this when we got it. Alex says we should play along and paint the top of the wall yellow so that it looks like an Easter egg."

Mr. O'Donnell pointed to the hangings on the wall. "See those bamboo scrolls? Kitty and I got those from a tea shop on Okinawa in Japan. We hung out at the shop all the time when I was stationed overseas, and the owner presented them to us when he heard we were being transferred stateside. I don't suppose you can you read them?"

"No," said Kateri, repressing her sarcasm with difficulty. "I'm Vietnamese. They're, uh, very different languages."

"'Long life, prosperity, and luck,'" Mr. O'Donnell translated, undeterred. "Beautifully done, eh? I love the brushstrokes. I believe the owner did them himself. What a culture!"

"Alex was born in Japan—did he tell you?" Kitty maneuvered out of the bathroom on her crutches with surprising fluidity. "This is the kitchen. It's terribly small but that actually helps when I can't move around so easily."

"No, he didn't tell me he was born in Japan," Kateri said, following her. With Mrs. O'Donnell, Mr. O'Donnell, and herself standing in the cluttered kitchen, the room was unbearably crowded. Every surface was packed with dishes, cookbooks, utensils, canisters, and small appliances.

"I'm still a U.S. citizen: I was born on the Army base in Okinawa," Alex said, leaning on the doorpost. "Does it explain too much?"

Again, Kateri felt she should suppress her sarcasm. *Negative humor comes from hell: send it back*, her mom was always saying. "Somewhat," she managed to say.

"We usually eat on the screened porch," Mrs. O'Donnell said. The porch had storm windows enclosing it, and a brick floor half-covered with a floppy Asian carpet. There were still dishes from the last meal on the brick-red painted table. "I don't know what we'd do without it: we'd be really crammed into this house otherwise."

Kateri was thinking that the house would be so much less crammed if there was less stuff around, but she couldn't say that. She guessed that it was probably difficult enough for Mrs. O'Donnell to clean house on crutches, let alone declutter.

"Okay, so how did you survive in this house with three boys?" she said, hoping that didn't sound sarcastic.

"Thank God for the outdoors," Mrs. O'Donnell grinned at her.

"And there's upstairs," Alex said. "I'll show her, Mom. C'mon."

He pulled her past his dad, and Kateri was forced to sidle around him (Mr. O'Donnell was not a small person) to get through the kitchen and into the miniature hallway. Alex opened a door, revealing steps going upstairs.

"C'mon up." He gave her a hand and pulled her up the steps, which were steep and led up to a large open attic room.

Here, at least there was no congestion. An Oriental paper screen muted the light from one of the far windows ("Blocks the view of the telephone wires," Alex said). And there was no furniture. Instead, thick beige mats of springy hard foam covered nearly every surface, taped together with black duct tape. The walls were pale yellow, and neatly ordered rows of hooks held staffs, rings, wooden swords, and other Oriental weapons.

"It's our own dojo," Alex waved his arms around. "Dad and I made it together. This is where we practice."

"It's neat," Kateri breathed, giving the word its double meaning as she stepped out into the middle of the room, where the ceiling was the highest. Even with the slope of the roof, it still felt spacious. "But how can you do martial arts here? Don't you hit your head on the ceiling all the time?"

Alex unconsciously rubbed his head. "You learn to be very, very careful. It's actually been a wonderful discipline. I just repainted the ceiling, by the way. You won't believe how torn up the plaster gets when you have three guys attacking each other with wooden swords in here."

"I believe it," Kateri said, looking up. "I'm surprised the light fixtures are intact."

"Only sporadically," Alex said. "But during your stay, this will be a place for rest, not for war. Since we don't have a guest bedroom, I thought you might find it easier to sleep up here." He folded back the screen to reveal a cot bed, neatly covered with a red silk comforter embroidered with flowers. "It's small, but it'll get you out of the tumult."

"Thank you," Kateri said gratefully. She'd already pictured herself trying vainly to get to sleep in the jumbled downstairs living room. She couldn't relax in disorder. "It's wonderful."

He winked at her. "Let me go and get your stuff."

Kateri only survived for three hours in the O'Donnell's house before she began to clean. It was a nearly obsessive itch that oppressed her. The younger boys were still out, so she and Alex and his parents enjoyed a leisurely dinner out on the screen porch (with flowers and votive candles floating in a glass bowl on the table, and Japanese tea served in an iron teapot at the end of the meal) during which Kateri managed to restrain herself from helping. But when the meal was over and Mr. O'Donnell rose, saying he'd better clean up, Kateri blurted out, "I'll do the dishes!"

She attacked the kitchen with a fury, scrubbing and stacking and drying and putting away. It was all she could do to stop herself from cleaning out the refrigerator and re-organizing the cabinets. Alex, of course, was helping (after the table was cleared, Mr. O'Donnell had excused himself since there wasn't room for three people to work in the kitchen). Observing her energetic activity, her boyfriend remarked, "Making space, are you?"

"I can't imagine how you all live here."

"Like Mom said, we have the outside."

"Still!"

Shouts outdoors announced that the younger boys were home. They tore inside and pounded into the kitchen, then pulled to a halt to gape at her.

Alex intervened. "Ah. Here, Kateri, are the inhabitants of this house known collectively as the barbarian horde. As the Chinese treated the Mongolians, so we share the same territory, and attempt to control, educate, and eventually civilize, them."

Kateri surveyed the two younger boys, who were stocky, with wild blond hair spiking in every direction, and whose sports shirts and khaki shorts and sneakers bore the marks of mud, sweat, and slight ice cream stains. "Better give up and build the Great Wall."

The older one sputtered in laughter, and the younger one, with big blue round eyes said, "Are you really from the Far East?"

"No," she said with annoyance. "I'm from New Jersey."

"Cool!" He had clearly been waiting to say the word, regardless of her answer. "Can you do martial arts?"

"No," she said. "I just use clubs."

"Cool!"

Alex said, "Kateri, meet Sam and David. David is the older one and Sam is the smaller one. You'll quickly be able to distinguish them because David is funnier."

"He is not!" Sam said.

"Funnier looking, he means," David said.

"Ha ha."

Alex added, "I should also mention that David is completely unprincipled, particularly when it comes to video games."

"When it comes to video games," David grinned, "what fourteen-year-old has principles?"

"Democracy does not produce morality," Alex said. "Kateri, forewarned is forearmed."

They forced her to leave off cleaning and come and play video games with them, and Kateri, remembering her manners, managed to play two hours of *Super Mangan Brothers IX: Breakout of Jail* with reasonable politeness. Mrs. O'Donnell sat on the couch, crocheting something long and multi-colored, and Mr. O'Donnell had vanished.

"Dad's on his computer, as usual," Alex said, noticing Kateri glancing around.

"What does he do?"

"In the evenings, software programming," Alex said.

"Code name for hacking," David put in.

"He's not trying to do anything illegal," Alex said, a little sharply.

"Just because the laws haven't caught up with him yet," David said. "Pow! You're dead, Kateri! Again. See what happens if you get distracted by talking?"

*Distracted by talking, or even just thinking,* Kateri said internally. *Neither of which seems to be compatible with this game.* With suppressed annoyance, she waited for her character, a bouncing pink fish, to attain enough Life-Force Energy to revive.

"If we had the new Super Mangan X game, you could blast right through that wall with the SuperM add-on blaster!" Sam said, apologetically. "We haven't gotten that one yet. Yet! Right, Mom? We'll get it soon."

But Mrs. O'Donnell only looked worried, and Kateri gazed again at the door to the bedroom where Mr. O'Donnell had disappeared. What was he doing in there?

It occurred to Kateri that she hadn't been shown the bedroom. That was normal: many married couples didn't put their bedrooms on display. But now his behavior during the house tour struck her as odd. Was Mr. O'Donnell trying to distract her from something very obvious, and very important? *Why? Why was he afraid—?*

*Afraid.* Kateri closed her eyes. That was what she had caught in Mr. O'Donnell's eyes: fear.

But of what?

# Chapter Three

*Now, his older brother had started out as poor as he, but Cassim had taken care to marry a rich woman, and was now one of the wealthiest merchants in town.* The Arabian Nights

So what's going on?"

It was extremely late at night, but Kateri and Alex were still up and talking in the dojo. The O'Donnells were night owls, another contrast to Kateri's early-rising family. The younger boys were still playing a video game, Mrs. O'Donnell had taken her crocheting to the bedroom to watch TV, and Mr. O'Donnell was apparently still on the computer. Kateri herself was tired, but she was also worried, and worry had a way of not letting her sleep.

"I wish I knew," Alex said, sitting on the steps. "He won't tell us anything."

Alex had accompanied Kateri upstairs, but out of propriety, he was sitting on the steps. Since the dojo was now Kateri's bedroom, both he and Kateri had agreed that it wouldn't be a good example to the younger boys for them to hang out alone there together at night. The door to the downstairs was open, but the video game music obscured their conversation.

"So what did he say when the check showed up?"

Alex shrugged. "I didn't tell him until it cleared. I actually almost forgot about it. Mom does the books: she saw the amount."

Kateri, who was sitting on the bed, hugged her legs to herself and tried to imagine suddenly having a million dollars. What would that feel like?

"Yeah." As usual, Alex seemed to read her thoughts. "It's really a strange situation: having money, even if we're not able to use it. There're so many things we could do with it: well, you can see how we live."

"What would *you* do with the money?" Kateri asked, trying to avoid the mystery neither could solve.

Alex inclined his head. "Ladies first. Tell me what you would do."

Kateri shrugged. "Help my parents pay off the house, settle my student loan debts, donate large sums of money to the Church and the pro-life cause."

"Yeah, pretty much the same for me." He paused, and his green eyes looked distant. "Plus get a bigger house for the family. Get Mom some more physical therapy, maybe some of the treatments we can't afford. Help Dad start another business. We'd probably lose all the money that way, but I know he hates the government contracting job he has now."

Kateri nodded. She and Alex had that in common. They were religious, idealistic, and poor. She changed the subject. "Your mom is a real trooper with her illness."

"Yeah, isn't she great?" Alex spoke affectionately. "You know, she doesn't care about not being able to afford therapy. I think she just offers everything up. I know the disease is hard for her, but she keeps on trucking. And laughing. She can't keep up with the house and with all of us, but she's always finding something to smile about. Even before this happened."

"Yeah, I can see that. Wow." Kateri burrowed her chin into her hands and thought. Even though the disorder in the O'Donnell house was driving Kateri crazy, she really liked Mrs. O'Donnell. "I can see she has a tough time with the house. I can't imagine. Do you think she would mind if I helped her out a bit? I don't want to insult her…"

"Oh, even before she got sick, the house was never clean," Alex said. "I guess none of us are very organized. But to answer your question, I bet she'd love it if you helped." He looked at her shrewdly. "I can see the nervous twitch in your eyebrow, Kat."

She rubbed her eyes. "What nervous twitch?"

"That itch you get when you want to declutter things. I saw it every time you looked into my dorm room. Well, you'd better suppress it. I bet you can't wait to get your hands on this house and de-junk it. But you'd better not throw anything out. Both my parents are pretty sentimental about their stuff. And so am I. So lay off the downsizing mission."

She gritted her teeth. How could Alex know her so well? "Forewarned is forearmed," she said. "Fortunately for you, I grew up with nine messy brothers and sisters. Believe me, I've learned the hard way that you can't force people to be as neat as you want them to be."

Alex chuckled. "Having seen the chaos inside the Kovach family farmhouse, I'm amazed that you're still sane," he remarked, getting to his feet. "Well, I'm glad we have at least one clean room in the house for you to sleep in."

"You didn't clean it up especially for me?" she looked around distrustfully.

"Oh, no. Well, I did send a couple dozen crates to the Lock N'Store down the street for your visit. I figured you wouldn't want to sleep in the same room as the rowing machine and the hanging loom." He leaned over and kissed her, laughing at her expression. "See you in the morning."

The problem was, she decided as she slid under the quilted silk sleeping bag, she couldn't tell if Alex was teasing her or not. And he knew it.

Even though Kateri was an early riser, Mr. O'Donnell was gone when she went downstairs in the morning. Alex had mentioned that his dad, like most commuters of Northern Virginia, rose earlier than farmers in order to beat the traffic into DC. The rest of the O'Donnells slept in, so Kateri went downstairs, made coffee, and, unable to control herself, started straightening up the silverware drawer.

She was trying to stack all the forks and spoons neatly in the divider without making noise when she heard the squeak of crutches on wood, and she looked up guiltily, to see Mrs. O'Donnell, wearing a pink floral housecoat and leaning on her crutches with a pleased expression on her face.

"Good morning! Kateri, I can't tell you how nice it is to have another woman in the house. One who understands that forks and knives are utensils, not weapons."

"I hope you don't mind," Kateri murmured.

"I had to surrender control of my kitchen a long time ago, back when the MS first started." Mrs. O'Donnell waved her hands. "Please. I would be delighted with anything you wanted to do. Poor Alan and Alex. They try so hard to keep things ordered, but they just don't have a woman's eye for how things should be."

Gratefully, Kateri removed three chopsticks from the pile of silverware on the counter and tucked them into the side of the drawer. "Can I get you some coffee?"

"No, my dear, allow me. Oh, this is fresh! Did you make it? Alan must have been preoccupied this morning: he usually starts it." One bound with her crutches had landed Mrs. O'Donnell beside the counter where she started pulling mugs out of the tiny dishwasher. "Do you take milk? Sugar?"

"Both, thanks."

They chatted comfortably until Alex got up, already dressed with his long black hair in his usual ponytail. He kissed each of them. "Eggs, anyone? Mom, did you want a muffin?"

"That would be wonderful," his mother handed Kateri her coffee, and then sank into the one chair in the kitchen that had nothing stacked on it. Alex fixed his mother's coffee with milk, and set it on the windowsill beside her, then turned to the stove to make eggs.

*I like that he takes care of her,* Kateri thought before she could catch herself. *That's a good sign.* She growled inwardly. Why was she still scrutinizing Alex as a potential marriage partner, even as she was steeling herself to break up with him? Nevertheless, it was interesting to see this side of him.

He shook his head at Kateri, who was pulling matchbox cars out of the utensil drawer. "I warned you expressly and in great detail about cleaning," he murmured.

"I'm just curious to see what else you have in here," she said, pulling out directions for Yatzee, a plastic mouse, and six screws.

"CKTC," he sighed.

Alex was happy. Despite his rebuke to Kateri, despite his worry about his father, and despite the Mystery Money, the fact was that Kateri was here. And so far she hadn't exploded, and the house hadn't blown up. In fact, Kateri almost seemed to like it here. Perhaps he was being optimistic. But when he had been awakened by the sound of her voice conversing with his mother's in the kitchen, it had sounded so completely natural, as though the two women had been fated to be friends from time immemorial. And he had felt as though the two halves of his world were converging as smoothly as yin and yang.

It had propelled him out of bed a full half hour earlier than usual. Regardless of what happened with Dad and with the money, if Kateri could get along with his mother, life was bliss.

Breakfast was a cheerful affair. His mother and Kateri had seemed to have agreed that the topic between them was going to be the kitchen. Kateri was admiring the furniture, cups, and plates his mom had painted. (During the course of her illness, Alex's mom had covered just about every wooden and pottery surface with flowers and designs, bringing brisk business to both the ceramics and unfinished wooden furniture stores in town). His mom was saying that she really wanted to sort through the crowded shelves of cups and get rid of the sports mugs and joke mugs among them. "The problem is, there are mugs *all* over the house."

"You're not getting rid of my Ninja Monkey mug," Alex warned her, finishing his eggs. "Paul Fester gave that to me. And the Mercy College beer steins have got to stay."

Both women glanced at each other, and Alex knew that behind-the-scene negotiations had already commenced. "All right, I'll get the mail," he said, ducking out.

The younger boys derailed the kitchen summit when they woke up and actually wanted to use the kitchen for eating. Kateri furnished them with bowls of cereal and Mom sent them out to the porch to eat. Alex turned on the television and caught up with the latest inside-the-Beltway news. The younger boys ate fast, and perhaps sensing that they were going to be pressed into service, dashed outside as soon as they finished.

At last his mom came into the living room and settled herself in her usual spot on the couch with a sigh, looking tired but happy.

"I'll just go through the lower cabinets and bring out anything that doesn't match for you to make a decision on," Kateri said from the doorway. She was wearing his mother's blue apron with the pink roses and looked all mission-oriented. He was used to seeing that expression on her face when she was organizing a massive pro-life protest.

"Wonderful, Kateri. That sounds wonderful," his mom replied.

Alex decided that if his mother was going to back up Kateri in her campaign, he was going to surrender to the inevitable, like any wise general. Link, the orange-tortoiseshell cat, who had been hiding under his parents' bed since Kateri arrived, came out purring, and leapt up into Alex's lap to have her long black-and-orange fur stroked.

"All's right with the world," Alex said, and the cat seemed to agree.

"Did you get the mail?" his mom asked, picking up her crochet needle.

"Right here," Alex said, picking up the sheaf from the end table. "Do you want it?"

"Just the newspaper. Can you sort through the mail for me? Thanks!"

Whistling, Alex sifted through the mail, and slathered a large portion of it into the trashcan. "All that's left is the phone bill, cable bill, garbage collection bill, and one actual letter." He held up the last for his mother to see.

She looked at it, and then wearily leaned her head back on the sofa. "Can you open it for me?"

Obediently, Alex pulled out his penknife, slit open the envelope, and removed the folded piece of paper. He instantly recognized the handwriting of the curt, scribbled note and understood his mother's reticence.

"It's from Uncle Cass, isn't it?" she said. "I knew he would send something. We weren't able to make the payment last month. Dad already called him to ask for an extension."

Alex read the heated note, and felt a spasm of anger himself. "You know, it's a good thing we're related, because otherwise, I'd never do business with him."

She sighed. "We did borrow a lot of money from him when the insurance didn't cover my medical bills. He just needs us to repay. That's all."

"Yeah, but I just find it a little hard that's he's been charging us interest!" Alex said bitterly. Every month for the past seven years, they were supposed to send a check to Uncle Cass, and with the interest he charged, the amount they owed seemed to get bigger and bigger, because they weren't always able to pay every month.

"Well, at least he didn't call a collection agency," she said humorously. Then abruptly she lapsed into silence, and her face took on that far-off look that Alex also recognized. She was calculating, running figures in her head. His mother was as good as an MIT professor when it came to numbers. She had worked as an actuary before her marriage.

After a few minutes, she said, "Hand me the checkbook, will you?"

Alex found it near her yarn basket, and she opened the plastic-covered book, took out a pencil, and started making marks, then was silent again for a long time while Alex turned back to the TV.

When a commercial came on, he glanced at her and saw Mom had a small smile on her face. "I think it might work. If we can use our new financial status to get a loan from the bank with a better interest rate, we can pay him back, in full. After the end of the month."

"Really?"

"Yes."

"Why then?"

"Because of when the interest is paid. We wouldn't have to use a cent of the money. All we'd have to do is take advantage of the fact that we *have* the money. Actually, this opens up all sorts of interesting possibilities…" She buried her head in the checkbook, and did not look up until lunchtime.

Kateri pushed back a strand of black hair from her face and surveyed her work. She had spent most of the day re-organizing the kitchen: removing books, papers, toys, and Oriental weapons from the cupboards and thinning out the kitchen materials to what the family actually used. She tried hard not to be disgusted at the amount of junk in the kitchen. *My family is just as messy,* she said to herself. *But by golly, I'm not going to have a kitchen like this when I get*

*married*. It was another point against Alex: surely living with him would eventually produce a kitchen as cluttered as this one.

The two younger boys, covered with dust, yelling and sweating, had returned for lunch, which Kateri made them eat at the table in a civilized manner. They seemed to be intimidated enough to avoid her afterwards. Now that the afternoon heat had settled on the suburbs in earnest, the boys were engrossed in a video game while an ancient air conditioner roared away in the living room window. When Kateri finished putting the last promotional mug into an overflowing box marked "giveaways," it was shortly after three o'clock, and Alex had gone to the store for his mom. Mrs. O'Donnell sat on the couch next to the air conditioner's blast, her eyes closed, her fingers moving on rosary beads. Kateri didn't want to disturb her. So she escaped to her dojo bedroom and sat on the bed, thinking about Alex and why she had started dating him.

Kateri liked to think of herself as a person with high ideals. Whenever she imagined being married, it was usually to someone like herself: an activist, a missionary, someone who worked the land, or at the very least, someone Asian. That was an accurate description of her former boyfriends, who had been either friends from the Vietnamese Club, or practical, hands-on farm boys, or dedicated pro-life activists. They'd mostly been thin, earnest guys: short-haired, good workers, more inclined to pick up a book by Fr. Paul Marx than a sword.

In her list of qualities of a future spouse, physical attractiveness was very low on the list—if had even made her list at all. So it was utterly frustrating to her that the first thing she had noticed about Alex was that she found him *appealing*. Not handsome, not good-looking, just very…appealing.

He had first caught her eye when he and some of his roommates were climbing trees on campus: he'd been wearing a sleeveless shirt and had thrown himself at a branch above his head and swung up easily as a cat. As a farm girl, upper-body strength was something she tended to notice and appreciate.

So she had noticed him. End of story.

Of course, she hadn't liked him: given his tattoos and long hair, she'd assumed he was a biker-wanna-be, shallow and immature. Then, later on, when she knew him better, she still thought he lacked drive and character. But all along, she couldn't help noticing how her skin prickled every time he walked near her, how she was always aware of what he was doing in a room, even if she didn't want to be, how her eyes kept being pulled to him as he raced around campus with his friends from Sacra Cor dorm. It was extremely aggravating, and he was source material for not a few sessions in the confessional.

At that point in Kateri's life, Alex O'Donnell was just a distraction: a very physical distraction, and hence, annoying.

In any case, he hadn't picked up on her attraction. She kept him at arms' length and whenever they crossed paths, she made sure she found a lot to criticize about him. And he returned the favor. So it was astonishing to her, when she found herself embroiled in a dangerous situation, that it was *Alex* who stepped up to the plate to rescue her. That was the first time she guessed that maybe he had been pretending to be disinterested as well.

Of course, they both kept on playing the game of cool disdain, but eventually they realized that it was a game without a point. When their friend Rose was in dire trouble, saving her life had created a state of affairs where Kateri and Alex actually had to put aside their differences in order to work and strategize together.

And when it was all over, and Rose was safe, Kateri felt it was only fair to catch Alex alone to thank him for his courage and thoughtfulness, and to admit she had misjudged him. That was all she intended to do.

So at some terribly early hour of the morning after that adventure had ended, Alex had driven her and their friends back onto campus. He'd dropped off the others, and finally parked his car outside her dorm, and, gentleman-like, escorted her to the door. She'd discovered that was the difference between Alex and most bikers: Alex had impeccable good manners when it came to girls.

And Kateri, who had rehearsed her compliments in the car, found herself tongue-tied as she turned around to face Alex.

"I just wanted to say…" she began, and realized that Alex was looking at her with a curiously intense look in his green eyes. But he said nothing.

She swallowed, and tried again, "I wanted to say…"

He just kept looking at her quietly. She looked away from him, up at the sky, and realized that the stars were shining down on them, as though the angels had cued the lights. Hurriedly she glanced back at him, and that was no help. He was still looking at her with that intensely interested gaze, not saying anything. And now, she found she couldn't look away.

"…thank you?" Absurdly, it sounded like a question.

Alex took a step closer to her, and she found herself moving closer to him. And the next thing she knew…

Um, well…

She'd never thought of herself as a swooning heroine, but she came pretty close that night. And Alex certainly didn't seem to mind that she had melted like chocolate in his arms. But it was irritating for Kateri just the same.

From her point of view, marriage should be based on practical considerations, like compatibility and temperament and friendship. Well, sure, she was friends with Alex now, but she had always heard that a relationship that started out with passion was destined to fail. She was skeptical of romance novels, and now that she seemed to be trapped in one, complete with a swashbuckling and witty hero, she couldn't help feeling that she was miscast.

For one thing, she wasn't pretty, let alone beautiful. Strong, tough, idealistic, truthful: those were the words she reached for when she thought about herself. Not a quivering, feminine mass of nerve endings who was willing to forget about her ideals for a set of marvelous biceps.

It wasn't that she disliked Alex: it was just that he didn't match up with the kind of guy she had always visualized she would marry. And she didn't know if she should stick to her original ideas, or change the picture to fit reality.

Finally, unable to find her way out of the maze of her conflicts, she threw up her hands, and decided to check her email.

A bit guiltily, she took her little blue laptop from her backpack. It had been a graduation present, the first computer she had actually owned. Kateri didn't like to be dependent on electronic equipment: for most of her life, she had distained the virtual for the real. The laptop represented a compromise with modernity part of her resented. Compromise? Was this going to be the new theme of her life?

She booted up her email and checked her inbox. After the usual routine of deleting junk mail and organizing her folders, she went to her Facebook and began to write a note to her parents, saying she had reached the O'Donnells safely, and things were fine—when *it* happened.

An animated cat, dressed in samurai clothing with a headband, jumped right onto the screen in front of her letter, brandishing a Japanese sword. A bubble appeared over his head with writing.

Can I Has Swordfights?

# Chapter Four

*Having confided in his wife,*
*Ali Baba recommended that she keep*
*the treasure a secret from everyone else.*
*The Arabian Nights*

ateri stared incredulously at the supersized anime figure that was hovering in front of her text, blocking her view of the Facebook page.

"What the—" She tried to click around it, but the cat sprang into action, hitting her cursor so that it pinged off the sides of the screen crazily. She hit the ESC key, the CNTRL-ALT-DEL keys: nothing. The little monster had completely taken over her computer. It even laughed at her as she hit the keys.

De Kitty Wants Swordfights.
U R Giving Me Swordfights NOW.

Emitting a yell, she grabbed her computer and shook it, then dropped it into her lap and stared at the anime cat again. It was still grinning at her and posturing with its sword.

Can I Has Swordfights?

"How do I fight you?" she exclaimed.

"Click on its sword," David advised her, sliding next to her.

"Use the space bar too," Sam said, coming up the steps behind him. "I love this!"

"Did you two do this?"

"Us?" David said, his eyes fixed on the cat. "Nah, Dad built him. He's the most highly detailed override security program ever made."

"An override security program?" Kateri shouted.

"Yeah, he's our network security guy," Sam said. "We have wireless internet, and Dad was trying to secure it so that no one else can get onto it. Most security systems have popup boxes. Dad built this guy instead. The neat thing is, if you can defeat him, you can use the Internet. Otherwise he boots you off."

"But I was on the Internet!" Kateri said as the cat threw its sword rapidly back from hand to hand with a fierce grin.

"Just like the guy in Indiana Jones," David said happily. "I love it when he does that."

"Yeah, he'll let you use the Web for five minutes and forty five seconds," Sam said. "But then you have to fight him. Come on, fight him, Kateri, fight!"

Conned into playing a video game. Of course. This *would* be Alex's house. Snarling back at the cat, Kateri grabbed her mouse from her backpack and plugged it in. "What do I do again?"

"The cursor is your sword… so…what do you do with a sword?"

"Um. I don't know. Cut his throat?"

David shrugged. "That's a start."

Figuring this should be simple enough, Kateri aimed the cursor onto the cat's throat but the cat easily deflected it, sending her cursor bouncing. She managed to control it with the space bar (Aha.) and tried again. She couldn't get the cursor anywhere on the cat without hitting the cat's flashing silver blade.

"Go for his feet," David advised.

After a few seconds of fruitless effort, Kateri was reduced to banging the mouse on the side of her keyboard. The cat complained,

### U R Doin It Wrong!

"That won't do anything," Sam said. "Believe me, I've tried. Neither will breaking the mouse."

"How do I get this thing to leave?" Kateri demanded.

"Well, come on," David said. "You're Alex's girlfriend. Don't you know how to swordfight?"

*Swordfight?* Kateri blinked at him. "What are you talking about? I'm his girlfriend, not his sparring partner."

"I thought Alex always taught his girlfriends to swordfight."

"He didn't teach me. I'm a pacifist."

"Well, that's dumb," Sam said. "What do you want to be that for? You could be learning a valuable skill. For free."

"Because killing doesn't solve problems," Kateri said.

"Um, yeah it does," Now David stared at her. "I mean, it doesn't solve *every* problem. But it solves *some* kinds of problems. Like, it stops bad guys from killing weak people. The neat thing is you don't even have to *kill* the bad guys to stop them, just *threaten* to kill them. Don't you know that? I thought you graduated from college."

"Magna cum laude," Kateri growled.

"Well, then you should know about this stuff by now!" David said.

"David!" Sam was elbowing him. "David. Shh. She doesn't have a job. She hasn't gone out into the real world yet."

"Oh. Yeah." David focused his attention back on the screen. "Hey, Kat, shaking the mouse back and forth isn't going to do anything. Try swooping it."

"What's going on?" Alex appeared at the foot of the steps. "What are you doing, Kateri?"

"Reconsidering my position on taking human life," Kateri looked up and met his eyes. "I'm about to make two exceptions. Maybe three."

"Boys, what have you been up to?" Alex climbed the steps and looked over her shoulder. "Oh! Our little samurai security cat! Isn't he cute? I love it when this happens to guests."

"Uh, Alex. I wouldn't goad her. She's nearly catatonic," David said.

"And she doesn't know how to swordfight! What's up with that?" Sam said. "I thought this would be a cinch for any of your girlfriends."

"Let's not get into my dating history," Alex said. "Kateri, just swoop your mouse from side to side as though it's a sword blade. No, not so jagged. A little more graceful. That's it. Use the side of the screen for practice. Try diagonal— you're getting it! Okay, now go in at a right angle—there you go!"

The cat staggered to one side, blood flowing from his shoulder.

"Yuck!" Kateri exclaimed.

"Realistic, isn't it? Okay, go in from the other side, diagonal again…"

Another swoop, and the cat staggered back.

Ouchay!

"Don't worry, you don't have to kill him. Just wounding both sword arms will do it," Alex directed. "See?"

U Giv Me Good Swordfight!
U Can Has Interwebs Now.

The cat sheathed its sword and made a deep Oriental bow, then vanished. The three brothers cheered.

"You have won the privilege of using the Internet in our home," David rose and said ceremoniously, "Please resume your browsing pleasure." Cackling, he turned and hurried downstairs.

"See why you need to learn how to swordfight?" Sam said. He raised a finger. "Lack of effort is not a virtue," he said in a deep voice that was obviously imitating his father's. He turned and followed David.

Alex leaned against the stairwell wall, smiling. "So you're reconsidering your pacifism?"

"Reconsidering a *lot* of things!" Kateri grabbed her laptop and scrunched herself into the corner of the bed.

"Aw, come on Kateri, don't be mad."

For an answer, Kateri flicked hard eyes at him over the screen for an instant.

"Want some pistachios?" he held out a bag. "I got them just for you."

She ignored him.

"Kateri," He stretched out her name, cajoling. "Come on! That wasn't even a very hard fight! You should see when Dad is actually controlling the cat: then it's really hard to beat him. I once fought that thing for forty-five minutes while you were waiting for me in a chat box."

"What? You mean that one time at Christmas when we were chatting on the Sacra Cor website, and suddenly you vanished?" She remembered that incident. She'd been waiting at the keyboard, wondering what had happened, getting occasional messages from him that said, "Tech problems!" When he finally returned, he'd just said that they were having network security problems at the house and they resumed their serious conversation.

"You should have been here," he groaned. "The whole family was downstairs at Dad's computer, cheering him on while he fought me and I sat up here trying to reconnect to the internet. He made me defeat the cat no less than seven times, while Mom and the boys shouted, 'Go Dad! Go Dad!' That's the last time I ever buy my parents Tequila for Christmas." He made pathetic eyes at her. "So I'm a victim, too."

She couldn't help grinning at the picture of Alex so disoriented. "I guess that's what happens in this household when you start dating someone."

"Yeah, it goes with the territory." He shook his head, and crossed into the dojo. Taking a wooden sword from the wall, he stretched. "But I really should teach you swordfighting."

"Not now," she said, returning to Facebook.

"But soon." He bowed, stepped onto the mat, and began his *kata*, sword exercises she was already familiar with. She could sit there and watch him, but then she'd probably have to go to confession. Dating Alex hadn't made that part any easier.

For once, she buried herself gratefully in electronic distractions without a shred of guilt.

Alex finished his exercises, feeling alert and fully rested. When he was home, he didn't do his *kata* as often as he should: it was hard to keep to a schedule. *Eh, I need either full-time school or a full-time job to keep me organized,* he reflected. His natural tendency was laziness. It helped having Kateri there. He wondered again how long she was going to stay.

She was still on her computer, so whistling, he went downstairs to get a drink of water.

"Alex?" Mom called from the living room.

"Can I get you something, Mom?" He recognized the tone of voice.

"My burgundy yarn from the bedroom? It's in the pile next to the closet in a plastic bag," she said. "Alan picked it up for me last week."

"Sure thing," Alex said. He pushed the door to his parent's room open (it always stuck on the carpet: bad hinges) and squinted in the half-dark. His dad's computer was on, with a screensaver of family photos bouncing and dissolving across the screen.

As he made his way through the room, suddenly the screensaver quivered and went off. Alex glanced at the desktop which had appeared, with a photo of Zatoichi the Blind Samurai in the background. Maybe he'd creaked the room's loose floorboard and caused the mouse to move?

But no. Oddly enough, the cursor was slowly moving across the screen, on its own.

Intently Alex watched the cursor hover and then swoop down onto an icon and click it. A menu opened, and the cursor scrolled down through the options.

There was no hand on the mouse. But the cursor was definitely moving.

Thinking, Alex grabbed the mouse, which responded to his touch, and clicked a text program. He typed in the open box:

                    Dad? Is this you?


He waited. The cursor began to move again of its own accord and typed.

                    Yes. Alex?

Alex typed back.

What's my favorite color?

The cursor responded promptly.

Chinese red.

Alex breathed in relief, and typed.

You sure freaked me out.

A second later the cursor wrote:

Sorry.
Just accessing my home computer from work.
I do it all the time. Kitty knows.

Alex typed,

Okay, just checking!  See you tonight.

Shaking his head, he pushed the keyboard away.

Kateri guessed that Alex must have been watching her that evening during dinner, because when she tried to unobtrusively excuse herself from the table, she found her arm suddenly immobilized in a jujitsu hold. "No cleaning," he said firmly, looking into her eyes.

"I want to help," she said, with a mixture of amusement and annoyance.

"I want you to sit down and relax," Alex said. He nodded to the others at the table. "Hey, Kateri, you should tell them your family history."

She pushed back her hair. "I don't want to bore them."

He folded his arms behind his head. "It's better than hearing Dad describe the history of the O'Donnell clan, and much less fictional."

"Why don't you explain the differences between Vietnamese and Japanese culture?" Mr. O'Donnell suggested. "Set us all straight so that we don't mix things up and offend you."

"What about the difference between Vietnamese and Chinese too?" David asked.

"And I'm confused about the difference between China and Japan…" Sam said.

Kateri shook her head with impatience as she resumed her seat. "All very different. China is a huge sprawling mainland civilization, and Japan is a little island with a superiority complex. Vietnam is a long strip of coastland and islands on the southern tip of Asia that managed to get free of China about eleven hundred years ago and went on to develop its own culture." She looked around. "How about I just tell you about Vietnamese culture, and you use Wikipedia to look up the rest?"

"That works," Mr. O'Donnell said.

"Well," Kateri ran her fingers though her hair to try to collect her thoughts. "Vietnam used to be part of China, so I guess you could say that our culture is a lot like Chinese culture. But we're still very different! We've been independent from China pretty much since the tenth century, ever since we fought for the right to govern ourselves and won."

"Eleven hundred years ago, when America was just wilderness," Mr. O'Donnell put in. "Gives you some perspective, eh boys?"

Kateri went on, "And one thing I find interesting about the Vietnamese is that many of us really took to Catholicism."

"Well, it was a French colony back in the 1800s, right?" Mr. O'Donnell said.

"Yes, but that's not how Catholicism came to Vietnam. Try the sixteenth century. It was the Jesuit missionaries from Portugal who brought the faith over. One of the Jesuits created the first Vietnamese written alphabet and we still use it today. And Vietnam wasn't a French colony for very long, by the way. We kicked them out pretty fast. Catholics were persecuted before and after the time of the colonization, but many Vietnamese held onto the faith."

"And then the communists took over," Mr. O'Donnell said.

"And everything changed," Kateri said quietly. "That's when my family came over here." She'd never been to Vietnam herself, but she had heard her mother's stories of growing up there, and she felt she shared her mother's connection to her homeland. "My mom's taught us everything she can about the culture. I speak a bit of the language. She taught us girls how to cook all the major kinds of *pho*. And how to do the Fan Dance."

"The Fan Dance? What's that?" Sam asked.

"Just one of the more famous Vietnamese dances. We used to do it all the time for homeschool talent shows and other events."

"Wow! Can you do it for us someday?"

"Maybe," Kateri said. "But I warn you, I'm not very good at it." That was an understatement, she thought. She had liked doing it when she was the smallest and shortest of her five sisters, when people thought she was adorably cute for mimicking them. But when she grew to be a teenager, she suddenly became all thumbs and angles, and never seemed to be able to achieve the weightless energy of her siblings. Plus there was the whole lacking-beauty thing.

"When did your mom leave Vietnam?" Mrs. O'Donnell asked.

"After the war," Kateri said.

"Did she teach you any martial arts? The Vietnamese scissor kicks are famous," David took another helping of stew.

"No," she said, and thought *why did boys only think about fighting?*

"Shhh," said Alex. "She's just getting to the good part of her history. Don't distract her. Kateri, tell them how your parents met."

She glanced at Alex, who raised his eyebrows a bit pleadingly. Sighing, she gave in. "My dad was an American soldier in Vietnam during the war. They met when he was stationed near her village, and they kept in touch after he was wounded and had to go back to the States." Kateri took another helping of salad, and wondered if her mom had started out by finding her dad physically attractive. Probably. There was a language barrier that separated them—both of them spoke only a little French—so they couldn't have done much talking. It suddenly occurred to Kateri that her own parents might have started out having a more conventional romance.

She shook her head to focus back on the story. "Then, when the Communists took over after the United States pulled out, Mom's family was in danger of being killed, so they got a fishing boat together with a group of other families and tried to cross the Pacific to get to America."

"Really?" Mr. O'Donnell said. "So your family were some of the boat people."

"Some of the *lucky* boat people," Kateri said, trying to keep her voice cool. "My mom's mother and brother—my grandmother and uncle—died on the way over." Her mother had described the horrors of the journey to her, but Kateri didn't feel the need to go into them now. "My grandfather died after they were picked up by freighter on the shipping lanes. But my mother survived. The freighter that picked them up took them to San Francisco and there she wrote to my father, who was back in Jersey with his family."

She swallowed, "The very day he received her letter, he got on a train and came to get her. They got married within the month."

The O'Donnells were spellbound, and she could tell that Mr. and Mrs. O'Donnell were deeply moved.

"What a story," Mrs. O'Donnell breathed. "To have that in your background—that's so romantic."

Kateri shrugged, trying to avoid getting emotional. She liked the O'Donnells, but she wasn't ready to cry in front of them. "Yes, I come from a family of romantics. Combine Vietnamese and Poles, and that's what you get."

Alex squeezed her hand. "Kateri, relax and enjoy this romantic heritage of yours."

Kateri rubbed her eyes a bit irritably. "I just hate being the center of attention. It was my parents who were the heroes. I'm just their youngest daughter."

"So, with such a romantic history, why do you always try to be so practical?" Alex teased her.

A bit surprised, she shrugged. "Reaction, I suppose. But you can't call me a pragmatist. Otherwise I'd never be an activist."

"And never gotten involved with me," Alex supplied.

She inclined her head. "I was just going to say that."

"So can you do a Fan Dance for us?" David asked.

Alex pretended to biff him on the head. "Not until you learn a better sense of timing."

Alex had assessed his campaign and decided that an intervention was called for. So on Saturday morning, he hustled Kateri out the door early. "Today we are escaping from my messy house. It's time for me to behave like a decent boyfriend and take you to DC to enjoy yourself."

"Out of the frying pan and into the fire," muttered Kateri, but she let herself be pulled along to Alex's car. "I thought you said we were going to Mass."

"At the Basilica of the Immaculate Conception, of course," Alex said, opening the door for her. He was pleased that she was wearing her blue summer dress and a yellow sweater, with her ample wavy hair caught up in a flowered ponytail. "But first we'll take the metro and hit the Smithsonian museums. Then noon Mass at the Basilica. Sound like fun?"

"Definitely." Alex thought she sounded relieved.

They drove through the early morning light on a mostly-free Route 66, driving over the broad bridge across the Potomac just as the sun cleared the clouds. The low profile of the capitol gleamed in the early light, and Alex reflected that even DC didn't look so bad on a morning like this.

They parked at Catholic University and rode the metro train to the DC Mall to take advantage of the free museums. Alex relished the experience of holding hands with Kateri as they walked about the cavernous exhibits. It was like exploring a new world together, and he began to feel that this partnership with her was something he wanted to hold onto.

"Can't believe that you made the March for Life in Washington DC every year since you were three and never once visited the Smithsonian!" he chided her.

She raised her small chin to examine a model of a praying mantis. "I was out in the cold, doing what the March is all about: praying for the unborn, attending the rally, and marching."

"Yeah, but didn't you ever leave the rally at the beginning to at least visit the Museum of Natural History? You mean you actually stood in the cold for two hours listening to those speeches?"

"Yes."

"Didn't it dawn on you that the speeches are the same every year? Come on, Kateri. You should have gone into the museums at least once, just to warm up your feet."

She regarded him coolly. "To my family, the March is all about sacrifice. Making reparation. Not sightseeing."

"I guess you're right," he conceded. He stared at the insect display. "But I always thought it was a challenge to see how much of the Natural History Museum we could manage to squeeze in before the March began."

She made a face at him. "Disloyalist. Don't you know how hard they work to prepare those speeches?" But she smiled. "And this way, I can see it all for the first time, with you."

"Aww," he teased. But inside, he couldn't help rejoicing.

At noon, they returned to the Basilica, which towered into sight, massive and forthright atop its marble staircase. Alex challenged Kateri to race him up the countless steps to the top, while humming the "Rocky" theme.

"Hey, you're really in shape!" he exclaimed as she finally reached the last step while he waited for her. "You're not half as out of breath as my other friends usually are. And you hate exercising. I don't get it."

She folded her arms. "I don't exercise. I live. On a farm."

"Oh yeah. I guess that's a real workout."

"It's real *work*, if that's what you mean," she said. Despite his praise, she was slightly out of breath. "That's the problem with most Americans. They never really work hard, so they have to create artificial work—exercise—to stay in shape. So no, I don't exercise. I work."

"Ah," Alex said, and glanced behind him. "Let's go in and explore before Mass."

"I've been here before," Kateri said. "Remember? The March for Life?"

"Yeah," said Alex, "but I bet you haven't been in the *organ loft!*"

"We're not supposed to be up here!" Kateri scolded him as they peered down over the balcony.

"Probably not," Alex agreed. "But we're not bothering anyone." He looked appreciatively over the vast expanse of the church with its stone columns, barrel-vaulted ceiling, and gold mosaic of Christ in glory on the far wall. "This is my favorite view of the basilica. C'mon down this way."

He led her along a dark, narrow passageway that ran along the upper walls of the church, pierced with arched windows that allowed them to look down on the church below. The hallway was barely big enough for one person. Alex paused when they were opposite one of the mosaics in the cross of the basilica. "Beautiful, huh?"

"How did you figure out how to come up here?"

He shrugged. "I have a friend who plays the organ on some Sundays and he invited me up. You're right, we're not supposed to be here. I guess I'm showing off."

"You are," she accused. But she gazed through the small pillared archway at the lovely mosaic of Our Lady and smiled. "Though it really *is* beautiful."

He grinned. "Okay, I got my compliment. Now we can go down."

"Is that why you men do so many off-the-wall things—just because you're hoping you'll get a compliment?"

"You won't believe the things we guys'll do for attention," Alex said. "Consider it a compliment—to *you*." He made a slight bow.

She sighed, but she took his hand warmly, so he guessed that the sigh was mostly for effect. Holding hands, they went downstairs to join the congregation for Mass.

Just to enable Kateri to see as much of the museums as possible, Alex deferred the usual native's practice of leaving DC before three to beat the traffic. Like any pair of ignorant tourists, they went to lunch, then stayed till the museums closed at five, then squeezed into a packed restaurant to wait a half hour for dinner, then drove home at twenty miles an hour in bumper-to-bumper traffic while they talked intensely about life, philosophy, and politics.

"So do you really have to leave tomorrow?" Alex asked as they turned into his neighborhood. He had brought this up several times throughout the course of the day, hoping to wear down her resistance.

"I need to find a job," she said again, rubbing her eyes. "I need to be up north, pounding the pavement, knocking on doors…"

"Why don't you stay Monday and look for a job down here?"

She glanced at him. "I don't know if I could. At least up North I have some connections. Here, I wouldn't know anyone except your family."

"Well, it wouldn't hurt to try down here, would it?"

He picked up a slight hesitation in her voice. "I don't know if I'm ready to give up on being near my family yet. Don't you need to get a job?"

He shrugged. "I've already applied to work at Dad's office. They said they'll take me on in July. I already have my security clearance from last summer. Government contracting: it's a family affair."

"But I thought you hated desk jobs."

"A man does what he's got to do. But seriously, Kat, I just like having you around. I don't know how you feel about it—"

"That's just it, Alex. I don't know how I feel." She dropped her eyes.

He parked the car, turned off the engine, and regarded her, wondering if it were wise to let her continue. "Is it—anything in particular?"

She heaved a sigh. "Alex, I don't belong here. I can't stand Northern Virginia: I don't like the suburbs, I don't like video games, I don't like computers: I just don't feel I fit in anywhere here."

"So it's the place that bothers you."

"Yes, but it's more than that. I don't know—I just don't know. I don't know if I should move here."

This was a disappointment. He decided to make one last try, putting on his most wistful expression. "Well—can you stay till Monday? At least?"

Kateri pushed back her hair, and looked at him resolutely with her dark brown eyes. He became sadder, and saw her resolve waver. "I guess it wouldn't hurt to leave on Monday."

"Okay!" He opened the car door, wanting to change the subject before she could change her mind. "Let's go inside and see if the kids are still alive."

Sam and David greeted them affably enough: as usual, they were in front of the TV. His parents were gone.

"Where are Mom and Dad?" Alex asked.

"On their once-a-month date," David said.

"Aha." Alex knew his parent's routine. "When did they leave?"

David shrugged. "Sometime this morning, right after you two did."

"Long date," Alex remarked. "Did you two eat dinner?"

"We did!" they informed Alex.

"No one cleaned up the kitchen," Kateri growled, inspecting that room.

"We'll do it later," Alex said, but catching her glowering glance, he changed his mind. "Like I said, we'll do it now."

Kateri had wiped the last counter and he had just put the last dish into the dishwasher when the front door opened and the kids shouted, "Dad and Mom are back!"

Alex looked around the jamb. Dad was helping Mom through the front door. They were both gleeful, as though bursting with some guilty secret. Dad looked happier than Alex had seen him in a long time.

"Their 'day away' sure works magic," Kateri remarked.

But Alex knew that something more was going on. Suspicious, he planted himself in front of the faded purple couch and folded his arms. "Mom—Dad— what's up?"

His mom adjusted the plaid pillows, and looked at his dad, who had just sat down heavily beside her. He grinned, and spluttered. Then all at once, both of them were laughing, rolling back on the couch and throwing pillows at each other.

"Come on you two, cut it out! You've gone and done something. What is it?" Alex demanded.

Finally his mom stopped giggling long enough to burst out, "We bought a hotel!"

# Chapter Five

*Yet the wife was determined to be diligent
in returning to Cassim what she had
borrowed, and such was their undoing*

The Arabian Nights

"A hotel? You bought a hotel? What is this, Monopoly?" David said, scrambling to his feet and getting caught in the wires from the video game console.

"We bought a hotel," Dad said, wiping his glasses. Alex noticed that he looked both resigned and relieved at the same time.

"So—you decided to use the Mystery Money after all," Alex said.

Dad shook his head, and put an arm around Mom. "No, thanks to this financial master-maiden I married."

"I figured out a way to use the money as leverage to help us qualify for a business loan," Mom said, wiping her eyes—she almost always ended up crying when she laughed. "All we need to do is come up with a down payment of two hundred thousand dollars."

David was untangling his foot. "Um, but Mom, if we're not counting the Mystery Money, we don't have two hundred thousand dollars."

Alex had already figured it out. "We're going to sell our house," he said.

Mom nodded. "Which, according to my old college roommate, who does appraisals, is worth at least two hundred and seventy-five thousand. We've listed it with a real estate agent already."

"Okay, so we're moving," Alex said, feeling the need to sit down on something, and lowering himself onto a footstool covered with newspapers. "Uh—what hotel did you buy?"

With a sigh, his mom threw herself luxuriously into his dad's arms and he put a pillow on her head. "We bought the Twilight Hills Hotel."

"And what is that?"

"Just the place where we spent our honeymoon," Dad said, causing the younger boys to yell, "TMI! TMI!" and clamp their hands over their ears.

"We were just back there for our twenty-fifth anniversary a month ago," Mom told Kateri, who was standing in the kitchen doorway, open-mouthed. "It's a wonderful place."

Alex was putting this all together. "Wait a second. This is the place down south in Virginia."

"Yes," his mother said dreamily, running her hands through her blond hair.

"The place in the mountains near Roanoke. The place you two are ga-ga over."

"Yes," Dad said. "That's the place. Remember when we went on our anniversary trip? The old couple who've run it for the past fifty years told us they were going to sell it and retire."

"—so you drove down there today and told them you would buy it." Alex guessed.

"You never saw a happier couple," Dad said, swooping Mom into his arms again and kissing her.

Kateri was clearly more stunned than any of them. She folded her dishtowel over and over. "What are you going to do with a hotel?"

"Run it. As a business," Mom said, pushing herself out of her husband's arms.

"Do you know how to do that?" Kateri asked, her brow furrowed. "I mean, it's not like being on a permanent vacation or anything…"

"Kat, I guess you don't know this, but my grandparents, God rest their souls, used to run a motel," Alex said. "They ran the Red Roof outside Manassas."

"I grew up doing the accounts and helping to run the business," Mom said. "Every day after school I used to fold sheets and make beds and wash dishloads of coffee cups—Of course, the little Red Roof was nothing like the forty-room resort hotel we just bought, but still, I sort of know the business."

"And we'll help out, right boys?" Alex said. "I guess you don't remember Grandpappy's Red Roof, but I do." He had vivid recollections of running races in the laundry cart down the long hallway, helping to strip beds every morning, and sitting beside his grandfather at the desk, watching him take down reservations.

"The hotel we bought isn't really a very posh place," Dad said to Kateri. "Big, but not fancy or anything. Still, we'll be living in one of the most beautiful locations on earth. The mountains of Virginia. Canoeing, fishing, hiking…"

"*Will* it be like a permanent vacation?" Sam wanted to know.

Alex winked at him. "Jogging my memory," he said, "I think it will be almost the complete *opposite* of a permanent vacation. But that's all right. You'll build character."

Kateri was nearly in complete opposition to the Mad Hotel Adventure, as she called it. "This can't be good for your mom's health," she confided to Alex Monday morning, while his mom busily worked over charts and graphs, writing a business plan. "There's no way she can do this. Hotel work is exhausting."

"You don't know my mom," Alex said positively. "I think it's good for her to have something she can do. I like seeing her so energized."

"She's going to need lots of help," Kateri frowned. "It's not prudent." They were cleaning the kitchen together after supper. "Yes, your mom might know how to do the books—"

"My dad will be CEO of the company and night manager, I'll be the day manager, my brothers will be the wait staff and cleaning staff. We'll hire out what we can't take on ourselves. My mom's budgeting it all out. If we trim our personal expenses, live on the interest, we can put all the profits back into the business and make it work, even if we eventually do lose the Mystery Money. It's all figured out."

"But so many things could go wrong—at any part of that equation! Starting with your mom's health. Suppose she takes a turn for the worse? It's a terrible risk—and you have no backup."

Alex pushed away his annoyance with her. He could see that it wasn't in his interests to quarrel with Kateri right now. She was due to leave this evening, and he had a feeling that if they parted on bad terms, she would use the opportunity to break up with him. And under no circumstances did he want her to do that.

He tried to broker a compromise. "Okay, you're right. It's probably not very prudent. But you have to admit it's clever. It's about the one thing you can do with a million dollars without spending any of it."

"Yes," Kateri agreed. "It *is* clever." She shook her head, washing silverware. "It's completely unfair of you, Alex. Playing on my pro-life sympathies like this."

"Pro-life sympathies?" Alex asked, stacking plates.

"You know I've run protests all through college in defense of the most vulnerable: unborn babies, the sick, the elderly—you must have known that I'd find it impossible to leave your mother, suffering from MS, and under threat from mysterious money and mad hotel adventures."

He chuckled. "Genius that I am, I never considered that," he said. Suddenly wary, he leaned against the stove. "Wait a minute—are you saying that you've been extending your stay because of my mom, not because of me?"

"Sort of," she muttered, throwing down her sponge. "Oh, Alex! I can't help how I feel! Don't make me—"

"Wait," he said, putting a finger on her lips. "Just wait right there. Don't say it. Don't say anything." He put his arms around her. "This will all work out."

She tried to push away from him, but he didn't let go. "How can you say that?" she complained. "It's not working out! It's completely illogical. You're thinking with your feelings!"

"Thinking with my feelings?" he gave a small laugh. "How illogical is that? You can't think with a feeling. First law of logic: A is not B. You *must* be a girl. But seriously—" he released her but still held her hands. *She doesn't think it's working out. Between us.*

*…But she likes my mom.*

Very well, he could use that to his advantage: Kateri had just told him how to get around her. "You're right, it's a foolish, mad thing that we're going to put my mom through."

Kateri looked almost as though she were going to cry. "And I'm sorry, Alex, but I just don't believe that you and your dad and brothers are going to be able to do everything that your mom needs done in order to run a business and get the rest she needs. The details! The little things around the house women see that men don't! And now you're adding a hotel into the mix—I don't see how you can do this alone."

"Exactly so," Alex said, allowing a slow, inviting smile to spread over his face, trying not to feel wicked. "Which is why, of course, that we're going to hire you to come with us."

The expression of shocked bewilderment on her Asian face was precious. Then her brows, eyes and lips shot down with adamancy. "No."

"You are, Kateri," he said, drying his dish placidly. "You are your own worst enemy. You *know* you're coming. You almost can't help yourself."

With a grin, he tossed the towel over his shoulder. "And I know you'll be our most valued asset." Whistling, he stepped into the living room. "Ahem. May I speak to the CFO of the Twilight Hotel Corporation? Mom? Make sure you include an item in that business plan for an Assistant Manager. And make sure you include a generous starting salary." He returned to the kitchen and confronted her.

"This is bribery." Kateri was still struggling to regain power of speech.

"Call it what you will. You need a job, and I'm offering you one you're perfectly suited for. You can't refuse." He drew himself up. "And if you require it, I can even relate to you on a strictly collegial basis, if that's what you need to feel more comfortable."

She eyed him suspiciously. "So you're saying I can break up with you, so long as I work for your family?"

He inclined his head. "Of course," he said. "It won't be so much *fun* that way but…"

"Oh!" she threw up her hands. "Okay. I accept."

"Fantastic!" he exclaimed, but caught himself. "Wait: do I get to kiss you, or should we just shake hands?"

"Hands," she said, her face still guarded.

A little stung, he nevertheless grinned and shook her hand. "Welcome to the company."

On the bus, Kateri burrowed her head in her hands and closed her eyes. She could still see the receding figure of Alex in her mind: all in black, wistful, smiling, waving goodbye to her as she looked out the huge plate-glass bus window. How had she gotten herself into this? Every time she had steeled herself to have a serious talk with Alex about their relationship, something had happened to distract her from the topic.

No, she realized: *Alex* had happened. He'd change the subject, asked her about something else, or just kept up a stream of what her dad called Irish blarney—the gift of the gab—to keep her from pursuing the issue.

So now she was leaving Virginia, and the big item on her to-do list: *Break Up With Alex*: was still undone. Not only that, somehow she had promised to come back. To work for the O'Donnell family and the Twilight Hills Hotel. Only Alex could have machinated this.

Not only done this, but done it in such a way that somehow she wasn't mad at him. Part of her was relieved to get a job, and thankful to have some life direction. And, she had to admit that Alex was right: no, it didn't make *sense* for her to do this. But it would probably be *fun*.

Fun. Alex used that word a lot, and she didn't like it. Fun didn't necessarily lead to happiness. And she doubted that God's plan for her life hinged on it being *fun*.

And then there was the whole matter of where the Mystery Money had come from in the first place…

Leaning back in her seat, she pulled out her rosary. *Might as well pray for some discernment.* With Alex O'Donnell's family as her employers, she was going to need it.

Alex missed Kateri. The nagging uncertainty of whether or not she would actually return was an ache in his stomach that woke him up early every morning. Fortunately, things were moving so fast now that he didn't have time to dwell much upon it once he actually got out of bed.

Their house sold. They signed the seller's contract, agreed to vacate in a week, and then the next day drove down to the town of Hunter Spring where the Twilight Hills Hotel was located, and crowded into the cramped office of a mountain realty company to sign reams of paperwork that began and ended with a handshake.

Afterwards all the O'Donnells and the real estate agent went out to a local steakhouse to eat prime rib and clink glasses with the former owners, an ancient couple from India, Mr. and Mrs. Bhatka. The Bhatkas had immigrated to America as newlyweds and sunk all their family money into the hotel until it had become a successful and steady, if not a booming, business.

The two families spent the evening trading stories and sharing wisdom. Mr. and Mrs. Bhatka were moving to Florida to be near their children and grandchildren, who had gone into the tech industry. They were tickled at the reverse movement of Mr. O'Donnell leaving the tech industry for the hotel business. The Bhatkas insisted that they would be delighted to stay on for a week or two after the O'Donnells finished their move to help them transition into full owners of the hotel.

The Twilight Hills Hotel was, fittingly enough, perched upon a hill—a hill so high it could have been called a mountain, but since the hill was surrounded by mountains, the competition had disqualified it. It was a three-story modern block structure in the typical mold of windows-and-balconies along two sides. It had a wide front lobby in retro 70's décor, a pool, a sauna, a weight room, a hot tub, a small breakfast area that overlooked the view of the south side, a conference room, and on-site living quarters for the owners. As a hotel, it was small-to-middling, but for the O'Donnell family, and Alex in particular, it seemed like a big job.

*Nothing like a challenge to take your mind off things,* Alex told himself. He spent practically the entire next day talking with Mr. Bhatka about what it took to run a hotel, trying to gather as many pearls of wisdom as he could.

"As day manager," Mr. Bhatka said, indicating Alex's t-shirt, "never in your shirt sleeves. Always the jacket. It tells people that this is a quality establishment. Some things you always have consistent. No fingerprints on the countertop and front door. Always gleaming. The things the guests first see must always be beautifully clean. Even if you clean them twenty-six times a day!"

Mr. Bhatka was shorter than Alex, but he had an energetic stride. Alex had a hard time keeping up with him as he followed him up and down the hallways, which were papered in beige linen and carpeted with huge overblown abstract flowers, vintage 70's. The hotel owner pointed to the bank of cabinets in the breakfast area. "See scratches on the doors? Just old. You should replace. Soon. Too noticeable."

He swung through the door that led to the hallway of first floor guest rooms and guided Alex past the rows of identical blank doors. "Make sure there are no fingerprints on the doors," Mr. Bhatka instructed. "First thing the guest sees." He indicated the door, which opened with a regular key. "Needs to be upgraded. Most hotels now have key card locks. Upgrade soon!"

"I'm sure my dad will: he used to work in security systems," Alex said.

Mr. Bhatka unlocked the door with a brass master key, and threw it open. "What do you see?"

Alex took in the neat double bed with the floral spread, the mountains beyond a wall of floor-to-ceiling glass. "The view."

"What do you NOT see?" Mr. Bhatka paused for an answer, then smiled. "The window! They must NOT see the window!"

"Ah. Right. Of course. Let me guess—no fingerprints?" Alex said.

"You catch on quick," Mr. Bhatka nodded. "The guest cannot see the gorgeous view if there are fingerprints, correct?" He yanked a gray flannel cloth out of his pocket. "Always on hand. Polish, polish!"

He rubbed what seemed like a non-existent spot on the glass, then turned and solemnly handed the cloth to Alex, as though it were even more precious than the master key to the hotel. "Yours. Never walk the floors without it."

"I'll keep it on hand at all times," Alex promised, pocketing the cloth. Rising to the challenge of managing a hotel was keeping him interested. He just kept hoping Kateri would keep her promise to come back.

It was a most enlightening trip, and Alex pondered it as the O'Donnell family returned to Northern Virginia the next morning with lists of most-frequently ordered items from the Bhatkas, business cards for the best vendors, including a cleaning supply warehouse that stocked gray flannel cleaning cloths. They also brought all the cabinet doors from the hotel. In a burst of energy, Mom had made Alex and Sam remove every one of the wooden cabinet doors, scratched or smooth, from the cabinets in the lobby, breakfast area, and home kitchen. That week, in between packing the house, she made the boys sand them and paint them with several coats of bright green lacquer. She propped them, one at a time, on an easel near her couch, where she was finalizing the finances for home and business. "A decorating project to revive me when I start getting tired," she explained.

"I don't know what Kateri's so worried about," Alex grunted to himself as he carried another box out of the kitchen. "You have more energy than I'd know what to do with."

His mom looked up at him with a smile. "The painting is to keep me from fretting about all the things I *can't* do," she said. "I think Kateri would approve."

Alex could understand fretting about what he couldn't do: starting with, making Kateri Kovach fall in love with him and come back down here to work with him. Except instead of painting doors, he was coordinating the move.

Last night, Alex and his dad had picked up the rental truck, and all that morning Alex had kept the boys loading boxes and furniture. Now he was glad Kateri had already de-junked the kitchen: it made that one room so much easier to pack and load. When lunchtime came, the younger boys mysteriously vanished into thin air.

"Let them off the hook, Mom," Alex said. "They're going to crack from all this work."

"I suppose you're right," she admitted. She selected a long paintbrush and dipped it into first red and then white paint. Biting her lip, she poised the brush over the blank green cabinet door on the easel and slowly began to stroke out the wide petals of a cherry blossom.

Alex watched the petals take shape beneath her skill, and felt the tension inside him start to lessen. "You're really getting good at this, Mom."

"Nothing like a fresh start to give you inspiration," she said, adding light feathery pink pollen to the flower stamens.

"Where's Dad?"

"He got a call from a friend who has about a hundred of those key card locks sitting in his warehouse. He's willing to let them go for cheap. Your dad went to pick them up."

"That's awesome," Alex said. "Now we just need to get them installed."

"Your dad thinks he can do it himself. It's just some circuit boards. That way, we can save on the installation."

"Even better," Alex said, internally relieved. He'd been worried about the old-fashioned locks on the hotel room doors.

"Mom, can I ask you what you think about the mystery money?" he asked her abruptly.

Her eyes remained focused on the brush. "You can ask," she said. "But I say…" She dipped her brush into the paint again. "I say we should trust your dad."

"Are you sure he didn't do anything illegal? I know Dad sort of likes to push the boundaries of 'legal,' but—he wouldn't steal the money, would he?" The question had been bothering him for a while.

"I think," his mother poised the brush again. "I think that if he stole the money, he'd be a little more eager to spend it, don't you?"

"Plus he'd probably have covered it up more, tried to pretend he got it some other way." Alex had to agree with his mom. His dad might be too adventurous with the keyboard for his own good, but he wasn't a thief.

Slowly his mother lowered the brush, and began to stroke out another tiny blossom. "I think he's as mystified as to how we received the money as we are."

"But I wonder if he suspects," Alex said. "Do you think—?"

"Sitting on the couch all day by myself, I think a lot of things," his mother said frankly. "But I'm going to trust your dad. And I think we all should."

Alex nodded, and patted his mom's shoulder, being careful to avoid her painting arm. "I'll get back to work then."

Arching his muscles into a full backstretch, Alex caught sight of the blinking red light of the answering machine. "Oops. Who did we miss?" He pressed the button and an angry voice filled the air.

Recognizing it, mother and son exchanged a wry look.

"Uncle Cass," Alex said, hitting the "stop" button to halt the stream of profanity. "Uh, when did you say we could pay him off, Mom?"

She set the brush down and took the checkbook out of her catchall basket. "You know, if I delayed the payment on the credit card for just three more days…" She knit her brow, then smiled. "Yes. I think we can do it. Today. Right now."

"No time like the present," Alex agreed. "I'll drive you over."

# Chapter Six

Cassim threatened to turn his brother over to the authorities unless he revealed the secret of where he had obtained so much gold.
*The Arabian Nights*

While his mother called Uncle Cass, Alex jogged outside and located his brothers, who were at the local sandlot playing baseball with the neighbors. He told them to stay put and alive for a half hour.

By the time he returned, his mother was saying to the phone, "No, the check is not in the mail. I'm bringing it over to you. This minute. You'll be there? Fine."

She attempted a smile as Alex helped her into the front seat of the car. "He didn't yell quite as much as last time we were two months late."

Uncle Cass lived in a neighborhood of McMansions: large stone houses, each on a half acre to accommodate three-car garages and landscaped terraces. It didn't matter that most of the houses were cookie-cutter copies of each other: the model alone was imposing.

"Do you think he'll be suspicious that we're paying him back in full?" Alex asked as they pulled up to the smooth black driveway. A Hispanic worker on a riding mower crossed the lawn next door in fast, even passes.

"I don't know," Mom answered, folding and unfolding her hands over the checkbook. "I'm praying he'll just be happy to have the money at last. You know he's not as rich as he looks."

"Could've fooled me," Alex muttered, shooting looks at his uncle's Jacuzzi and elaborate outdoor kitchen fireplace, used for outdoor parties that Alex's family were never invited to. Alex helped his mom out of the car, and they both made their way up the long curved walkway to the front door, Alex glancing around warily, in case the dog would come out of nowhere and attack them.

Aunt Mona answered the oversized white door, dressed in designer jeans and a frothy turquoise green blouse, oversized shell earrings dangling from her ears. Even though she was older than Mom, her red-dyed hair and makeup made her look younger. "Why are you here?" was her greeting to Mom, who was still breathless from hobbling up the long paved walkway.

"I just came to pay Cass."

"I'll tell him you're here. Come in, if you want." She peered over their shoulders and walked away, leaving the door open. Alex guessed she had only invited them in because she didn't want the neighbors to notice her embarrassingly poor relatives on the doorstep.

Alex helped his mother into the slick marble hallway. She started to sit down on the wide padded bench in the entranceway, but Aunt Mona stopped her.

"Oh, don't sit there—that's the dog's place. Persia gets out of sorts if a stranger uses it. Come into the home office."

The home office looked barely used: a palace of shining mahogany with massive bookshelves holding two or three volumes artistically interspersed with abstract glass sculptures. The air conditioner was set to freezing, and as they sat down, Alex wished he had taken Mr. Bhatka's advice and started wearing a suit jacket at all times.

Then there were steps echoing on the staircase outside the door, and Uncle Cass came into the room. He resembled Alex's dad, except Uncle Cass was tanned and shaven, his bristling black hair was cropped short, and his arms were muscular. He obviously exercised.

"Well?" he snapped. "Why so late? Another credit card crisis? What did you overspend on this time?"

Mom rose on her crutches and held out the check to him with dignity.

"I'm very sorry, Cass. I didn't mean to set you back. I know you have expenses you have to meet, too."

"You're right," he growled, sitting down behind the desk and not taking the check. "Look, Kitty, for the eightieth time, I just have to say that I feel taken advantage of. I mean, I think you and Alan know I'm not a bank who's going to take away your house and throw you out on the street, so you just put off paying me—put me off—put me off—'Hey, Cass's rich. He can spare it.' Well, listen: I'm not going to stand for any more of that."

"Cass, I just—"

"I know, I know. Always something with your health, or with the kids. Don't know what you were thinking, having all those kids."

"All those kids," Alex muttered. "I'm dating a girl who's one of eleven."

Cass scowled at him. "More crazy Catholics? Environmentally irresponsible. Overpopulation."

"I'll agree, if you agree to be part of the overpopulation," Alex said.

"There's nothing wrong with being generous in having children," Mrs. O'Donnell, who looked a bit pale, said resolutely. "Any more than there's anything wrong with being generous with money. Speaking of which, I'm happy to say that we're able to pay you back in full now for your generosity."

Cass looked even more startled, and took the check from Mom. "What's this?"

"The rest of what we owe you. With interest."

Cass stared at the amount, and turned it over in his hands, just as Alex had done with the Sundance Fun Foundation check, as though he were sure it was a fake. "That's everything?"

"Everything. I checked it with the payment plan you gave us."

"Everything?"

"Everything."

He stared, and a suspicious gleam came into his eyes, and he gave a barking laugh. "No good."

"What's no good?"

"You don't have that much in your bank account. I know Alan's paycheck and I know your disability payments. Heck, I could hack into your computer and check them if I wanted. There's no way that check is real. I get what you're doing. You're just making a play to put me off. I'll deposit this, it'll bounce, you get yourself another week before you have to pay off. Nice try, but I'm not buying it." He threw the check back at her.

Alex jumped to his feet, but his mother's hand stopped him.

Uncle Cass pointed a finger at him. "Alex, you try anything with your karate, I'm calling the police."

His mother spoke quietly, her hand still on Alex's arm. "Cass. I promise you: that check is good."

But Cass leaned back in his seat. "Bring me cash," he stated. "Cash, or nothing."

There was silence, and Alex felt his mother's patience transforming into cold Irish fury.

"Okay." She staggered to her feet with her crutches. "Cash you want? Cash it will be. Alex, bring me to the bank."

With barely controlled anger, Alex drove Mom to the bank and helped her inside. His mom, a true Irishwoman, was stolid, polite to the clerk, withdrew the money, and hobbled back out to the car.

But when they reached Uncle Cass's house, his mother's reserve finally broke. "Alex. I think I'm going to need you to bring this inside to Uncle Cass for me." She wiped her eyes and handed him the stack of bills in a large manila envelope.

"That's fine. I'll do it." He got out of the car.

"Don't kill him."

"I'll try not to." He strode up the walk to the door, opened it, and went into the home office. Uncle Cass was there, watching TV on his computer screen. He looked up at Alex sharply.

"You could have knocked."

"Here, sir, is your cash." Alex placed the envelope in front of his uncle, opened it, slid out the stack of bills and counted them out in piles of ten. "And thirty-nine cents." He stacked the quarter, nickel, and four pennies on top of the last pile and pushed it towards his uncle. "Would you like to check the bills to make sure they're not counterfeit?"

His uncle was staring—not at him, but at the money. Gingerly, he touched one corner of a crisp thousand-dollar bill.

"What is your dad up to?" he said quietly.

"Nothing that concerns you. Any more. Fortunately." Alex gave a slight bow. "Thank you again for all your help. Have a nice day."

He showed himself out, jogged down the walkway, and jumped into the car. As he pulled out in reverse as fast as he could, he bellowed, "Free at last, free at last!" Their car shot out of the cul-de-sac and he roared, "Thank God Almighty, we're free at last!"

His mother began to giggle, and they both laughed for several minutes as they breezed down the highway.

"Alex," Mom said, blowing her nose and opening up the checkbook. "Where's the bank receipt? I have to deduct this from our savings."

Suddenly Alex's hands felt cold on the steering wheel. "I left it in the envelope."

There was silence as his words sank in.

"Maybe he won't notice it," Mom said at last, trying to sound hopeful. "Maybe he'll just toss it, without looking at the amount."

But Alex knew they were both fooling themselves.

It took less than two hours for Uncle Cass to show up at the house.

Alex's dad pulled up shortly after they got home, followed by his friend with a vanload of the new keylocks. The boxes were the size of a PC and felt like they were made of bricks. And there were a hundred of them. Not to mention some oversized circuit boards in boxes the size of small refrigerators.

Transferring them to the moving van took an hour and involved unpacking and shifting around nearly all the boxes that Alex and the boys had packed that morning. So it was after five o'clock by the time the keylocks were all in the van, the friend had shaken hands with Dad and said goodbye, and the family could all go back inside the house.

No sooner had Dad wearily settled himself on the couch next to Mom to admire the six green doors propped against the wall, displaying a spray of cherry blossoms stretching over them, when the doorbell rang. Alex went to answer it.

Uncle Cass stood on the doorstep, hands balled into fists on his hips. His eyes were snapping with suppressed energy.

He barely glanced at Alex. Instead, he just looked over his shoulder and yelled into the house. "Alan? I want to talk to you."

Slowly, Dad rose and came outside. Feeling a mixture of guilt and suspicion, Alex stood behind his father on the roofless porch, both to back him up and listen in.

Uncle Cass spoke low, but his voice was charged with excitement. "Alan. I think you have something to tell me."

"Do I?" Dad shifted his weight to one foot, and looked at the ground. Despite being the older brother, Dad had always deferred to his younger sibling. Maybe because Cass always *acted* like the older brother.

"Yeah. We hackers know each other. The fact that I went legit and started working for the Federal Banking Commission just means that I'm really good at picking up scams. And I know one when I see one."

"What are you talking about?"

"You should know."

Dad looked confused, so Alex murmured into his ear, "Mom paid Uncle Cass the rest of what we owe him today. I guess he thinks we have a money printer in the basement or something."

"She did? Why did she—?" Dad started to explode, then bit his lip as Uncle Cass laughed.

"Yeah, a money printer. Wouldn't surprise me, but I know these bills are real. So, where did she get the money from?" Uncle Cass prodded.

"We took out a loan with a better interest rate," Alex attempted to put his uncle off.

But Uncle Cass went for the jugular. "A loan for over one million dollars?" He leered, dangling the left-behind bank receipt in front of his brother's face. "I don't think so."

It was all there: the savings account clearly showed the balance as well as the withdrawal. A balance of over a million dollars.

Uncle Cass leaned in closer. "Now, quit lying to me and show me how you got this money. Or I'm making a call to the office, and you're behind bars."

Alex was suddenly aware of the crickets, the cars, the hundreds of sounds dotting their neighborhood as the two brothers stared at one another in silence. Cass, arms folded, standing in his designer golf clothing; Dad, sweaty in his rumpled shirt and tie, beard messy, shoulders slumped, eyes defeated.

"All right," he said at last, putting a hand to his beard and stroking it. "You win, Cass. I'll show you."

There was an intake of breath from Cass. "Right now?"

"Right now. But not here."

"Fine by me. We'll go to my house." Cass looked at Alex and addressed him as though he were a dog. "You stay here."

"Dad?" Alex tried to meet his dad's eyes, but his father had turned to follow his brother to his car. He looked caught, beaten.

Secret or no secret, Alex didn't like leaving Dad at this moment. Thinking quickly, he darted back inside. He grabbed his keys from the rack and said to his mom, "I'll be back."

"What's going on?" Mom was starting to struggle to her feet.

"Can't tell you. Not now. Pray." He gave her a quick kiss and sped back outside.

Dad and Uncle Cass had driven off together. Alex got into his own car and followed them.

By the time he reached Uncle Cass's neighborhood, he slowed down and waited until his uncle's car had vanished into the yawning garage and the heavy paneled door had slid back down. Then he pulled over to the curb.

He rummaged around the back of his car (fortunately, despite Kateri's attempts, it was still a mess) and found a baseball cap and a new pair of hedge clippers his mom had asked him to pick up at the store the other day. None of the omnipresent immigrant landscape workers were in evidence now, but hopefully the residents wouldn't look too hard at a spare one working after five.

Jamming the hat on his head and pulling the clippers off of their cardboard backing, Alex got out of the car, and carelessly strolled up the lawn to the bushes that surrounded his uncle's house. He worked his way to one side, making judicious cuts and hoping Aunt Mona was out shopping instead of sitting inside looking at her shrubbery. When he thought he was out of sight of the windows of the opposite houses, he slipped into the concealing foliage and made his way to Uncle Cass's office window.

Sure enough, his uncle and dad were in there. They were both huddled over a computer, and he could hear them talking.

His dad's voice, "Are you sure this computer is secure?"

Uncle Cass laughed. "It's secure."

"How's it connecting? Is it using your static IP address? If so, it could be tracked—"

"Don't you worry about that. Just go ahead and hack."

"I wasn't hacking when I found this site," Dad said, a little defensive. "I was just watching." There was a pause. "Look, all I have is the sessions log from when I went in. In order to get in, we'll have to get into two different web servers ourselves to access the Sesame program. I don't feel comfortable…"

"You'll hack in there if I tell you to. And if you get stuck, I'll take over." Uncle Cass flexed his fingers and cracked his knuckles.

His dad sighed. "Well, let me show you the session logs first. I stored a copy on my web email. Here."

There was silence. Alex slowly looked over the windowsill and saw both brothers leaning over the computer screen.

"At first, I thought that Sesame was the program that cracked the password for the site," his dad said. "But when I looked at the session log, I realized it wasn't calculating that. It was finding the IP address." He shook his head. "In other words, the address for this website changes constantly: maybe even hourly. The Sesame program is what tells you where to find it. See? The program looks for a post on a microblogging site, and decrypts it to tell your browser where to go."

"Interesting," Uncle Cass said. "Probably proves the site is run by criminals. They don't want anyone to find them. Let me see that microblogging site."

His dad typed on the computer for a moment. Then his uncle pushed him aside and stared at the screen.

"I bet that's the encryption key right there. See that symbol in the logs? Ha! With that, I can reverse-engineer this thing myself," Uncle Cass said. "Move over. Let me take over."

"What are you going to do?" his dad asked.

"Crack this code."

"But if you do a brute force… No John the Ripper is going to work here."

"Shut up."

Alex shot a glance in the window to see his uncle commandeering the keyboard while his dad inched out of the chair. After a few minutes, his uncle beamed.

"How do you like that? Three minutes! Pretty good, eh? My job gives me access to a distributed cluster of rainbow tables. There's nothing it can't crack." He pointed. "And see that? Not only does it give the IP numbers to tell us where to find this site—it also gives us the username-password combination. We don't even need the Sesame program. All we need to get into the website is right here." He began to type.

"I hope you're right," Dad said, sounding unsure. "But I wonder why the other guy took the trouble to use the Sesame program? There must be something in there you need. If you don't use that program, I wonder if…"

"Hey, what happened? I just sent my information, and the screen went black."

"Guess it worked!" Dad said.

Uncle Cass glowered. "You don't have to sound so surprised. What's this?"

"Security questions," Dad said. "I think I remember the answers…" There was a pause, more typing.

"Wow!"

Silence. Alex glanced in and saw his uncle transfixed, looking at the screen. His dad sat back, scratching his beard and looking worried.

"So what are these piles of things? Is that where you can get gold, jewelry, things like that?"

"I don't know. The guy I followed didn't go there. But he did go to the room with windows—there."

"Real estate too?" Cass whistled.

"I wouldn't click on any of that," Dad cautioned. "Remember, there are menus here you can't see."

"So what did the guy you followed do?"

"He clicked on a puddle of water."

Cass laughed. "I get it. Liquid cash. Okay, take me there."

There was silence.

Now Uncle Cass chuckled. "The stone is their ATM. This is the bank. Let's see if I can make a massive withdrawal."

He typed swiftly.

"Are you sure that's a good idea?"

"Just seeing how much they have," Cass said.

"Are you sure you want to use that snail mail?"

"Should be fine! Can't you tell this is an off the record system? It probably sends the address straight to the printer and deletes it. These guys don't want anyone to know where they're sending their money to: that's obvious." He seemed to relish his cleverness. "And the site just thinks I'm one of them."

Silence. Alex saw his dad shifting, a worried expression on his face.

His uncle was typing rapidly and clicking. "I'm encrypting the data for safekeeping. Then I'll send it down my reverse DNS UDP tunnel. No trace I've been here. Did you do that?"

Alex's dad shrugged. "I didn't think to."

Uncle Cass laughed. "You didn't know *how* to, is what you mean. I've kept up to speed, Alan. I've kept up to speed." He cracked his knuckles. "So what happens now?"

"We got a check in the mail at the address I had entered," his dad said.

"For the full amount?"

"Yes."

"Wild," Uncle Cass said. And chuckled. "You did the smart thing, showing me that site, Alan. I got the whole thing in here." He tapped the laptop. "I can get in there any time I want, now."

"Hey!" His dad leaned forward. "You just closed out!"

"Yeah—so what? I thought we were done."

"I just remembered," his dad said. "The man I followed pushed a button on the cave wall to log out—and he logged out of the Sesame program on the SSH too."

"So what?" Uncle Cass shrugged. "We're out, and there's no trace we've been there."

"Cass, I'm sure we tripped some kind of alarm when we were there…"

Uncle Cass waved his hand. "You have no idea how far removed my machine is from that destination. There were over ten authentic-looking hops. I've got the number one security system in the country: the same one our spies in the field use. No one's going to be able to find me."

"Cass—"

"Alan, I know what I'm doing. And don't try to pretend you know more than me. I got tired of that game a long time ago."

His dad pulled a phone out of his pocket. "Well, if we're finished, I'll call my son to come and get me."

*Shoot.*

Alex grabbed in his pockets for his phone. *Should have seen that coming.* He yanked it out and turned it off just as the *Gladiator* theme song began.

"Is there someone…" he heard his uncle say.

Inching away from the window, Alex scuttled beneath the shrubs, grabbing the hedge clippers.

He backed out of the bushes and started making his way around the house when he heard the flap of a dog door. *Oh crap.*

All at once the barking began. Realizing that there was no way to escape notice now, Alex faced the snarling Alaskan husky.

"Hey, Persia—good doggie—hey girl—" he whispered.

Sensing someone behind him, he raised his forearms and swung round to meet his uncle's fists.

Alex blocked the blow easily, but didn't return it, his idea being to get away instead of starting a fight. But his uncle was evidently spoiling for one. He grabbed Alex by the back of the neck. "Get in here!"

"If you're finished with Dad—" Alex twisted around but his uncle clamped down painfully.

"Get in here!"

"Alex, come in," Dad said from the back door. "Let go of him, Cass!"

Alex lowered his arms and obeyed, but his uncle took advantage of this to yank the clippers out of Alex's hands and push him inside. Alex ducked, but since he was in the doorway, he couldn't get out of the way soon enough as his uncle viciously smashed the clippers on his shoulder.

With difficulty, Alex restrained himself again from striking back as he stumbled forward. It would have been easy to go straight for Uncle Cass's throat, but Alex couldn't see that any good would come of it.

"How dare you," his uncle growled, and raised the clippers again. This time Alex dodged to the side, and his uncle only succeeded in putting a gash into his drywall. Alex aimed a quick kick at the side of his uncle's kneecap, and, stunned by the pain, his uncle dropped the clippers with a curse.

"Stop!" Dad said, making a dive for the clippers.

"I'm not finished," Uncle Cass said, breathing hard, getting to his feet and lunging at Alex. "Alex started this, didn't you, Alex? What were you doing, spying on my business?"

"What were you doing, threatening my dad?" Alex retorted, hotly, circling his uncle. He didn't want to fight, but he didn't want to get hit again, either.

Uncle Cass laughed, pushing aside Dad, who was fruitlessly trying to hold him back. "Your dad is a thief."

"Then so are you," Alex said. "What were you just doing?"

"Doing my job as a federal banking commission employee," Uncle Cass said, closing in on Alex. "Investigating a fraudulent website. Nothing illegal at all. Unlike your family."

He threw another punch at Alex but Alex ducked to one side and avoided it. Uncle Cass struck again, and again Alex dodged, blocking the punch and directing his uncle's momentum. His uncle stumbled and narrowly escaped falling. He spun around and tore back into Alex, who evaded the punch again.

Seeing as he wasn't getting anywhere, Uncle Cass pulled himself together. "I could still have you both arrested—your dad for hacking, and you for assault—get out of here!"

"I'd like to see you make the assault charge stick," Alex said.

"Okay, Cass, we're going." Dad ducked between the two combatants and pulled his son out the door with him. They hurried out into the summer evening air.

Alex didn't break the silence until he and his father were safely inside the car and had pulled out onto the highway. Driving with one hand, Alex felt his shoulder gingerly and was glad that at least his uncle hadn't broken the skin. Then he took a deep breath.

"Dad, tell me what happened in there. You know where the Mystery Money came from, don't you?"

His dad groaned. "Okay. I've told your mom most of this, but you might as well know too. It was this funny website I found with the MouseCatcher."

Alex listened intently as his dad described how he had followed a user who had turned out to be a hacker. His dad had watched him hack into a website and use a program called "Sesame" to get into a mysterious private website.

Dad rubbed the lines in his forehead. "I guess whoever runs that changes the website address—the IP numbers—about every hour. That's why the user I followed used the Sesame program to calculate the web address." He groaned. "It might sound stupid, but I didn't even realize I was asking for money the first time I went. I just entered a number sequence to make the form go away. But the computer sent me a check for that exact amount."

"One million some dollars," Alex murmured. "Okay. That makes sense. So they sent you a check."

"Yes. And the computer must erase the address it's sent to automatically, because otherwise I don't know why they haven't come looking for me. But I'm not sure they'll do the same for Cass."

"You showed Uncle Cass how to get into the website?"

"Yes," his dad said. "He decided to get in without the Sesame program. He used some fancy password cracker he got from his job. And he didn't log out correctly. Plus he gave them his home address to send the check to. That was a terrible risk." He shook his head. "Alex, why'd you follow me?"

Alex winced, rubbing his shoulder. "You expect me to hear him threaten you and stay behind? Sorry, Dad. I was raised to be loyal."

"And raised to be a fighter, too. Are you hurt?"

"Just my shoulder. Serves me right for turning my back on a known enemy," Alex said.

"Cass isn't our enemy," his dad said sharply. "We're brothers."

Alex shrugged. "So were Cain and Abel."

Dad fell silent, then said, "Cass *might* just be doing his job. For all I know, he's doing research on cybercrime and will use the information to turn them in. But he made an awfully large withdrawal."

"How much?"

"Five million."

"Five million—! That's some research he's doing!"

"He swore his machine was untraceable, but I'm not so sure. I know he's treated us like dirt, Alex, but I'm really worried for him. If that stash I found has five million dollars in it—all I can say is—I'm really worried for Cass."

"Then, Dad, you're a better Catholic than me," Alex said. "Because all I can say is 'just desserts.'"

# Chapter Seven

*But when the robbers found their cave
disturbed, they realized that someone
must have discovered their secret.*

The Arabian Nights

This time when Kateri got off the bus, she was exhausted. Even though the bus ride was now four hours longer due to the O'Donnell's move south, she hadn't been able to sleep. Her parents had thought taking the job at the hotel was a wonderful idea. Her older brothers and sisters seemed to think it would be good experience for her. But Kateri herself wasn't sure. *Am I making the right choice? Moving down here when I'm not even sure I'm meant to be with Alex? Is this what God wants? Or am I just acting on my feelings?*

"Kateri's back! Hooray!"

Kateri blinked as she stepped off the bus. The entire O'Donnell family, clad in red and black shirts, was waiting for her at the bus depot, and set up a collective cheer, waving long-stemmed red roses, as she appeared. Staring at the laughing, cheering group, she felt unexpected warmth rising in her cheeks. Had they really missed her this much?

"Welcome to Hunter Springs!" David and Sam swooped around her, hugging her. Alex parted the waves and came to her, kissing her cheek and taking her luggage.

"So glad you came," he said, as though he had doubted she'd show up for some reason. Even though she'd called him to say she was coming. "How was the trip?"

"Endurable," she said. "You look like you have something to tell me."

He smiled, a little less broadly than last time. "I sure do. But it can wait till later."

"Good to see you, Kat," Mrs. O'Donnell said, leaning forward on her crutches to accept Kateri's hug. "I've missed you!"

"Good to see you, Kitty," Kateri said, and smiled. "Glad to be back. How are you holding up?"

"Ready to see our new home?" Mr. O'Donnell asked cheerfully. He was wearing a red cap that said "Twilight Hills Hotel" in black letters.

Kateri regarded him a little grimly: he was the troublemaker who had generated this whole mess she was in. "Guess so!"

The O'Donnells piled the six bags of clothes and personal effects she had brought into a white van with the Twilight Hills logo emblazoned on the back. "The owners threw it in with the sale," Mr. O'Donnell explained. "It's helped a lot."

"I think we should have it painted red, myself," Alex said.

The road led over and through mountain passes that revealed one beautiful vista after another, marred only by billboards advertising caves, water slides, and resort hotels. "Here's our new palace!" Mrs. O'Donnell exclaimed as Mr. O'Donnell turned up a long, steep black driveway.

The road wound up and around, up and around, until Kateri wondered if they would ever reach the top. For a hotel, this place was remote. But at last the building came in sight.

"There!" There was a collective sigh from the O'Donnells, who, Kateri saw, all had a sort of bemused rapture on their faces. The building coming into sight didn't look nearly as impressive as the mountains. Three stories of concrete block and steel, the narrow side walls painted a jarring blue, its windows obscured by balconies, it looked like a slightly dilapidated 1970s hotel. Which it obviously was.

It wasn't exactly Kateri's idea of a romantic honeymoon getaway. She had expected a grand old Victorian bed-and-breakfast, or a wooden lodge house. But the O'Donnells apparently loved it.

"I can't tell you how much fun it's been to fit this place out," Mrs. O'Donnell said. "We can't afford to completely update the décor, but I'm almost not sure I want to."

"We're closed for business right now while I upgrade all the locks on the doors," Mr. O'Donnell said. "But we'll have the grand re-opening this weekend."

Alex opened the glass doors to the lobby with their retro spiral-metal handles for her. As Kateri stepped inside, she felt physically assaulted by the violent yellow, pink, red, green, and purple of the carpet. The wallpaper was beige plaid, and the bank of counters that greeted her were lemon-yellow tile with green linoleum on top. Metal tube lights of yellow and green hung from the beige ceiling.

She stared around her in bewilderment.

"See? Mom painted the doors on the cabinets!" Sam pointed to the left, where a breakfast area stood beneath an alcove canopied by a sweep of chrome.

The bank of cabinet doors were painted bright green with a tree branch of red and pink cherry blossoms sweeping across it.

"Oh yeah, that makes it better," Kateri said under her breath.

Mrs. O'Donnell settled herself into the black wheelchair which stood waiting by the doorway. "I want to cover the seats of the chairs in pink satin, but Alan thinks red would go better," she said to Kateri. "What do you think?"

Kateri made a disorganized shrug, and allowed herself to be propelled by Alex towards the double doors at the other side of the lobby.

"Here's the conference room." Mr. O'Donnell threw open the doors. The room was wallpapered in red, and bamboo scrolls of Japanese calligraphy lined the sides of the room around the massive brown table. "We bought those scrolls off of eBay," Mr. O'Donnell said. "Doesn't it look neat?"

Alex pulled Kateri away through a side door before she could comment and continued the tour. "Weight room—in yellow. A little jarring, but Dad likes it. We're going to ditch most of the stuff so we can use it as a dojo. Sauna—in wood, of course. Pool!" He threw open a door to reveal a dazzling square of blue sparkling in the sunlight, surrounded by a white patio, backed with a tall black iron fence. Beyond the fence were cedar trees, and the side of the mountain.

"Beautiful trees," Kateri said, glad to be able to say something.

"Guess what? I can climb that fence, even though it's eight feet high!" Sam bragged. "Wanna see me?"

"Yes, we all know you barbarians like scaling walls," Alex said, steering Kateri back inside. "So that's the pool. What's left? Guest rooms. Forty of them."

The hallways were carpeted in the same garish oversized pattern that made Kateri dizzy as she walked over it. Alex led her down the hallway. "It's pretty much the same wherever you go," he said. "All we've really done is change the pictures."

Of course, the pictures were Oriental—mostly flowers and landscapes.

"What did they have before?" Kateri had to ask as Mrs. O'Donnell, who had come up the elevator on her wheelchair, rolled over to meet them.

"Pictures of hunting and Civil War scenes," Mrs. O'Donnell made a face. "I think the Eastern art fits better with the décor, don't you?"

"As well as anything could," Kateri managed to say.

They took the elevator up to see the third floor to show Kateri the admittedly impressive mountain view from the top floor windows.

"It's even better from the roof!" Sam said, pulling her towards the stairwell. "Come on! We've got to show you."

"We'll wait down here!" Mrs. O'Donnell called as her sons escorted Kateri away.

*What is it with the O'Donnell boys and high places?* Kateri shook her head as she followed Alex and his younger brothers up the side stair to a service door. Alex unlocked it, then pushed the door open.

"This view is for the privileged few," David intoned, leading her onto the flat gravel-covered rooftop of the hotel.

Kateri shivered at how low the roof ledge was, but Alex pulled her aside. "Look out this way to the east," he said softly. "I assure you, it's nothing like DC." He turned her around.

She gasped at the magnificent vista of the Blue Ridge Mountains stretching off into the horizon, with clouds drifting softly over their woody peaks.

"And nothing like New Jersey," she admitted. Alex chuckled, squeezing her shoulders.

"Hey!" Sam said. "Wanna know something else? I bet I could jump right into the diving well of the pool from here! Want to see if I can?"

"Absolutely not," Alex said. "Are you trying to get our hotel insurance revoked? Don't let the CFO know you even thought about it. She'd have a heart attack. Now, get downstairs!"

Grumbling, the boys followed Kateri and Alex back down the steps to rejoin the O'Donnell parents, who were discussing whether they could afford to upgrade the lighting fixtures in the hallway.

"Mr. Bhatka said we should expect to upgrade things constantly," Alex said to Kateri.

*They've obviously never upgraded the color scheme since they bought the place,* Kateri thought.

Alex continued, "Incrementally, so we never have to close down the hotel again for repairs. You know, we'll just do one floor or one room at a time."

Kateri shook her head. "Sounds like a lot of money," she said. "You think you can afford to keep this running, on just the interest of the Mystery Money?"

"Maintenance is in the budget," Alex said. "We have one year to sink or swim. But the first three months should let us know if we're going to make it."

"Plus I got a great deal on the new security locks from a former colleague," Mr. O'Donnell said. "They open with keycards—you know, those plastic keys that look like credit cards. I've been installing them on all the doors in the hotel. Hopefully it'll be the last time we have to close the hotel for repairs."

Together the family took the elevator back to the lobby, Kateri bracing herself for the shock of retro color this time. It wasn't quite so bad. *But I hate the idea that I might get used to it.*

"And here is where we'll be living," Alex said, opening a side door leading off the lobby. He led the way down a hallway to a suite of rooms at the back.

Kateri drew in her breath: it was completely different from the O'Donnell's old house: as open and organized as the old house had been cramped and cluttered.

It was an open floor plan with kitchen, dining room, and living room all in one area, the long, large kitchen separated from the rest by an island with black metal bar stools. The walls were white and pale blue. There was a TV in one corner, but the main area was done in traditional Japanese style: sisal mats, small tables, large throw cushions in subdued patterns scattered about a low coffee table containing one black shining vase, round as a large marble, with a spray of artificial cherry blossoms in it. A black brocade futon couch sat against one wall, near a low chest where the family statues of Christ and Mary stood, a round grass basket of colored enamel-beaded rosaries between them. The emblematic glass fishing weights and potted plants hung from the ceiling, but the room was distinctively clean, fresh, and uncluttered. Link the Cat lay on a cushion in a sunny spot, looking even more relaxed and contented than usual.

Kateri gradually became aware that all the O'Donnells were watching her amazed expression with wide smiles.

"See, Kateri? We learned from you. I thought we'd use the move to phase out of a lot of things," Mrs. O'Donnell said. "I told the boys that if we got rid of almost everything, I'd treat them to new furniture and a new game system."

"Of course we did it because of the new gaming system," David said, running to the corner where a gleaming silver console stood by the TV and stroking it lovingly.

"It's amazing what you can do when you have more room," Mr. O'Donnell admitted. "What do you think?"

"She doesn't know what to say," Alex said. "We've completely shocked her. I don't think she thought it was possible."

Kateri could only stand there and nod.

Just as in their old house, the O'Donnells were making do with two small bedrooms—one for all three boys and one for the married couple. "But we're used to small bedrooms," Sam assured her. They had brought their bedroom furniture from the old house. But in one corner of the master bedroom, Mr. O'Donnell's laptop computer sat on a new desk of gleaming red lacquer.

The home computer was in its own niche in the kitchen. Kateri noted the kitchen had the same green doors with pink flowers, but they weren't quite as jarring here.

"We just can't figure out where to put our swords and weapons," Alex said. "Right now they're in an umbrella stand in Dad's room, which isn't at all dignified. Let me show you your room."

He was still holding her hand, and now guided her back down the hallway, through the lobby, and over to the first of the guest doors. "We figured this would be the easiest setup," he said. "But if you don't like this room, we can always change it for one of the thirty nine others."

He took out a key and pushed open the heavy door. Inside was a typical hotel room—queen-sized bed, boxy end tables, round table, thick boxy chairs with wooden arms. "Since you're a special guest, though, I gave you the upgrade," Alex said. He pointed to a spray of red roses on the end table, and a pair of chocolates on the pillowcase. "Welcome to the Twilight Hills Hotel, Kateri. I hope your stay will be long, and pleasurable."

She couldn't help smiling as she pushed back her hair. "Thank you, Alex."

They stood in the doorway and looked at each other. Alex was more groomed than he had been when she last saw him. He wore a black button-down shirt instead of his typical t-shirt, his beard was trimmed and his hair neatly combed back. Otherwise he looked just as relaxed and competently muscular as usual.

With a flush of warmth, she realized that she hadn't had a moment to take in the reality that she was going to be spending a lot of time with Alex O'Donnell. He seemed to realize that as well, and cleared his throat.

He waved a hand. "Feel free to do anything you want to the room. We can change out the furniture if you want. But don't do anything too permanent: if we get overbooked, we might have to kick you out for a night."

"That only makes sense," she said. "So—" she was about to ask him what he wanted to tell her, but Sam and David were pushing a brass luggage cart into the lobby, piled with her baggage. She changed the subject. "So when do we open for business, Mr. Day Manager?"

"Two days," he said. "Want to have a swim to cool off before dinner?"

That actually sounded wonderful. "Sure," she said gratefully. Despite the air conditioning, she felt hot and sticky.

He bowed. "We'll leave, and let you get settled."

After the O'Donnell brothers left, Kateri looked around the room, feeling a bit helpless. At least the carpet wasn't that horrible yellow-and-red tulip pattern, but the green plaid wasn't much better. No matter what she did to it, this room was going to feel like a hotel and not a home. But she had agreed to get involved. And to spend the rest of the summer here. Getting to know Alex and his family. How had this happened?

Resigning herself, she began to unpack, looking for her swimsuit.

She met Alex at the pool a short time later. He had changed into a swimsuit and tee, and was sitting on a lounge chair, checking email on his laptop, while Sam and David cavorted in the water.

"Want to talk now?" she said.

Alex glanced at his brothers. "Nah. It can wait."

"At least they're outside more," she indicated the boys.

"Yes. They'll have a lot less free time now," he said wryly. "Good thing it's summertime. In the fall, when school starts and they have to work the hotel *and* do school, they're going to value their recreation time."

"But things should be slower then," Kateri pointed out.

He cocked his head. "According to Mr. Bhatka, fall was one of their busiest times. The tourists come to admire the fall foliage and attend festivals. It's not so hot and muggy then."

"Well, the winter should be pretty slow."

"Would you believe there's skiing, even this far south? It's amazing what kind of business you can do with a good slope and a snow machine."

"So when *do* you slow down?"

"Spring, maybe? Or perhaps this *is* the slow time. I can't tell." He closed his laptop and got up. "Ready for the water?"

"Sure." She felt a little awkward and self-conscious in her blue swimsuit with the floral swim skirt. Her suit had good coverage, but she felt more on display than usual, and wished she had worn a t-shirt.

She resolutely averted her gaze from Alex's sleek biceps and chest muscles as he pulled off his shirt, but she gasped as he turned around to dive in.

"What happened to your shoulder?" There was a large black-and-blue bruise running across his back.

He glanced at it and blinked. "Oh. It probably looks worse than it feels."

"Did you—drop a dresser on it or something?"

For an answer, he dove into the water, and, feeling misgivings, she jumped in after him. It wasn't like Alex to answer a question with silence.

The shock of the cool water was relaxing, but she didn't forget her question as she surfaced.

"Alex, what happened?"

He had started to do a lap, and she thought he hadn't heard her, but reaching the far side of the pool, he paused, and she caught up with him.

"Alex?"

He stared at the opposite end of the pool, water dripping from his face and ponytail. A long loud ringing was echoing over the courtyard.

"What's that?" Sam said, pausing in his act of holding a spluttering David under water.

"I bet it's the house phone," Alex said, and then laughed. "Mr. Bhatka probably set it so loud so that he could hear it ring even when he was out swimming."

The ring continued, loud and insistent.

"Will someone get that?" Alex bellowed.

No answer except the ringing.

"I'll get it," he started to get out of the pool, but Kateri grabbed his arm.

"No escaping," she warned.

"Sam, David! Race to the phone!" he shouted. "Winner gets to use my computer!"

Sam and David instantly scrambled out of the pool and pelted inside, spraying water everywhere.

"Once we have guests here, I'll have to yell after them, 'No running in the pool area!'" Alex said ruefully. "But for now it's okay."

"Alex, I want an explanation for why you have a massive bruise you're reluctant to talk about," Kateri said.

The ringing stopped, and Alex blew out a sigh and sat on the side of the pool. Kateri grabbed his shoulder to pull herself up beside him and he involuntarily yelped.

"It *does* hurt you," she accused.

"I guess it does," he admitted. "I must be getting out of shape."

"So what happened?"

"Just had a run-in with Dad's younger brother. Uncle Cass."

"A run-in? How?"

"He hit me with a pair of clippers. He's a jerk. That's all."

"He hit you with a—Alex, what were you doing? Was it an accident?"

"Sorry to say, no. Just in line with how he usually treats me."

"You two usually fight?"

Alex shrugged. "He's always slapped me around. Bad temper. He's probably the reason I got into martial arts in the first place, come to think of it. I was so sick and tired of being knocked down and sat on at every family reunion."

"He would bully you like that?" Kateri exclaimed, sitting up. "Didn't your parents know?"

Alex shook his head. "I don't think I told them. Stupid of me. But I was smart enough to make sure he kept away from my kid brothers."

Kateri was so horrified she almost didn't know what to say. "What a jerk! He must have problems."

"Yeah, I don't know why a grown man would go out of his way to be so mean to a kid like me. I mean, I was probably annoying, but nothing to justify how he would treat me when no one else was looking." He spoke nonchalantly.

She was still processing. "I don't understand people like that. Even after four years of studying mental health, I don't understand why some adults will beat up kids."

Alex put his head to one side and scratched his chin. "I've sort of tried to analyze him, and I think it might have been a holdover from when he was a kid himself. He's Dad's younger brother, and they probably fought a lot. I guess when he found himself in the presence of a short fat little kid who looked just like his big brother, it put him in touch with his inner thug."

Kateri looked at Alex critically. "You were fat?"

He shrugged. "Sure. I was pudgy, just like my brothers are. And not good at sports. But one day when I was ten, I saw an old Jackie Chan movie where Jackie takes out this guy who's three times bigger than he is, and I thought, 'Wow, I got to learn how to do that!' So I pestered my parents until they enrolled me in karate, and the rest, as they say, is history."

He tugged at his ponytail, wringing it out. "But that wasn't the end of my battle with Uncle Cass. Soon as he found he couldn't throw me around the same way—I gave him a nasty surprise at the family reunion when I was fourteen and he tried to knock me into a pond—he started in on the psychological battle. God, the Church, values, current events—he had to prove I was stupid somehow. So I had to learn to think and argue to defend my beliefs. In some ways, I've actually learned a lot because of him."

Kateri pushed her damp hair behind her ears. "You amaze me. If it were me, I'd be so angry with him, I couldn't even talk about him. You're incredibly calm about this. And *you're* supposed to be the fighter."

Alex's smile was quirky. "Well, I've learned how to deal with him now. And I don't exactly trust him, and we'll never be buddies. But in a way, he's made me who I am today. So I guess I have to be grateful, don't I?"

"He made you what you are today? I can't believe that."

He stretched. "Well, I almost had to define myself in opposition to him. Even in how I cut my hair. We're just diametrically opposed on everything—religion, family life, politics—you name it. Even Dad is more middle of the road than I am. Cass is a raving liberal, so of course I got interested in conservative politics." He shook his head. "And our lifestyles are different too. He's rich—we're poor. Well, we *used* to be poor, and he used to be poor too. He wouldn't have gotten through college without Dad's financial help. But when Mom got sick, Dad asked him to help cover the bills so we wouldn't lose our house. And—" Alex waved his hand. "He's been a jerk about it."

"Sounds like he's one splendid uncle."

"He's a piece of work." Alex shoved himself into the pool. "But doesn't everyone have at least one screwy relative? Anyhow, I'm glad we paid off the loan and we don't have to deal with him any more."

Kateri was quiet, thinking this over. It was hard to imagine Alex as a helpless, chubby awkward boy, facing up to a mean older relative. "So you've forgiven him, Alex?"

Alex glanced at her. "I think I have. Actually I prayed the rosary for him last night. Dad's worried about him. I mean, more than usual."

"It amazes me that you can talk about him making you who you are today."

Alex laughed. "I'm sure if Uncle Cass had ever thought his actions would have produced a guy like me, he'd have given me lollipops and bought me hashish instead of always trying to sock me and then ask me about the dumb things I learned in Catholic school." With a quick tug, he easily pulled Kateri into the pool. "C'mon. Race you to the other side!"

Giving up, she threw herself into the water beside him and swam as fast as she could. She managed to tie with him, but he grinned and leapt sideways. "Race you back!"

She swam after him but gave up after he pulled three lengths ahead. He waited for her to finish, and planted a kiss on her head as she bobbed up from the water on the last stroke.

"Did I ever tell you that you're beautiful when you're wet?"

She was about to make an acid reply when she spotted David. He had come out of the courtyard door and was standing on the pavement, staring at them with a horrified expression on his face.

"David?" Alex said, following Kateri's gaze. "What's wrong? What happened?"

David seemed to be struggling to speak. At last he came out with it. "Uncle Cass is dead."

# Chapter Eight

*Thus the robbers discovered the unhappy
man and slew him as a warning to all those
who might dare to pilfer their treasure.*
*The Arabian Nights*

*L*ess than an hour later, the entire O'Donnell family and Kateri were
in the Twilight Hills Hotel van and speeding back up the highway to
Northern Virginia.

Alex had taken the wheel. His father was in no state to drive. Kateri was
riding shotgun, and Alex knew she was praying silently as she sat, fingering her
scapular. Sam and David, more quiet than usual, sat in the back seat, not
playing video games. Alex's dad was sitting in front of the boys next to Mom, his
head in his hands. Alex could hear his sobs as they drove.

Aunt Mona had called them, after she had looked up the hotel number on
the Internet. She was in hysterics, and she had been ever since Uncle Cass had
dropped dead in the hospital emergency room.

Aunt Mona had just thought her husband had the flu. He'd been
complaining of a sore throat and headache for a few days. But then he started
having trouble breathing, and Aunt Mona rushed him to the hospital. While
they were filling out the paperwork, he went into shock, and fell backwards onto
the emergency room floor, ballpoint pen still in hand. He was dead fifteen
minutes later.

Alex wasn't feeling anything just now: just concentrating on driving the van
and getting his parents there safely. But a steady tattoo of questions was running
through his mind.

"It's so bizarre," Mom said, breaking into Alex's thoughts. "To die of the
flu—in this day and age."

"It's like God's judgment," Kateri said, and then quickly looked at Alex. "I'm
sorry," she said, a bit husky. "I didn't know him. I guess from what you told me
about him, I don't like him very much. Maybe he was nicer in person?"

Alex found himself wanting to laugh. "No. He wasn't." He silenced himself.

"Guess he didn't get his flu shot. Too weird. Too random." David shook his head, in a fourteen-year-old's attempt to come to grips with the tragedy.

Alex looked into the rear-view mirror, and met his father's red eyes. Instantly he knew that he and Dad were thinking the same thing. Uncle Cass had not died of the flu. And his death was not random.

When they arrived at Aunt Mona's house, she met them at the door. Her red hair was disheveled and she was missing one oversized earring. "Oh Alan! Oh Kitty!" she exclaimed, and fell into his dad's arms, sobbing while his mom patted her on the back. It was as though all the bad feelings between them had evaporated, and they were back to behaving like a normal family. Had his parents and Aunt Mona ever gotten along? Maybe a long time ago? Alex wasn't sure.

He stood to one side a bit awkwardly, with Kateri and his brothers, while his mom and dad helped Aunt Mona to the massive oak kitchen, where his dad started making tea at Mom's suggestion. After a moment or two of standing around while the grownups fell to talking and weeping, the younger generation drifted back into the living room.

"Keep quiet so they can have some space," Alex said in a hushed voice to Sam and David, who obeyed with unusual attention.

In the living room, Sam sank onto the white leather couch, while David stood around fidgeting, hands in his pockets. Kateri sat down carefully on a white satin antique-looking chair.

"Nice house," Kateri said, looking around, apparently wanting to say something.

"If you like this sort of thing," Alex said, his eyes traveling over the opulent room with its glass coffee table showcasing marbleized Venetian glass paperweights that probably had never held down any paper. *Vanity of vanities*, he thought randomly, and made himself say another prayer for his uncle's soul. It was odd to think that Uncle Cass, his enemy for so long, was dead. And no longer an enemy.

He noticed a picture hanging very low on the wall, and recognized that it was probably covering the place where the drywall had been punched in during the fight. Although he was sorely tempted, he decided not to mention it to Kateri.

But now that he had started thinking about that night, Alex couldn't stop. In a moment, he had crossed to the door of the home office and tried it. It was open.

Glancing around, he made a decision and slipped inside.

The office was in more disarray than the last time Alex had seen it. Books and papers were scattered everywhere. He stepped cautiously, looking around carefully.

"Hey, what are you doing?" David said, pushing open the door. "You trying to get onto their computer or something?"

"Shh! No."

Kateri was behind him. "Alex, why are you in here?"

"Just curious."

"CKTC!" Sam piped up from behind her.

"You shouldn't be in here," Kateri warned, hands on her hips.

"I'm not touching anything! I'm just looking," Alex rounded the corner of the desk. The laptop was open, but it was off. He looked carefully over the large mahogany surface.

At last he spotted what he was looking for, in the wastebasket: a torn envelope from the Sundance Fun Foundation. But it wasn't a paper envelope: it was a red padded envelope that looked as though it had been heavily taped.

*So Uncle Cass had gotten his check.*

He reached down for the envelope and found his hand caught by Kateri's.

"You just said you weren't going to touch anything," she reminded him.

Now he was annoyed. "I'm just looking in his trashcan!" he whispered.

"Doesn't matter! It's in his office!"

"Look, will you stop picking a fight?"

"*I'm* picking a fight? You're the one who's poking around in someone's private papers!" she hissed. "Leave it alone, or I'll call your aunt!"

"Fine," he retreated from the trashcan. "If you want to be pigheaded about it…"

Just then, the doorbell rang loudly, right behind them.

All of them jumped. Hurriedly, they all exited the office. Feeling guilty despite himself, Alex attempted to open the door calmly. "Can I help you?"

Two men in dark suits stood on the doorstep. One was short, with blond, bristling hair and a stiff, wooden expression, the other was tall, dark haired, and thoughtful-looking. Behind them, a police car was quietly pulling up to the curb. The taller man produced an ID. "I'm Agent T. Furlow of the Federal Bureau of Investigation. We need to speak to Mrs. Cassidy O'Donnell."

Hearing the doorbell, Aunt Mona had staggered out from the kitchen, trailed by Alex's parents. "I'm right here," she managed to say. "What—?"

"Mrs. O'Donnell," the agent said, looking sober. "Agent Furlow of the Federal Bureau of Investigation. This is my partner, Carter Randolph. May we speak to you?"

"Come in," she said, backing up.

"Actually, I'll need to ask you to step outside," Agent Furlow said apologetically. There were police officers coming up the walk. Aunt Mona didn't seem to like this idea, but the FBI was the FBI. She came out onto the walk, holding her arms around herself, trailed by Kateri and the O'Donnells.

The agent glanced around. "Are these people your relatives?"

"Yes." Aunt Mona started to shake. "Oh God. What did Cass do? Is he in trouble?"

"Not any more," Agent Furlow said. "But perhaps the rest of us are. The medical examination showed us the cause of your husband's death."

"It wasn't the flu," Alex guessed, speaking aloud before he could stop himself.

The agent gave him a keen look from his blue eyes. "No." He turned back to Aunt Mona. "He died of ricin inhalation, a biohazard contaminant. I'm afraid we need to quarantine this house in order to search for the source of the contaminant." He looked at the rest of them. "Also, for your own protection, everyone in the house needs to be given medical attention immediately. We have our biohazard unit coming to escort you all to a medical facility for decontamination and observation."

*He didn't mention that it was going to be a top-secret medical facility*, Kateri thought to herself hours later as she sat in her windowless room, staring at the cinderblock wall. After the agent's pronouncement, what had followed was something out of a science-fiction movie. An eighteen-wheeled truck had backed into the cul-de-sac and a team of men in puffed-out yellow suits with masks descended on the house. The O'Donnells and Kateri weren't allowed to return to the house, not even to get Mrs. O'Donnell's purse. Instead, they had all been asked to get inside the truck, which turned out to have a complete decontamination facility inside of it.

After being shown to a private shower, Kateri was instructed to wash twice with a decontamination solution and rinse, scrubbing for at least five minutes for each session (she did ten). At some point during her third shower, she became aware that the truck was moving, and realized, with a tremor in her stomach, that she was completely in the hands of the US Government. As someone who had been raised by her parents to be a conscientious objector, this was fairly terrifying.

She wasn't allowed to get her clothes back: in fact, she suspected that her entire outfit—her vintage blue peasant blouse from mom, the jeans she had borrowed from her sister Teresa, and her favorite wooden clogs—was gone for good. They said she might get her medal of St. Catherine back eventually. They had strongly suggested she should unwrap the thread from the thin braids in her hair, and, Kateri, juggling in her mind between dissenting again government interference and the possibility of contracting a biohazard disease, submitted.

She'd had those tiny braids wrapped for the past four years of college, one for each time she'd been arrested for leading a protest. With a few furtive tears, she acknowledged that that time in her life was probably over for good as she unwrapped the braids and handed the tangled thread over to the female agent monitoring the shower unit. *Another compromise. Great.*

When the agent gave her a pair of Wal-Mart sweats to wear instead, in pink and purple, it didn't make her feel any better about her surrender.

After she was dressed, she was shown to another small cubicle somewhere in the bowels of the truck, and FBI Agent Carter Randolph, who, Kateri quickly discovered, had the personality of a two-by-four plank, came to interview her about what had happened at the uncle's house. Of course, he was wearing a face mask and rubber gloves, which probably inhibited his personal interaction.

Kateri, who, due to life experience, knew a thing or two about talking to the feds, matched her behavior to his and answered his questions without any elaboration, just telling him what he wanted to know and not giving any extra details. She hoped she wasn't sweating.

*If they dig up my records and do a background check, I bet I'll be their prime suspect.* After all, she had willingly disobeyed abortion clinic access laws repeatedly during her college years, and her older siblings had been labeled as terrorists because they had organized nonviolent protests against abortion.

But the agent didn't ask her any questions about her past, and after a while, Kateri realized that all the O'Donnells, who had been questioned as well, would probably corroborate what she'd told the agent: she'd never met Uncle Cass. She'd been in his house only about fifteen minutes. By the time she'd even heard of the existence of Cassidy O'Donnell, he was already dead.

It took about two and a half hours for the truck to reach its destination. That destination turned out to be some sort of massive bunker of a medical facility with no windows and no identification. She'd been examined by a doctor wearing a HEPA filter, her vital signs were taken, and then she was shown to a private bedroom, hooked up to an IV, and left alone with a stack of fashion magazines and a television.

Even if they didn't know about or care about her activist background, how could she possibly trust these people who had locked her into this concrete bunker like a prisoner? For someone who was used to having her civil rights infringed, it wasn't exactly easy to relax. And the thought of being killed by biohazard exposure: well, to the daughter of an organic farmer, this was nothing but ironic. *Serves me right for coming to Northern Virginia…*

She didn't open the magazines or turn on the television, just stared at the concrete block wall, trying not to give into paranoia and wondering what in the world she'd done to get herself involved with Alex's family and this crazy mess.

As the son of a Beltway employee involved in security, Alex had always known that the US government had many resources when it came to terrorist attacks, but he'd never dreamed that he'd be able to benefit directly from them. During the decontamination process and medical exam, he'd looked around as much as possible and, after estimating the direction of the truck and the length it took to arrive at their destination, he'd figured out that his family and Kateri were being treated at a facility somewhere west of Mt. Weather. That was the demarcation line for the estimated blast zone of a nuclear attack on Washington DC.

Once he was left alone in his hospital room, he'd gotten out of bed and examined what he could of the room, including the mattress, which was premium (his tutorial with Mr. Bhatka had included what to look for in a good mattress), and concluded that they were in a pretty nice medical facility.

*Maybe we're at the same place where they'd treat the president if he was exposed to a biohazard. Cool.*

"Feeling okay, Alex?"

Alex restrained his reflexive urge to jump and casually looked up at the tall FBI agent who'd just opened the door. "Yeah, I am." He hopped back into bed and straightened out his IV line.

"Better not kink that tube or the nurse will get teed off," the man said, sitting down in the chair next to the bed. He pointed to the facial mask he was wearing. "Sorry for this. The medical team's making everyone wear one."

Alex grinned. He figured he should try to get off on the right foot with the agent. "That's okay. Your name is Furlow, right?"

"Yes, Agent Thomas Furlow." For an FBI agent, he looked surprisingly friendly. "My partner and I are the ones they call in whenever there's a biohazard investigation."

"How often does that happen?" Alex asked.

Agent Furlow shrugged. "Enough so that it keeps us on our toes. But usually the cases aren't fatal, as this one unfortunately was." He cleared his throat. "We're probably going to ask you not to tell too many people how your uncle died. The public tends to panic over these sorts of incidents."

"Yeah," Alex said quietly. "So—how's my mom doing?"

"She's okay," Agent Furlow said. "Seems like quite a lady."

"She is that," Alex said. "Can I go and see her?"

The agent hesitated, toyed with his blackberry. "I'm not sure if that's possible."

*Ah.* Alex cocked his head. "How long are we going to be here?"

"I'm afraid that ricin has a long incubation period. To be absolutely sure you're safe, the medical team is probably going to want to keep you under observation for seventy-two hours."

*Three days.* Alex whistled. "And during that whole time, we're not allowed to talk to one another? Is there such a big risk of infection?"

Agent Furlow paused. "Well, it's not exactly infection. I'm afraid that's Bureau procedure after there's been a biohazard incident that might be intentional."

Alex absorbed this. "So you think that Uncle Cass's death was the result of a deliberate assault with a biohazard weapon? Did you find something in his office?"

The agent's eyelashes flickered, but he didn't say yes or no.

Alex pressed on. "It wasn't in that weird red envelope in his office, was it?"

Agent Furlow coughed. "I see you had your suspicions."

"Yeah," Alex said. "I mean, his dying of the flu was too strange. He was such a big, healthy guy. So was the ricin he inhaled in that envelope?"

Agent Furlow tilted his head with a slight smile. "Okay, I could deny it, but I think it'll come out in the investigation. So do you have any idea of how it got there?"

Alex shook his head. "Like I told you earlier, we had just arrived at the house minutes before you guys showed up. I was looking around his office and saw the envelope, but I didn't really put anything together. I guess you're working on finding out who sent it?"

"We will be doing that," Agent Furlow promised. "I'm sorry you're going to have to be stuck here for three days."

"Yeah, that stinks. But you know, it won't be so hard on us if—listen, are you *sure* I can't talk to my family?"

"Bureau procedure dictates…"

Alex spread his hands. "Think about it. We just lost our uncle, suddenly and tragically. We'd had no warning: my girlfriend had just arrived from New Jersey an hour before we got the news. We dropped everything, drove up north and rushed up here to be with my aunt. I know my aunt's a mess. There's no way any of us could have had anything to do with his death. I mean, my kid brothers are going to be traumatized by this, and I'm sure my girlfriend's freaking out. I understand why you have to quarantine us, but can't you let us at least talk to one another?" He put his head on one side. "Can't you talk to your chief and find out if you can make an exception, in this case? Otherwise, I'm sure the psychological pain of this on top of losing Uncle Cass is going to be too much for the rest of my family to handle." In these situations, you had to know just what to say to get around the red tape. Gently hinting at civil lawsuits—more red tape—was sometimes a good strategy. So he'd heard.

Agent Furlow paused. "I can see your point, but standard protocol is…" he shook his head. "Well, you're right. I can at least talk to the chief and see what he says, in this case."

Alex smiled with all the Irish charm he could muster. "I really, truly appreciate it."

But after the agent left, Alex didn't relish his victory. He sank back onto the bed pillows, feeling his hands go cold at the thought of his near escape.

So the ricin that had killed Uncle Cass had been in that envelope. *And I almost picked it up.*

He really hoped the FBI would let him see Kateri soon.

Kateri was starting to feel herself shift into prison mode—not a good thing. She wondered if the FBI would let her tell her parents where she was, at least that she was safe. Or suppose they discovered that she had been exposed to some freak biological virus? Suppose that it was fatal—or worse, chronic?

Slowly, all the government conspiracy movies she'd ever seen began to knit together and replay themselves in her mind. The US government erasing every trace of their existence in the outside world, while keeping them alive in a secret laboratory for study and observation…

Several times she had to snap out of it, tell herself that she was living in America, not Communist Russia, but as soon as she started drifting off, the entire movie would start again, in bad 60's Technicolor: Agent Furlow somberly telling her parents that they would never see their daughter again … A desperate fight in the bunker for freedom … Alex in a yellow space suit escaping from the feds, leaping over tombstones …

"Kateri!"

Snapping out of it, she blinked to find a completely real Alex staring in her face and grinning. He was wearing bright red sweats and an IV tube was still taped to his arm, but that was the only Technicolor thing about him. "You okay?"

"Just replaying *Capricorn One* in my mind for the fortieth time," Kateri said, rubbing her eyes.

"Serves you right for watching such lousy movies," Alex said, hopping onto the side of the bed next to her. "How do you feel? No flu symptoms? No strange sore throat?"

"No, thank God," Kateri said. She knew she didn't have any symptoms, even though her brain had been doing its darndest in her paranoia to convince her otherwise.

"Hey Alex! Hey Kateri!" David and Sam tumbled in through the door. "Isn't this a cool place? When do you think they'll let us out? Do you think we're underneath the ground?"

"Pipe down, barbarians," Alex said. "So they let you guys out too? Where're Mom and Dad?"

"Right here," Mr. O'Donnell said, maneuvering Mrs. O'Donnell's wheelchair through the door. "Good to see you all again!"

His hearty greeting made Kateri take a deep breath and try again to switch back to normality. People in conspiracy movies spoke in grim whispers, not in loud, cheerful voices. Besides, all the O'Donnells were wearing the same bright, terrible colors of sweatpants, and life was starting to feel more like an episode of Teletubbies.

Alex shut the heavy door behind his parents and they all settled themselves on or around Kateri's bed. "So," Alex said, "now we can talk."

"Are you sure?" Kateri looked around her room suspiciously. "Are you sure this room isn't bugged?"

"Highly doubtful," Alex said, and his father nodded.

"I'm sure they have the capability to..." Kateri said, pointing at the light fixture where she had been positive that a camera was hidden.

"Oh, yeah, sure, they do. But I doubt they are," Alex said.

"How do you know?" Kateri said sharply.

"I don't know," Alex said with a shrug. "But at some point, you have to trust. Otherwise, civilization and sanity break down." He patted her on the shoulder. "Look, I know you've had some rotten experiences with law enforcement in the course of your career, but don't let it poison your mind."

"Besides, everything I'm going to say to you, I'm going to tell to the FBI myself in a few minutes anyhow," Mr. O'Donnell said unexpectedly.

They all stared at him in silence. Mr. O'Donnell removed his glasses from his red-rimmed eyes, wiped the frames, and put them back on again.

"Not that it's going to solve any problems," Mrs. O'Donnell said resignedly. "Otherwise, we would have told you all earlier.

"You're going to tell us everything?" Kateri asked Mr. O'Donnell, trying not to sound as skeptical as she felt.

He nodded. "I will," he said huskily. "I will. I never thought I would hurt anyone. I was just taking a risk..."

Kateri was stolid. "Curiosity killed the cat."

"Yes," Mr. O'Donnell bowed his head. "But in this case, it killed my brother," he whispered.

Telling herself not to be so harsh, Kateri said, "I'm sorry."

Mr. O'Donnell sighed heavily. "Okay. So here's what happened."

Alex edged closer to Kateri, who had fixed her entire attention on his dad. She didn't seem to like what she'd heard thus far. There was a deep furrow between her dark eyes.

"So that's the whole story, so far as I can understand it," Dad said, a bit wearily. "And I think at this point, I'd better tell the authorities everything I know."

There was silence as this sank in.

"So that's the end of the million dollars," Sam said.

"It looks like it," Dad said.

"Alan, I'm so sorry—" Mom began to say in an agonized voice but he shook his head abruptly.

"No, Kitty, stop. Don't blame yourself. I absolutely forbid you to blame yourself. We needed to pay Cass what we owed him. No matter how we did it, he was going to be suspicious. He chose to do what he did." His voice started to break, but he managed to steady it.

After a silence had passed, Sam said, hesitantly, "Dad. Are we going to have to give back the hotel, too?"

"Not necessarily," Mom said, drying her eyes with a tissue. "What we have to do is make the hotel work. If we can make money with it, we can continue to pay off the mortgage. It'll be tight, but we'll get by." She squeezed her husband's hand, and said steadily, "Well! It's been an interesting adventure, being rich, but I had a feeling it wasn't going to last."

Dad looked at Kateri. "I'm sorry you had to be part of this madness."

She shrugged, with what Alex knew was pretended nonchalance. "These things happen." She didn't say anything else.

There was a knock on the door, and a nurse, still masked, poked her head inside. "Excuse me. I'm afraid we need everyone to return to their rooms for a medical checkup. It will only take a few minutes."

"That's fine," Dad said, and Sam and David, possessed by restless energy, got up and began fighting almost immediately.

As his mom began to remonstrate with them, Alex pulled Kateri aside.

"Look, I need to apologize," he said. "You were right. You saved my life back there in Uncle Cass's office. If I had touched that envelope, I might be dead now."

"Don't say that," Kateri muttered, shivering. "I'm completely paranoid already. We won't be given the all-clear for another forty-eight hours."

"But do you forgive me, for being—well, pigheaded, to choose a word?"

"Yes."

"Thanks." He squeezed her hand and kissed her lightly on the cheek.

Alex had intended to be in the room when his dad confessed to the FBI, but during the medical checkup, the doctor found some sort of noise in Alex's lungs that concerned him and ordered another set of tests to be run. "After all, you were in that study where they found the ricin longer than anyone else," he said testily when Alex argued with him. Alex insisted that it was probably just his seasonal allergies, but the doctor was adamant. Irish charm might sway the feds, but not the already-heavily litigated against-medical profession.

So Alex had to sit and have his blood drawn (again) and wait for the tests to come back. There hadn't been time to talk to Dad earlier. And by the time Alex was pronounced free to move around again, Dad's room was empty and Mom said he had gone speak to Agent Furlow.

Mom was really worried about Aunt Mona, so after wheeling her into his tearful aunt's room, Alex went back to see Kateri, where he confided his fears.

"Well," Kateri said, with some hesitation. "Sometimes doing the right thing will get you in trouble. And your dad is willing to risk that."

"Yeah," Alex conceded. "I guess it's just the O'Donnell clannishness rising up in me. I was raised to be loyal, I guess." He scratched his arms fitfully. "I wish I could be there with him," he said again.

Kateri didn't say anything but Alex knew she was thinking the same thing he was: CKTC.

Having secured permission for the O'Donnells and Kateri to see one another, Agent Furlow continued to make himself popular when he recommended, over Agent Randolph's objections, that the family be allowed to have access to a video game console. So while Alex waited for his dad to return, he relieved his anxiety by creaming Sam and David in a Japanese anime game involving crash-testing tanks. Kateri even consented to watch them, so they were all piled on the bed in Alex's room. Eventually they were joined by Mom, who had been allowed to have crochet needles and yarn (again, thanks to Agent Furlow's thoughtfulness). She sat in her chair working on a potholder in red and black and making cheerful small talk with Kateri. So they were all there when Dad finally returned, after speaking with the FBI for nearly three hours.

Dad told them that he had had to reconstruct his visits to the website verbally, since computers that could connect to the internet were disallowed in this facility. "Once we're given the all-clear, I told them I'd come to the FBI headquarters and show them more. But I think I gave them what they need in order to investigate Cass's death." He put his head to one side. "Also, I'm not sure about this, but I get the idea that Agent Furlow thinks he knows who the website belongs to."

"Who?" Sam asked.

"He mentioned there's a ring of cyberthieves the FBI has been after. He seems to think I might have stumbled onto their website."

"Cyberthieves?" Kateri repeated.

"Criminals who hack into banks, steal personal identities, run internet scams, that sort of thing," his dad explained. "Most of them are small operators, but apparently there's a group of them who work together to commit larger crimes."

"Like stealing millions of dollars? But where do they steal the money from?" David asked. His dad shrugged.

"There are different ways cyberthieves have of harvesting money. Sometimes they hack into a banking system and deduct a half-cent from each account. That can translate into a lot of money, depending on the size of the banking system."

David whistled.

"So you didn't just find their website," Alex said. "You found their online bank. Where they store their money."

"I'm just hazarding a guess," Dad said. "You know how federal agents are: they never want to tell you anything for certain. But Agent Furlow seemed to feel comfortable telling me a little more."

"So these criminals have millions of dollars, and they don't mind killing people," Alex was thinking hard.

Dad nodded. "By the way, Agent Furlow told me that the ricin did come in an envelope from the Sundance Fun Foundation, just like our check did. But this envelope was red, padded, and heavily taped."

Alex, his brothers, and Kateri exchanged glances.

Dad put his head to one side. "I'm wondering if the red envelope was meant to be a warning: in other words, if you're using the online bank and you do something wrong when you're making a transaction—such as not logging out correctly—the site administrators will send you a red envelope of ricin. Someone who's part of the ring of cyberthieves will know they've done something wrong, and would know not to open it..."

"But Uncle Cass was an outsider, so he didn't know," Alex finished.

Dad didn't say anything, just touched Mom's hand. She shook her head and gave him a familiar look, saying softly, "The luck of the Irish saved you that time, Alan."

"Let's hope that luck holds out," was all Dad said. Kateri narrowed her eyes. Alex recognized too well what she was thinking: *what was his dad going to do next?*

*Now the Forty Thieves knew that
Cassim had had an accomplice, and their
chief vowed to discover and destroy him.*
The Arabian Nights

*T*he man looked around one more time to make sure he was really
alone, then stepped into the mahogany office and softly closed the
door.

It was after three in the morning: everyone was asleep. No one could
possibly know what he was up to.

He fumbled in the briefcase he'd brought with him from home, and opened
up his laptop.

In the middle of the night, something had suddenly gelled into a resolution.

Arguing with himself, he opened the black SSH screen, and then, with a
deep breath, went to the online folder that contained the program he had
secretly downloaded from the helpdesk website several weeks ago. He'd
promised himself that he'd never go back there, never take advantage of the
passwords he'd collected with the MouseCatcher. But…

His finger hovered over the enter key. *Should I? Is it wise?* He reminded
himself that he had neglected to mention to the FBI that he'd copied the
program and hidden it in his web email.

He took a deep breath, and opened up the "Sesame" program.

Darkness.

The verification process. The security questions.  And then the cave
materialized around him. He wondered if he would be visible to other users or
not, or if he'd have to attach the MouseCatcher to someone in order to become
invisible.

But the questions were irrelevant, he realized at once. He wasn't alone in
the cave. Someone was waiting for him.

The ninja.

Unlike last time, the ninja was facing the camera, and his dark eyes seemed to bore through the screen. The man had no doubt that this time, the other user could see him, or at least, some online representation of him.

A transparent veil dropped over the screen, and words appeared.

*You again. I thought you might come.*

*I kept that portal open and waited to change my login information*

*just to see if you would try this door again.*

*And you did.*

*Very clever of you to get in. You must be a hacker of exceptional skill.*

*Would you like to tell me how you did it?*

*I'm sure we can come to some sort of an understanding…*

# Chapter Nine

*And the chief robber directed his thieves to
search far and wide for the unknown person
who had stolen their secret, and kill him.*
*The Arabian Nights*

ateri woke up on the plush mattress of the guest bedroom where she
had been sleeping since their release from the decontamination
facility. Unable to shake her farm upbringing, she had woken early,
even though she'd gone to bed far after midnight. There was no falling back
to sleep again, even in a bed as comfortable as this one.

Her fears of being pinned for the crime on some sort of flimsy grounds had
not materialized: actually, those fears had evaporated in the face of more
reasonable fears that the FBI would take Mr. O'Donnell into custody. But
apparently the FBI didn't think that was necessary: or else, they weren't ready to
prosecute. So after making a copy of Mr. O'Donnell's laptop and warning all of
them to not to talk to others about their experience at the decontamination
facility, lest they accidentally jeopardize the security of their country (blah blah
blah), Kateri and the O'Donnells and Aunt Mona were released and allowed to
go wherever they wanted.

And much to everyone's surprise, Aunt Mona insisted the O'Donnells and
Kateri all come home with her, now that her house had been decontaminated
and given the all-clear.

It only made sense, from a certain point of view. There was a funeral to plan
and a will to figure out, and a story to keep out of the public eye—at least for
now. So the O'Donnells moved into Aunt Mona's various guest rooms, and
camped out to help her through the trying days that followed.

Aunt Mona told all well-wishers that her husband had died of the flu, and
explained the presence of the police and the biohazard team to her neighbors by
saying that her husband's job involved sensitive government information.
(Apparently so many of her neighbors were government contractors that they
accepted this story without asking much more.) Since Aunt Mona was so good
about not saying anything, Kateri didn't feel right about telling her own parents

what was really going on, despite her distrust of the federal government. She knew Alex was having a hard time stopping himself from sharing their latest adventures with their college friends, too. So for now, they were all keeping quiet and sticking to the 'official' story of a rogue flu bug.

Uncle Cass had left a will, and it turned out that he had made Mr. O'Donnell the executor. So there were financial details to go over, and all sorts for financial difficulties to manage. Apparently, Uncle Cass was not as rich as he pretended to be. Fortunately, Mrs. O'Donnell was not only good at numbers: she was good at explaining to bereaved wives that their husband had been hiding the credit card statements from them for a reason. After some understandable histrionics, Aunt Mona was starting to think reasonably about what the next step should be. Her own parents were wealthy, and once she had (at Mrs. O'Donnell's suggestion) talked to them, it seemed as though they would be willing to help bail her out and settle Cass's remaining debts.

All in all, given the O'Donnell's history with Aunt Mona and her husband, it was amazing that there wasn't more animosity over the money.

It probably had something to do with Kitty O'Donnell. Kateri had previously noticed that when tragedy strikes, people tend to reach out for those who've already been living with suffering. So Aunt Mona apparently wanted Alex's mom to stay near her, listening to her and helping her. And Mrs. O'Donnell, true to character, was happy to help out. She managed to keep Aunt Mona calm and even make her laugh. And even more surprising, Mrs. O'Donnell somehow persuaded Kateri to help her.

So it was that Kateri found herself sitting at the kitchen table at night long after the boys and men had retired, drinking Irish coffee and listening to Aunt Mona and Mrs. O'Donnell reminisce about the past and discuss the future. Mrs. O'Donnell drew Kateri into the conversation, and on their second late night, Kateri found herself talking about pro-life protests, and Aunt Mona, unpredictably, approved. She told Kateri that she'd protested against nuclear power plants in the 1970s and had a roommate who knew Karen Silkwood.

Most surprisingly, Aunt Mona disagreed with her late husband on abortion. She was pro-life, at least by default. "My sister had an abortion, and never got over it," she said, tearing up again. "I'm glad you had the guts to stand up to the system." She poured another shot of Bailey's Irish Cream into Kateri's mocha latte.

Kateri felt a lot more warmth towards Aunt Mona after that.

So now Kateri lay in a pink plush canopy guest bed, wearing a designer nightgown Aunt Mona had insisted on buying her. Aunt Mona had taken everyone shopping for new clothes, and had even bought Kateri some vintage outfits to make up for her lost clothing. Sitting up in bed and leaning against the down pillows, Kateri ran her hands through the tangles in her thick black hair, jerking out the knots, she worked her way through the unruly facts of the O'Donnell Mess, which now included not only Mystery Money, but murder.

It still bothered Kateri that Mr. O'Donnell was the sort of person who would follow people into locked websites. It was just inviting trouble.

*Sure, some of my brothers are risk-takers, but I doubt they'd sneak into websites out of curiosity,* she thought. *How would you even know if you were breaking the law?*

She'd broken the law before, but deliberately, openly, in the name of upholding the moral law, as part of pro-life protests. Hacking, cyberpranks—this was a completely different sort of thing. She didn't know if she liked Mr. O'Donnell's conscience very much.

And Alex? She doubted Alex would ever hack websites, but he didn't seem to question what his dad had been doing. As in many things, Alex was casual and off-the-cuff about it when she would have been passionate and driven. It was enough to make her insane.

During the past few days, Alex's job was keeping the younger boys entertained, which wasn't too hard in a house like Aunt Mona's. The only difficult part was dragging them off of Uncle Cass's gaming system at the end of the day. Alex was doing a lot of gaming himself, and Kateri suspected he was still processing everything, including the death. She could tell he was as antsy as she was to get back to normal life. Well, whatever the definition of "normal life" *was* for the O'Donnells these days.

Then there was the question of this supposed gang of cyberthieves. Did they know that Mr. O'Donnell had hacked into their website? And if they knew, what were they going to do next? Especially now that he'd confessed to the FBI?

Something inside Kateri tensed. She'd been the target of criminal activity before, but she doubted the O'Donnell family had. They might not know what to watch out for. She had to be ready.

Right now, everyone seemed to be acting as though things would be fine as soon as today's funeral was over and the O'Donnells returned to Hunter Springs that afternoon. But would it?

She heard someone moving around downstairs, and got up. Pulling on a robe, she tiptoed down the steps to the living room to find out who was awake.

It was Alex, up unusually early. Wearing grey sweatpants, his hair loose about his shoulders, he stood in the center of the living room, his back to her, illuminated only by the soft light of dawn. In his hands he held a long wooden stick. With practiced moves, he struck, lunged, and stood, then struck, lunged, and stood, moving easily through one stance after another. He was practicing his *kata*, the exercises that kept him prepared for combat.

She didn't interrupt him, just watched, and felt a bit reassured that on some level, Alex was on his guard as well.

Despite the fact that Cassidy O'Donnell hadn't been a practicing Catholic, the funeral service was held in a Catholic church. That was Dad's doing, Alex knew.

During the service, Alex stood in the pew next to Kateri, not looking at the urn that held his uncle's ashes, and praying with the priest that Uncle Cass would find some mercy as he faced his Maker. It was fortunate that Cass had asked to be cremated, as his death from biohazard contamination had made cremation mandatory anyhow.

It was a sunny day, ironically, and Alex hoped that the future would be kinder to Aunt Mona, who had turned out to be a nicer person than Alex had suspected. He even felt sorry for her when the husky dog Persia, the only other casualty of the ricin poisoning, had been put down at the animal shelter a few days ago. Though it would have been easier to sympathize if Persia hadn't bitten him more than once over the years.

The Mass was over, and the priest, carrying the ashes, left the church, followed by a strangely sober Sam and David, who were altar servers. Behind them, Dad escorted a sobbing Aunt Mona. Mom followed in her wheelchair. Behind them, Alex genuflected to the tabernacle, took Kateri's hand, and started down the aisle.

Something caught his eye: a man in the back corner of the church holding up an iPhone towards the procession. When he saw Alex, he quickly thrust his phone back into his pocket, and left the church.

At last, their family obligations were over: Aunt Mona thanked them profusely for all their help, hugged Kateri, and even kissed Alex, Sam and David, and they were back on their way to Hunter Springs. Alex had never thought he'd be so happy to leave Northern Virginia.

Once they were home, they threw themselves into hotel work, taking reservations and reorganizing the office and service rooms, fixing and updating and cleaning. Dad went to work, installing the new electronic locks on all the doors, which meant removing ceiling panels to install circuit boards and wiring.

The Mystery Money still sat in the bank account, collecting interest, but it seemed to Alex and the O'Donnells that any day, the government would seize it as evidence. So they did all they could to save money.

Alex was determined to find a suit jacket, but combed the thrift stores fruitlessly for one he liked in his size. After sending up a prayer to St. Anthony, he remembered that Mr. Bhatka had given him the keys to the storage room in the basement, and decided to look down there. The storage room was a veritable treasure trove. There he found not one, but an entire rack of red jackets. He showed them to the family, and Mom remembered that the entire hotel staff used to wear them. So Alex decreed that all of them should follow suit (no pun intended), over Sam and David's loud protests.

After a family council, the staff of the Twilight Hills Hotel decided that the new uniform for male staff should be black dress shirts and pants with the red jackets. (On weekdays, the waitstaff and bag carriers—Sam and David—were allowed to wear black t-shirts.) Mom found some black and red patterned blouses for herself at the thrift stores. But Alex found an outfit online for Kateri, and in a burst of extravagance, bought it and had it shipped to the hotel.

He brought the package in to her when she was hard at work putting the finishing touches on the organization of the kitchen that serviced the breakfast area. "Open it."

She removed her rubber gloves and pushed back her scraggly hair. "Why? What is it?"

"I bought it for you."

Giving him her characteristic look, she opened up the white box, and removed the tissue paper. "What is this supposed to be?"

"Your uniform," Alex said proudly. "As assistant manager."

She lifted the black sleeveless dress with the Mandarin collar from the package and shook it out. "You've got to be kidding."

"What's wrong with it? Look, it comes with this little red shrug."

"Alex, I'm going to be cooking. And cleaning rooms. And running around all day long. I can't wear a dress like this."

Alex shook his head. "You shouldn't be cleaning rooms. That's what the 'Maid In Time' service is for: maid service. It's a great deal. We signed a contract with them: they clean as many times a month as we need it at a reduced hourly rate."

Kateri looked adamant. "But it's an awful lot of money. We can save if we do the cleaning ourselves."

"But there's no need to. Besides, they know this hotel inside and out: they've cleaned it for years."

"They have to impress me first." She shook her head at the dress. "But how am I going to chase after them in that dress?"

"I'll do the running around," he urged. "Wear it, Kateri. You'll look great."

She held it up to herself, and then glanced at him. "Is this a trophy Asian girlfriend dress?"

"Possibly." He felt deflated. "Well, if you really don't like it…"

"I didn't say I didn't like it," she said, running her hand over the fabric. "It's lovely. I'm just trying to say it's impractical."

"Oh," he said, "I got you two matching ones."

"Alex!"

"I figured it's worth it to have a great-looking assistant manager on duty."

"You're the only one who thinks I'm so great looking," she said, shaking her hair at him. "I'm no beautiful Lotus Blossom of the South East. Ask my family. For a Viet, I'm pretty plain."

"Speak for yourself," he said, running a finger down her cheek. "You're so very beautiful."

She groaned and started to push him away.

"Kateri," he said, in some frustration. He didn't want to badger her, but he had to say something. "When I give you a compliment, what terrible thing is going to happen to you if you just accept it?"

She flushed. "It just makes me feel foolish, that's all."

"Well, when you shoot back with a sarcastic remark, then *I* feel foolish. What about if you just start saying, 'thank you?' Just to humor me?"

"Thank you," she muttered.

"Much better."

*Alex is a hard worker*, Kateri noted to herself. It wasn't something she'd expected: at school, Alex had always seemed to be the perennial lounger, never far from the video game console or his weapon toys. The only time he seemed to be energetic was in a crisis or when organizing an elaborate prank.

But now for the first time, she saw him working hard, and she had to admit she'd misjudged him. He spent the day dashing here and there, checking off things on endless lists, taking inventory, answering the phone, entering data in the computer, organizing supplies, and always polishing something with a gray cloth.

He was inventive with what they had. When they needed something, he scoured the storage rooms in the basement and came up with new uses for old things. When his mom wanted planters for the pool area, Alex discovered a bunch of old brass waste cans that would work for planting herbs and annuals until they could afford something more permanent. And when Kateri had let slip a complaint about having to live with hotel décor, he took the Oriental rug that had graced the O'Donnell living room in their old house, and installed it in her room to cover the plaid carpet she hated. Then he brought her an armful of old Indian-print cotton curtains with rich patterns that he had found in a box in the basement to spruce up her room.

He only kept one, and used it to make a place for the O'Donnell arsenal on the long drab wall of the hallway stretching from the door leading to the hotel lobby back to the living suite. With the help of Sam and David, he installed hooks for hanging all the various deadly implements his family owned: swords, throwing stars, knives, nunchucks, and other more obscure weaponry that he and his Dad had collected.

"Hm. Impressive." Kateri said, when he dragged her away from cleaning the office to view his project. "It's, um, odd to be friends with a family who has the ability to kill people so many different ways."

"I think it's good for you," said Alex. "And us, too. Every band of warlords should always have a pacifist around to say, 'war is not the answer' in a deep tone of voice when the battle cries get too loud."

"Is that why you keep me around?"

"One reason."

She pointed to the large Oriental fans hanging in the top corners of the curtain. "Something tells me those two are not simply innocent decoration."

"Ah. No." He pulled one down, and showed her the razors on the other side of the printed cloth. With a deft move, he closed the fan and shook it out again, apparently enjoying the *ching!* of steel as it snapped open. "Fighting fans. I wouldn't advise cooling yourself off with them."

"I see," she said. "I'm learning. Now, shouldn't we return to getting the hotel ready for its first guests under our regime?"

Alex made an expansive gesture. "No hotel can afford to open unarmed."

"No hotel run by your family, that is," Kateri said, resigned.

Then there was the matter of the new locks. Mr. O'Donnell proudly demonstrated the new keycards for the entire family. He gathered them around Room 101, where the new brass card lock with a slot for inserting the keycard gleamed on the door.

"This is a RAC system, 'remote access system,'" he told the family. "The circuit boards above each door are powered by an e.e.p.r.o.m. chip, so that we can set these doors to operate in any way we desire. For instance, when a room's taken off of the rental list—say, because we need to touch up the paint—the room keycard won't open it until it's put back on the rental list."

"So how are we going to open it to paint?" David asked.

Mr. O'Donnell smiled. "Ask me," he said, "or use the master key." He held up what looked like a red credit card. "This master key I now hereby bestow on our day manager, my son Alex." He formally handed Alex the red card, and Alex pocketed it and bowed as his mom and Kateri clapped. Kateri thought he looked rather proud.

"And now," Mr. O'Donnell said dramatically, "our new keycard system in action!" He held up what looked like a cell phone, placed a gold room card in the slot, and punched in a number. "Now this card is activated for this room. Sam, why don't you be our first honorary guest and try it out?"

Sam took the keycard, pushed it into the slot on the door, and the doorknob clicked open. Everyone cheered. With a flourish, Sam stepped inside the room and closed the door.

As the applause died down, they heard Sam say, "Um, Dad, how do I open the door from this side?"

"Use your keycard," Mr. O'Donnell called. The door clicked, and Sam opened the door again with a huge gesture.

"Hey, no one cheered now," he said, disappointed.

"Wait a second," Kateri said, stepping inside the hotel room and examining the inside of the door, which had another keycard slot instead of a handle. "You need to use a keycard to get *out* of the hotel room? That doesn't make any sense. You should be able to just turn the knob to get out." She turned the knob on the inside of the door, but it didn't turn: it was completely stationary.

"Uh, well—" Mr. O'Donnell seemed embarrassed. "My friend didn't have any of the inside doorknob hardware. But we had more than twice the right amount of the keylocks. So—I just kept the old interior knobs on the door but added keycard locks to the inside."

"Yes, but what mom checked into our hotel is going to want to have to get up and open the door with a keycard every time one of her kids wants to run out into the lobby for something?" Kateri frowned. "Not to mention if there was a fire…"

"If any of the fire alarms go off, all the doors in the entire building will automatically open." Mr. O'Donnell assured her, holding up the handset. "That's why it's compliant with the fire code. But you really think it will bother people to have a keylock on both sides? I thought it would feel more secure. It's a double lock."

Kateri folded her arms. "Speaking as someone whose parents had eleven kids, I think it would be more annoying than anything else. Can't you change it?"

"She's probably right, Alan," Mrs. O'Donnell said.

Mr. O'Donnell glanced at his wife. "Okay. Well, we'll have to downgrade—I mean, change over to regular interior doorknobs, but we'll probably have to wait until we can afford it."

"In the meantime, why not just set the interior lock as 'always unlocked' for now?" Alex suggested.

"I guess I could do that," Mr. O'Donnell said, but he looked a bit deflated. "If we wanted to lock them, we could do it with this key, by the way." He held up a purple card. "When you slide this through either the exterior or interior lock, it locks both sides until the master key opens them."

Kateri shook her head. Again, she felt that Mr. O'Donnell's technical expertise was almost more of a liability than an asset.

That is, until that evening, when her laptop took ten minutes to boot up. She was sitting on the futon in the living area, trying to get it to work, when Mr. O'Donnell came through on his way to grab a snack, and heard her groan of frustration.

"Something wrong?" he asked.

"It's just very slow," she complained, staring at the "Wanted" page of the FBI website, which she had added to her homepage tabs. The photos of the five Most Wanted Cyberthieves were downloading nearly pixel-by-pixel. "Are you trying to put an Internet security cat on it or something?"

He chuckled. "Haven't gotten around to that yet. Do you want me to take a look at it for you?"

"Sure," she said, handing the laptop to him. "I'm going to help Kitty make dinner anyhow."

He took it with him to the lobby, and in a half hour he was back. While she stir-fried dinner, he showed her what he had done.

"Your problem was spybots." He held out the computer to her, and pointed to her program files. "Little programs that downloaded themselves to your computer as you browsed the internet. I installed software to keep them out. But here's what will make it easy." He opened a yellow notepad file on her desktop. "Here's how many programs you should have in these key folders. You should only have 173 programs in this file folder, unless you install something else. If you have more, then you know you've got more spies. See? I did it for all your folders."

"Gee, thanks," Kateri said, taking her laptop back with more than a twinge of gratitude. And she sighed. It was true, perhaps. Compromise was becoming the new theme of her life.

But regarding Alex? She groaned. Too much of a paradox to think about. And she was fairly sure that a quick overhaul of the control panel wasn't going to fix *him*.

On the night before they officially started to accept guests, she and Alex drove down the mile-long driveway to the long wooden sign that stood by the county highway. While Kateri held the banner, Alex hammered in the nails until the large red letters reading "GRAND RE-OPENING" stretched across the bottom of the oversized hotel sign. Alex trimmed the grass around the sign, pulled some weeds, and stood back to admire it.

"What do you think?" he asked Kateri.

"I think we're all crazy," she said.

"Oh well," Alex said with a shrug. "What else are we going to do?"

# Chapter Ten

*The servant girl who worked for Ali Baba*
*was quite clever, and she resolved to be on her*
*guard against the plots of the Forty Thieves.*
*The Arabian Nights*

eing somewhat of a pessimist, Kateri was sure that the launch of the Twilight Hills Hotel was doomed. But much to her surprise, business in the first few weeks was good, which bore testimony to the Bhatka's hard work in customer service over the years. The hotel phones rang in a steady stream. Mrs. O'Donnell worked the reservation desk from her wheelchair, answering the phone in a polished manner, taking down guests' information, and entering it into the new software Mr. O'Donnell had installed. The same software accepted online registrations with a credit card, and made their lives easier.

Alex adopted the dress of a day manager from the Grand Opening onwards. When the guests arrived, they invariably found Alex, surprisingly debonair in his black dress shirt and red jacket, his hair smoothed sleekly back into a neat ponytail, there to meet them. He asked how their trip was, handed out room keys, asked if they had any special requirements, and directed them to their rooms. Kateri had wondered if any guests would look askance at the ponytail, but after a week she had seen so many Southern men with long hair and goatees coming through the hotel doors that she figured that Alex simply fit right in. But it helped that he kept his overall appearance so neat.

Sam and David took luggage to the rooms. Alex had to do a lot of on-the-job training about how NOT to carry bags, but once Sam and David learned to walk at a normal pace without flinging suitcases around, it became much easier.

Unfortunately, the younger boys weren't always around. When a group of retired police officers arrived at the hotel for their annual golf weekend, Kateri was incensed when neither boy was to be found.

"I'm sorry they're not here; I'll go get them," she told the sandy-haired man she was checking in.

He chuckled. "That's okay. I can carry my own bags up." The other men, all burly retirees, said the same thing.

But Kateri could barely contain her rage. When the last policeman had been checked in, she stomped into the living area to find Sam and David focused on the huge TV screen, working their joysticks furiously to counteract an alien attack.

Growling, she marched to the corner and pulled out the TV plug, heedless of the horrified wails from the two boys.

"No more video games during work hours!" she bellowed over their protests.

Alex and Mrs. O'Donnell were soon on the scene, and when they heard the story, agreed with Kateri.

"No iPods in your ears either," Mrs. O'Donnell said. "It's very unprofessional."

"But we waited around for three hours with nothing to do," David whined. "We just came in here for our break to see if we could get 5000 points in fifteen minutes. We were at 4890 when you pulled the plug, Kateri," he said accusingly.

"Oh, I am sooo sorry," Kateri said, giving free rein to her sarcasm at last.

"From now on, there will be no computers, video games, or iPods used during work hours," Alex decreed. "And that's final." He turned to his dad, who was standing in the bedroom doorway, the fuss having woken him up. "Does the Board agree?"

"Agreed," Mr. O'Donnell said.

"Agreed," said Mrs. O'Donnell. "And it's about time."

Sam threw down his console. "What are we going to do, sitting around here for hours waiting for something to do?"

"You can read," Kateri interjected. "That's what my brothers and sisters did."

"But that's boring. Too much like school," David grumbled. The boys, who were enrolling in the local schools in the fall, had already gotten their required reading lists.

"Then it will make you so happy to leave it when a guest comes and needs your help!" Alex said. "When you're on the job, I never want to hear the words, 'Just let me finish this level' again!"

Mr. O'Donnell weighed in. "It's about time you boys started becoming serious readers anyhow. A good book is a great pleasure. So think of it this way: while we're going to ban video games from the job site, you are always permitted to enjoy a book when you're temporarily off duty."

"Cruel and unusual parent," David muttered.

As they walked back down the hallway, Kateri complained to Alex, "Why does your family even own video games? I can't think of anything that's less likely to ever be useful!"

"Well, I don't know," Alex said, scratching his chin. "Life has a way of making certain skills useful."

"I'm not holding my breath," Kateri said, stomping back to her desk.

Mr. O'Donnell worked the night shift, being available for any emergencies that occurred between the hours of eight o'clock at night and eight in the morning. Fortunately, there weren't many, so he spent most of his time sitting at the front desk, figuring out the bugs in the new security system at the hotel or working on his software projects. (The ban on personal computer work during job hours did not apply to him.)

Guests of all stripes came to the Twilight Hills Hotel: many of them seemed to have stayed at the hotel for years. They inquired about the Bhatkas, welcomed the new management, and seemed pleased that nothing much had changed beyond the addition of homemade cinnamon buns to the breakfast menu.

Then there were guests who came to the hotel through an internet search, and who had picked it because of location or cheapest rate. (The O'Donnells had shaved a penny off the going rates, which kept them towards the top of the search engines.)

All in all, the O'Donnells seemed to take to hotel work like fish to water. The only one who was having a hard time fitting in was Kateri.

This was because hotel management was, simply put, a lot of work. She ran the breakfast area, kept it clean, and invariably did the cleanup too. Every evening she made the dough for the buns and set it to rise: first thing in the morning, she baked them. She cleaned up after breakfast. After one week, she abandoned the black dress and red shrug for white scrubs. She wore sneakers and pants: there was just too much mess involved.

As for the "Maid In Time" service, they were a more a Pain In Time, at least in her book. The Maids were mostly Hispanic women who spoke Spanish and seemed to resent her oversight. To Kateri, the speed with which they cleaned rooms was in direct proportion to how many times Kateri poked her head in during the job.

Kateri took to following them around to ensure that rooms were properly cleaned, and found that sure enough, some of them never vacuumed in the corners, or didn't bother to dust all around the windows. Demonstrating the "right way" to do things took up too much of her time and energy. So on slow days, she took to sending them home and doing the job herself. It was easy enough to change bed sheets and clean bathrooms. She pressed Sam and David into service whenever she could to strip beds and vacuum.

After a while, she persuaded the O'Donnells to redefine the terms under which the maid service was used. Occasionally a riotous party of guests would trash a room, and then Kateri gladly called the service. The Maids seemed to take exception to being made to do the dirty work, and she had a difficult time with the murmurs in Spanish that seemed to erupt whenever she gave them an order.

No one could say she wasn't doing her job as Assistant Manager and earning her salary. But even so, Alex found fault with it.

"You're not enjoying yourself, Kateri," he said, one evening when he had gotten off duty and she was still cleaning the kitchen, since a number of unexpected guest departures meant that she hadn't had time to clean it earlier. "I almost get the idea that you don't like the guests."

"The guests are what cause all the trouble!" Kateri said, feeling like the hotel manager from *Fawlty Towers*. "If we didn't have them, things would stay clean!"

"And we'd be out of a job," Alex pointed out.

But it didn't look as though they would be out of a job any time soon. Reservations came in daily: for a wedding. For a business conference. For a football team traveling in the fall. Looking ahead at the calendar, Kateri had a feeling the O'Donnells would be doing just fine by September. Alex had already told her he wasn't going back to finish his college degree in the fall: he was going to stay and help his parents run the hotel.

But would she still be here? Did she want to be? That was one question she still couldn't answer.

One night in the middle of the week a month into their stay, Alex realized there were no guests expected for the next twenty-four hours: the hotel was empty. Having looked at the reservation bookings, which showed several guests arriving tomorrow for another wedding, Alex was actually relieved to have some respite.

"Taking the night off, Dad?" he asked, when his dad came into the lobby wearing khakis and a polo. His dad usually took over at eight o'clock and worked till eight in the morning.

"Hardly," Dad said, and touched his arm. "Alex. I've been working on something."

"The new security system for the hotel wireless network?" Alex said, shrugging out of his jacket. "Sam showed me. The Security Cat is back, eh? The upgrade looks great. Love how he's wearing a red jacket now."

"No. Something else. I've decided to take a risk. For Uncle Cass's sake."

Dad had an intense look in his usually pleasant green eyes.

"Dad…" Alex said, a little warningly. "What?"

"The cyberthieves' site. I think I can hack it."

"What?"

Dad took a deep breath. "I've been going back there a lot. They changed all the settings, even the Sesame file. I used the old version of Sesame to sort of guess what the new program would look like. And after a lot of work, I managed to hack into the login portal for the site and I trojaned it. I mean, to make a long story short, I did the equivalent of modifying the login files so that all the passwords that were entered were secretly copied and sent to me. Make sense?"

"Yeah, Dad. Um—did the FBI know you had the 'Sesame' program?"

"Uh—I sort of forgot to tell them I had it. Probably not completely above-board, but they didn't ask me, so I didn't tell them." He wiped his forehead. "Last night, I got lucky: I snagged the password of the site administrator. When I used it, I found a private key for the portal to another server. I have a feeling that if I can get in there, I'll find out a lot more about this website."

"And find out who runs it?"

"Most likely."

Alex whistled. "I bet the FBI could use that information. But wait a second—don't they have their own computer experts working on it?"

His dad shook his head. "I talked to Agent Randolph the other day, and he said they've hit a brick wall. So I think they could use some help."

Alex looked over his shoulder, feeling a little spooked. "Okay. So you're going to try to get the goods on the cyberthieves. Uh—what do you need me to do? Run the desk, distract Sam and David, or something?"

"No. I—" Dad hesitated. "I guess I'd just like you to know."

Alex stared at his dad. This was obviously something that Dad had been thinking about and working on for a long time. *And he wanted me to know.* Alex recognized that his dad, who spent so much time alone in his work, was asking for moral support.

It was an easy decision from there.

"I'm going to watch your back," Alex said. "What can I do? Let me help."

Dad hesitated, but Alex could see he was grateful. "How about you monitor the home network? I'm going to bounce through several other servers to hide my approach, but just in case they figure out where I'm coming from, it might be good to be on the alert. I'm going to start in an hour."

"Can Kateri sit with us?"

"If she wants to."

Alex could guess what Kateri would want to do, but he decided she didn't have a choice this time. He hung up his jacket, slung his tie around the hanger, and went to find her.

She was upstairs on the second floor changing sheets on a bed, and looking very out of sorts.

"Kat. Hey. How are you?"

"You want a serious answer to that question?" She lifted up the end of the mattress and tucked two flat sheets underneath.

"Not really. Hey. Dad is going after the cyberthieves tonight. I'm backing him up. You need to come and watch."

She dropped the mattress with a thud. "I thought you and I were going out shopping tonight. You said we could take a break."

He had completely forgotten about this. "Uh. Yeah. But I didn't know about this. Dad just told me."

Frowning, Kateri methodically began to pull the lower sheet to the top of the bed and tuck it around the sides of the mattress. Alex knelt down to help her. "What do you want me to do?" she asked.

"Just be there."

She finished the last tuck then stood up to spread out the top sheet. "So you want me to sit by the computer and admire you both as you type and click?"

Alex grinned at her. "That would be awesome. I knew you were a quick study." He threw an arm around her. "But seriously, this could be dangerous. If the hackers pick up that Dad is after them, they might start coming after us."

She dropped the pillow she had been snapping into a pillowcase. "Uh. Oh. So—you want me to pray."

He nodded. "Possibly starting now."

The mood was tense in the small office of the Twilight Hills Hotel as Kateri sat down between Alex and his dad. Mr. O'Donnell was on his laptop: Alex was on the hotel office computer, which was now linked to the laptop. Cables and electronic implements were scattered around the office she'd just cleaned that morning. Apparently the operation Mr. O'Donnell was preparing for required some hardware reconfiguration.

"How are you connecting?" Alex asked his dad.

"Just using a modem I had on hand. The problem is that it only works with Windows, so I just routed our connection through the front desk computer. But it might help to hide my approach as well."

The lobby outside was deserted, silent except for the humming of the front desk computer, and the rest of the family was in the residence suite. Mrs. O'Donnell and David were to answer the phone and the door buzzer if any guests showed up. The summer night was silent: the stars outside glimmered overhead in distant tranquility.

Kateri shifted in her seat as Mr. O'Donnell plugged in a USB port and said, "Here we go."

*I guess I should start the Rosary now.*

And she did.

The first part of the hack was fairly interesting, because it involved going into the cyberthieves' cave, which Kateri and Alex had never seen. The gleaming stone walls and piled jewels gave Kateri an inkling of the curiosity that Mr. O'Donnell must have felt when he first discovered the treasure trove, but they didn't stay there long. Mr. O'Donnell moved quickly through the cave and clicked on a shape embedded in the wall: an "O" with a slash through it, which glowed faintly and then sank into the wall.

"What was that?" she asked as the screen vortexed into black.

"Looked like a number zero," Alex said.

"It was. The universal symbol for 'super-user,'" Mr. O'Donnell said. "Once I logged in with the site administrator's password, I spotted it right away. It's his shortcut, a portal to the root account of the cave's storage server. This is where the data for the main operations of the site should be found."

When a password box came up, Mr. O'Donnell hit 'zero' on the keyboard, and the password box dissolved into darkness. They all waited.

What eventually emerged from the black vortex was something much less spectacular: a list of files and numbers and symbols. But apparently to Mr. O'Donnell, it was truly amazing. He exhaled in wonder. "I can't believe I made it in here," he said. "Now, I can actually get to work."

From that point on, Kateri found it much more difficult to follow what was going on. Hacking a computer, she recognized, was not a very dramatic project. It seemed to mean maneuvering through screens of numbers. Alex had screens of charts and graphs he was constantly checking through. She could only follow what was going on through the conversation, when it didn't involve numbers and technical terms.

For a long time, Mr. O'Donnell was silent, clicking through screen after screen and analyzing data. Finally he said of one column of endless numbers, "You know, this is interesting. I think it's the password file. But there's a lot more passwords than the ones I collected. I can't tell if they're all active users or not."

He typed something quickly. "I'm pulling up the logins from the last three months." Then he whistled. "Hundreds of logins. This is a pretty active site. How many unique users?" He typed again, murmuring, "Sort by unique... Oh, wow. Like I said, this is a pretty active system. Exactly forty accounts are in use."

"Forty different people use this site?" Alex asked.

Mr. O'Donnell shrugged. "Assuming one password per person, and that Admin doesn't have two passwords. Safer to say there are forty passwords used to get into this site." He shook his head. "Okay, I'm logging this session. But there's bigger data out there to capture. Got to hurry!"

"Can you find out who the users actually are?" Alex asked.

"Possibly. If personal data is stored on this site, this is where I'll find it. But I better move fast. There're hundreds of files in this root directory."

A few minutes later, he whistled again. "Bet this is the personal data. It's encrypted, but there are thirty-nine entries. I get it. Admin's got personal data logged on all of the other users, but none on himself. I wonder if the users even know one another? I bet none of them know who he really is."

He typed. "Logging this session."

"Are you copying everything that's in that file?" Kateri asked, squeezing her rosary beads. The realization that Mr. O'Donnell was accessing personal information on dangerous criminals had hit her now.

"Yes. I'm just copying the files onto a tarball—sort of a zip file—connected through the cave site—compressing the data, bouncing it back through the servers I went through—not as fancy as a reverse DNS tunnel, but it's safer because it's just using the connection I already opened." He glanced at Kateri. "Hope you understood at least some of that. The important thing is that it's all going to be written to a CD-R on the drive right here." He pointed to a flat box connected to the computer. "I'll get a copy to the FBI, but I'm going to make a few dozen copies myself just to make sure."

"Great," Kateri breathed. "Just checking." She reminded herself not to bother Mr. O'Donnell while he was hacking. Not good to be distracting him when time was of the essence.

She concentrated on her rosary, and she was on the Fourth Joyful Mystery when Mr. O'Donnell spoke again. "Okay: I found the bank. This is where the money is funneled into the site."

Alex leaned forward. "From banks?" Kateri squinted at the screen, but she couldn't understand it. It was just more numbers and data.

His dad was nodding his head. "From banks, and from other places. There's a lot here. And the withdrawals are mostly electronic transfers, but a handful of checks like the one we were sent. Yep, the checks are issued to unknown recipients and locations: only the amounts are recorded here." His fingers flew over the keyboard. "Okay. Logging all of this. It might take some time." After half a minute, he said, "Once I get everything, I'll start transferring all the data to my computer, and writing it to the CD-R for safekeeping."

"That's going to be pretty incriminating evidence. Stealing from a bank is what—mandatory ten years in federal prison?" Alex asked. Suddenly his eyes fixed on his own computer screen. "Dad. Don't mean to distract you, but someone's onto you. Intrusion detection system says we're being portscanned."

Kateri wasn't sure what it meant, but she could tell from Mr. O'Donnell's tensed back and increased finger speed that it wasn't good. But all he said was, "So they found us already."

Alex's eyes were glued to the screen. "I'm checking our security: looks good…enhancing security…well, guess I can't enhance it any more… Okay, now the computer says that someone's attempting a brute force SSH login."

His dad didn't answer, but continued to click and type, click and type, the screens flickering by so fast that Kateri couldn't believe he wasn't dizzy. "For what it's worth, I'm gumming up their processes while our data downloads. If this works, their banking system's going to start shutting down, and the more they try to fix it, the more it'll get confused."

"In other words, you're stopping them from stealing money? Go for it," Alex said, still watching his screen. "I can't tell that this guy who's trying to get in is making much headway."

"It'll just take me a few more minutes," his dad murmured, his fingers still flying on the keyboard.

Then Kateri saw a bright red security box open on the computer. "Dad, he's in!" Alex exclaimed.

"How'd he get in? Run diagnostics. Find out and shut off the portal."

Alex quickly clicked on some menus. For a few seconds he searched and then groaned. "The front desk computer! He got in through there!"

His dad moaned. "Of course. Probably got in through some lousy Windows bug that Microsoft hasn't got around to patching."

"Kateri, shut down the computer at the front desk," ordered Alex, and Kateri jumped to obey, but his dad said, "No, wait! You can't! Our connection is coming through there. If you shut it down, what I'm doing is going to be cut off." Saying something unflattering about Bill Gates, Mr. O'Donnell continued to click and type feverishly.

"Dad, he just established a reverse command.com shell prompt on the network," Alex reported, reading from the screen.

"Close down his processes!"

Alex hit the control-alt-delete keys simultaneously on his computer, scrolled through the menu that came up and hit "delete." "It's not working. I can't shut him down. Looks like we just got a new administrator for this computer too."

"He's already made himself admin." Mr. O'Donnell said softly.

"What does that mean?" Kateri queried.

Alex was grim. "It means he can do anything he wants, including disrupting the CD record, so Dad loses everything he's just gotten. And we can't do anything to stop him—" All at once he sat up, "except—wait a sec—this!"

He suddenly hit several keyboard commands in a rhythmic sequence, and the most colorful Internet Security Override program that Kateri had ever seen leapt onto the screen.

The Samurai Cat was seen from behind, facing into the screen, but the same familiar balloon appeared over his head.

### Can I Has Swordfights?

Alex attempted a cocky smile. "Bet our intruder doesn't have privileges over de Cat."

Dad glanced at the screen. "He doesn't. It's prioritized over everything on the system by hooking into the Windows kernel's system calls. A rootkit, but a good one. He can't get around it."

Alex took up the gamer's posture. "Until he defeats me."

"Um, yes. That's the problem," his dad said, his tone falling.

"*Not* a problem!" Alex exclaimed, maneuvering his fingers to make the cat leap back and forth with his sword. "My plan is to be undefeatable!"

Kateri swallowed. Despite Alex's usual bravado, she could tell he felt the pressure.

A large, spiral-shaped drill appeared hovering in the air over the cat's head and jabbed towards the cat, who swatted it away easily with his sword. "That's the other guy's cursor," Alex said, tapping the arrow keys to maneuver the sword. "Everyone always does that first. He definitely sees the Security Cat, all right."

The cat threw his sword from hand to hand, then paused, the same way Kateri had seen Alex pause before a fight, waiting for his opponent's first move.

"Bet he's pretty ticked off," Alex said. "He's trying to shut me down. Ah. He discovered he can't. So bet he decides that the Cat Are Worth Fightings."

The cursor quivered in the air suddenly, and dove down. Swiftly Alex parried via keystroke, and the huge drill bit went spinning away. But it quickly dove down again, like a massive hornet and jabbed, over and over and over again, slashing at the cat from every side. But the cat's sword met it every time.

The cursor pulled back, and then suddenly came in from the side, pushing the cat towards the side of the screen, but Alex parried every blow and finally, hitting two keys, gave a tremendous clout that sent the cursor flying and ricocheting off the corners for several seconds.

"Ooh, bet that ping-pong action sequence made him mad," Alex said, as the cat's sword momentarily changed to a paddle and he sassily leapt from side to side. "Better get ready for a counterattack. I think this guy's a gamer."

The drill finally stopped bouncing and drove abruptly down at the cat, stabbing and withdrawing, stabbing and withdrawing, switching from one side to the other. Alex rapped quickly in a constant staccato on the keys.

Suddenly the cat staggered back, a red gash appearing on his arm. Kateri winced. "That's not good."

"Just a flesh wound," Alex said, parrying and striking back, sending the cursor flying again. "Dad? How are you doing there?"

"If you can hold him off for ten more seconds, I'm going to grab the log of online activity," Mr. O'Donnell said.

"Can do," Alex said. "Oops!"

Blood spurted from the cat's other arm. "Isn't there an option where you don't have to die?" Kateri begged.

"Nope," Alex said, squinting at the screen. "Dad made the cat tough to beat, but not impossible. Fair is fair."

The cursor came down again. Undaunted, the cat swept his sword again, dodged and kicked at the cursor, landing a few karate blows on its point.

"He might hurt me this way, but I get health points for doing it," Alex murmured, continuing his patter on the keys. "If I can get in one good kick—there!"

Again the cursor bounced off the side of the screen crazily and bounced from corner to corner while the cat danced with a ping-pong paddle.

All at once, the cursor vanished.

"I got it," his dad breathed hard. "I got it all. Written to the CD-R. Secured it by generating a signature checksum for the archive, and I'm keeping the hash for that offline. Okay, let's shut down and get out of here." He unplugged the box from the computer, then set back to work on the keyboard, working his way back through the menus.

Alex remained poised at the computer, fingers over the keys, waiting, while the little cat on the screen held his katana at the ready.

Kateri became aware of the faint whine of the computer's cooling fans in the silence.

"Is he trying to get around you some other way?" she asked.

"Maybe," Alex said. He flicked his eyes at a corner of the screen where the intrusion detection box was still open. "No, he's gone. He's shut down his internet connection to get rid of me."

"In that case, let me shut down Windows and patch that hole," his dad said, closing down his computer. He got up, and patted Alex's shoulder. "Good work, son. Thank you."

"No problem," Alex said, as he continued to watch the screen. He tapped the keys, and the Samurai Cat leapt back and forth, sword ready.

"Okay, I was wrong," Kateri said. "Maybe video game skills can be useful, sometimes."

"Every once in a while," Alex said lightly. Both of them continued to stare at the computer.

"I think he's not coming back," Kateri said at last.

"But they know where we are," Alex said, almost to himself. "And they know what Dad stole from them. Sooner or later, they'll be back."

And for once, Kateri didn't doubt him.

# Chapter Eleven

*Yet as time passed, the life of Ali Baba's family was busy and productive, and they began to wonder if they had escaped the thieves after all.*

*The Arabian Nights*

For the next few days, Mr. O'Donnell was working on the data he'd captured from the cyberthieves' site every moment he could spare.

He had delivered a copy of the raw data to Agent Randolph at the FBI, who almost betrayed a sign of surprise and appreciation. But Mr. O'Donnell continued to sift through the information on his own, hoping to unearth more evidence for the FBI, and Agent Randolph had encouraged him to keep at it.

Kateri was nervous. As far as she was concerned, Mr. O'Donnell couldn't get that processed information to the FBI fast enough. But even then, as Alex pointed out to her, what was going to happen? Even if Mr. O'Donnell could pinpoint the identities of each of the users of the Mystery Site, what good would that do? The forty users, if that's what they were, could change identities and move. They probably did it all the time. And Mr. O'Donnell said it could easily be one person with forty different usernames. Or a thousand and two hundred, with thirty people each sharing one username.

In any event, Kateri was expecting something to happen. So the events of Wacky Wednesday undid her completely.

A week had passed since Mr. O'Donnell's hack, and once again, the hotel was bereft of guests. The last one checked out at nine. So Alex had switched places with his dad to take his mother out shopping, and Sam and David, in a fit of stealthy rebellion, had managed to go along.

So it was that Kateri found herself left alone to do all the rooms.

Granted, there were only three rooms to do, but that didn't help her mood. She pulled out the laundry cart and began to trundle down the hall to rooms 103 and 109. The guests had left these in relative disarray—they'd used all the towels, unwrapped all the soap for some reason (maybe they had a toddler?), and the wastepaper baskets were overflowing and smelly. Kateri took a practiced whiff and wrinkled her nose. Yes. Diapers.

She emptied the trash first and doused the cans with scented disinfectant. Then she washed down the solid surfaces, and on a hunch, did a deep-cleaning check and found plastic zoo animals thrust into the cracks of the mattresses. She removed them all (she was keeping a Lost and Found box whose contents grew increasingly interesting) and checked the ceiling light and found a burst balloon. Great. She would recommend replacing the fixture with something more impenetrable. Another thing for the To-Do List.

Then, starting from the back of the room and moving forward, she dusted the furniture, made the beds, and cleaned the bathroom. She swept the bathroom, pushing the dirt out onto the carpet. Finally, starting from the window at the rear of the room, she vacuumed, saving her last pass to clean up the bathroom dirt pile on the way out. Door closed, room done, and ready for the next guest.

Onto room 109. It took her a half hour longer to clean this room, where someone had apparently gotten sick. The bed mattress smelled disgusting, and she hurried back to the janitorial closet for additional cleaners. She decided no one was staying in this room for a while as she scrubbed the mattress and yanked it off the bed to let it dry in the sunlight from the undraped window. She'd tell Alex to take its keycard off the reservation list.

It was much later than she expected by the time she wearily pushed the cart up to room 310 for the last cleaning. This one, at least, was fairly standard, but there was a curious smell in it that she couldn't place and couldn't get rid off. After searching every corner for the source, she finally located it beneath the solid box bottom of one of the dressers: a molding hamburger. It had left a round dark spot on the carpet. She tossed the offending item, overturned the dresser and scrubbed the bottom, and applied carpet cleaner to the carpet. Actually, she should probably shampoo the entire room. Another room that would have to be taken off the roster for a day or so.

By noon, she finally pushed the laundry and cleaning cart downstairs, sweating and irate, and had only one thought: she needed a swim. She put everything away, glanced at the clock and wondered what was taking the O'Donnells so long? Well, she'd just have to hope that someone else would answer the phone or the desk. In her room, she changed into her swimsuit and coverup, and then hurried to the pool. Maybe she could get at least a five-minute swim?

She ran to the glass door, slamming into the bar to open it, and was crushed against the glass. It hadn't opened.

It *wouldn't* open.

Puzzled, she checked the handles. They wouldn't budge. She needed the keycard.

Hoping that if someone came to the desk, they'd mistake her for a guest, she ran to the office in the lobby in her bare feet. Mr. O'Donnell, who was supposed to be taking over Alex's shift, wasn't there. The office was locked, and Kateri's blue staff key wouldn't open it.

She remembered she had a copy of the red master key in her purse, which was in Alex's car (Alex had taken the van to the store). She decided to dash out the front door and grab it.

The glass front doors wouldn't open either.

Now she was worried. Feeling panicky, she ran to the closest fire exit and tried it. The door wouldn't budge. She sprinted to the O'Donnell's living quarters and tried the door there: locked! She pelted back to the delivery entrance. Locked!

Eight exit doors from the building, all locked.

Now she began to panic in earnest. She ran back to her room and grabbed her cell phone to call Alex, and that's when she began to lose her mind. Her cell phone wouldn't connect. No matter what she did—turn it on, turn it off, it wouldn't connect. She couldn't get service.

She picked up the phone at the front desk, and found it was dead.

It rapidly dawned on her: *I am trapped inside this hotel. I can't get out.*

This did not make sense. What if there was a fire? What about building codes? Surely there had to be some way out of this building! The elevator wouldn't work. And the doors to the stairwells were locked.

Desperate, Kateri ran to the janitorial closet where the fire extinguisher was, next to a fire ax. She grabbed the ax, and ran towards the front door, raising it as she went.

"Kateri! Wait!"

Mr. O'Donnell stood in the lobby, waving his arms. He was holding a handset.

Shell-shocked, Kateri halted, lowering the ax and trying to catch her breath.

"There's nothing wrong." Mr. O'Donnell said.

"Nothing wrong?" Kateri couldn't help spluttering. "None of these doors will open!"

"Uh," Mr. O'Donnell suddenly began clicking on his handset. "Which door do you want open?"

"All of them. Now." Her joints suddenly collapsing, Kateri dropped the ax and fell into a chair. "Don't tell me *you* did this."

"Um. Yes. I, uh, did. I've been working on the door locking system while I wait for the analysis scripts to finish processing. I guess I must have locked all the access doors accidently. I'm sorry."

Kateri took this in, and then flew to her feet. "Do you realize what would have happened if we had guests here and there was a fire? People could have been killed! And it would have been *your fault!*" She yanked her hair, trying to contain herself.

Mr. O'Donnell didn't try to defend himself. "You're right. I'm sorry."

"Did you block the phone lines too?"

"Yes. That's what I was actually trying to do," Mr. O'Donnell said. "I was trying out this cell phone jammer."

"You were TRYING to jam the phones?" Kateri yelled. "Why in the world would you need something like that? For Pete's sake, we run a hotel, not a fortress!"

"I don't know. It just seemed like it might be useful," Mr. O'Donnell offered.

"You—you—you…" she ran out of things to say. "You think just like Alex!" she finally burst out.

"I suppose I'm guilty of that, yes," he admitted. "Or, to be precise, Alex thinks like me. Uh. Let me go and get things unlocked. Before any guests show up."

"And before your assistant manager quits," Kateri muttered to herself. "Never, ever do that again!"

She stalked back to her room and threw herself on the bed.

Alex's Thursday was going fairly well, except that Kateri seemed to be unusually uptight. He had called the Maids In Time to come and clean, since there were twelve rooms being vacated: several families en route to a reunion had experienced a car breakdown and had checked in after midnight. It took most of the morning to check the guests out, but they all left on time, which had to be some kind of record.

Then a minor medical crisis occurred: a guest who had arrived last night called to say he was having an allergy attack. After finding out the guest was allergic to cats, Alex guessed that Link had been illegally sneaking around the halls that night. With profuse apologies, Alex relocated the guest to the top floor, where the exploring tortoiseshell cat was least likely to prowl.

He called Sam and David to help the guest move his luggage, and was just giving them final instructions when Kateri stomped into the lobby.

"Let me guess," he said quickly. "The Maids."

She thrust out her hand. A cigarette was dangling from the end of it. "One of them was SMOKING while cleaning the room!"

He helpfully held out a trashcan for her to dispose of the cigarette.

"I told her I was completely disgusted by such unprofessional behavior, and all she did was mutter something in Spanish, when I know she speaks *perfectly good English*!" Kateri ranted.

Alex listened to her, and, when she paused for breath, said, "Was she cleaning one of the smoking rooms or the non-smoking rooms?"

"The smoking rooms," she said. "But what difference does that make?"

Alex shrugged and reached for the phone. "I'll call their manager and tell them our complaint."

"You'd better," Kateri growled. "If I catch another one of them…"

Alex tapped her on the shoulder. "Shh. Someone's coming in." Kateri shook her head, trying to change her expression from peeved to pleasant, and turned to face the couple who had just walked into the hotel. She and Alex both gasped at the same time.

"Excuse me, is this the legendary Twilight Hills Hotel?" the man asked, taking off his gray flat cap as he came into the door, escorting his smiling wife on his arm.

Kateri was frozen. "Rose!"

The redheaded girl grinned, tossed her blue scarf over her shoulder and threw out her arms to her friend. "Kateri!"

The two girls hugged and began jumping up and down in excitement. Grinning, Alex came around the desk to greet his own friend. "Ben Denniston! This is a surprise! What brings you down here?"

Ben pulled off his grey cap and glanced around the hotel. "Business trip, but we couldn't pass up a chance to come by."

"It's really good to see you. Why didn't you let us know you were coming?"

"Well, it's not as though we thought you wouldn't have room for us," Rose said playfully, still holding Kateri's shoulder. She was wearing a multicolored coat that was almost too bright to look at. "We were on our way down to North Carolina and we thought we'd stop by to stay the night—that is, if we can get a room."

Alex immediately moved to the hotel computer and briskly typed. "One honeymoon suite available—with the hotel's compliments."

"Oh, you don't have to do that," Rose said, blushing. "It's been a year since the wedding."

"I don't see a problem," Ben said, squeezing his young wife's arm. "But there's no need to make it complimentary."

"Absolutely there is. We couldn't charge friends and comrades-in-arms," said Alex. "Please. We'd be honored."

The other O'Donnells happily agreed to cover for Alex and Kateri so that they could take their shifts off to spend time with their friends. The O'Donnells knew Rose, who had gone to the same college as Alex, and had come down to visit during the March for Life. And Rose had grown up in the same town as Kateri, who counted Rose as one of her oldest friends. They'd both gotten to know Ben through Rose, and he'd become a close friend of theirs as well.

"So how are things with Alex?" Rose asked, sitting on the bed while Kateri changed out of her work clothes.

Kateri sighed, "That's a large question."

Rose shrugged. "We've got time. Tell me."

Kateri glanced at Rose, who'd taken off her coat and was wearing a simple blue shift dress that matched her embroidered blue scarf. As usual, Rose was dressed with style and flair. Rose was beautiful, adventurous, a diehard romantic: in short, she was everything that Kateri was not.

"Rose, the problem is that Alex should really be hooked up with someone like you, not someone like me."

"What makes you say that?" Rose put her head to one side so her long red hair fell down her back.

An image flashed into Kateri's mind of a lovely, forlorn Rose fainting on Alex's shoulder while Alex slashed his way out of a band of enemies. But she couldn't explain that. "It's a mystery to me why you never fell for him."

Rose laughed. "I was just never interested in him. Sure, we have a lot in common, but I've never felt for him that way. Not like I felt for…" A faraway look came into her eyes, and Kateri rolled her eyes and turned to her hairbrush. She'd seen that look on Rose's face quite a lot whenever the subject of Ben came up. *Thank God they're married at last.*

"What do you think about Kateri, Ben?" Alex said abruptly, as the two friends stood in the weight room, talking about some adventures of the recent past.

"You've mentioned her quite a bit in your emails," Ben said, staring out the window with a smile. As usual, he looked battle-scarred and older than his age, but Alex thought to himself that marrying Rose had been good for his complexion. "She's quite a character. You know I have a world of respect for her."

"Just don't know if it's going to work out between us sometimes," Alex said, and found himself rambling on. "I'm crazy about her, even still, but she's always holding me at arms' length. I feel I'm trying too hard to make something happen, and I don't like that. I've always thought, if it's meant to be, it'll happen. No matter what I do. And if it's not meant to be… nothing I can do will change that." He shrugged.

"Spoken like a fatalistic Irishman," Ben said, with a hint of irony. "Well, perhaps it's good for you to be trying too hard. It might keep you from taking her for granted. You know, I always took Rose for granted. Until suddenly, one day, she wasn't there." He raised an eyebrow and turned away.

Alex was silent, recalling those dark days of the past when it had seemed that Rose was beyond their reach. They'd never given up hope, particularly Ben, but it was far easier to be on the far side of that trial.

"I hope I'm always there for Kateri," Alex said quietly.

"Yes," Ben said, fingering his hat. "I hope you can be. None of us ever intend to go."

"The thing is," Rose said unexpectedly, "is that Ben isn't really flamboyant and romantic like me. At least, not on the surface. I think I bring out the romantic in him."

"Huh," Kateri paused in trying to tame her hair. *Is that what Alex does for me? Is that why I like him so much?*

"Well, we all need that," Rose shrugged. "Otherwise, we'd just be stern-faced Puritan Platonists, all morals and ideal forms."

"I don't know why *I* need it," Kateri said, sitting down. "I'm not an intellectual, like you. And we Kovachs have always been romantic idealists. It's the Polish in us. How else could we be activists?"

Rose shook her head. "But you're idealists. That's the problem. And in this fallen world, ideals are easily shattered, and then you have a disillusioned idealist, which is almost worse than a cynic. In fact, they're probably the same thing. No, I think you need to be a romantic in order to survive, because it doesn't make sense to be one. It never does. That's the whole point."

Kateri stared at her. "So you're saying I should flutter and faint in Alex's arms sometimes?"

Rose giggled. "It would probably do you some good. It's hard to keep trusting a man, Kat, but you have to trust him. And distrust those high ideals of yours. I'm not saying don't believe them. Just don't take them quite so seriously. Laugh a bit at yourself, especially when you fall short. Ideals are fine things, but they can't be the only things, or they turn into idols," Rose said reflectively. "And don't forget: 'Satan fell through the weight of his own gravity.'"

Kateri groaned at the familiar words. "Okay, stop confusing me with your literary brilliance, Miss Bookworm! So who are you quoting?"

"You should know!" Swinging her legs mischievously, Rose grinned, and added, "You obviously need to read him more often. Don't you remember? 'Angels can fly because they can take themselves lightly.'"

"Do I really want to read him? He sounds too much like Alex," Kateri grumbled.

Rose threw up her hands. "It's all in G.K. Chesterton. Look him up sometime."

Kateri shook her head wearily. "I could never stand that guy."

"This is the problem, Ben," Alex said, later on that evening. They had gone out to dinner at a restaurant attached to a local cavern. The girls were prowling about the gift shop, trying to find a present for Rose to bring home to her new niece. The two men were sitting at the table, finishing their wine. "I guess Kateri feels our relationship is too random. She and I—let's face it. We were thrown together during all of that stuff that happened with you and Rose. If that hadn't happened, we probably never would have started dating. I bet that's why she feels it's too odd for us to be together."

"Well, God can use anything," Ben said philosophically. "After all, Rose and I were thrown together as well. I suppose that's one reason I kept writing her off for a long time. She was just this appendage I had picked up during a bizarre quest. I never thought that there might be something more to it than that."

"An inconvenience that turned into an adventure," Alex said with a smile. "So, what happened to you that changed your mind?" Alex asked.

Ben toyed with his wine glass, and a slow smile came over his scarred face. "Losing her," he said quietly. "Let's hope it doesn't take that for you and Kateri."

# Chapter Twelve

*Now Ali Baba was a generous man, and
if any traveler needed a place to stay the night,
Ali Baba would welcome him into his home.*
The Arabian Nights

Busy week ahead," Mom announced to the family at breakfast a few days later. "I just took reservations for a business conference. They booked every room we have for one overnight Tuesday next week. Then on Thursday, the Tietjen-Namod wedding will take up one-third of our rooms, and the Wood-Heesch wedding will take up another third. Let's hope we don't have an influx of tourists all of a sudden! There're a couple of one-night reservations in between these two as well. Kateri, I've already booked the Maid In Time service for the day after the business conference so you can relax."

"Busy indeed!" Alex said, pushing back his chair. He could already think of about ten things that needed to be attended to before this surge of guests arrived. "Barbarians, look alive. There are great opportunities for civilization ahead."

David looked nonplused, but Sam said, "Guess this means that we're making the hotel work, aren't we?"

"It certainly does look like it," Mom said, putting on her reading glasses. "This quarter has gone remarkably well so far. If we can manage to build up a little bit of a cushion, well and good."

"A cushion we need, just in case our hefty king-sized mattress is snatched out from under us," Alex reminded her.

"Wait a second," David said, pausing with his fork in midair. "If we've booked every room for this Tuesday, does that include Kateri's room?"

"Um. Yes," Mom said hesitantly. "Kateri, you can move into our suite…"

All eyes were on Kateri, and she colored.

"That's okay," she said, and picked up another forkful of eggs. "I'll book a room at the motel down the street."

"And give the competition business? Absolutely not," Alex said firmly. "We'll upgrade you to our living room couch."

"Upgrade? You should get your sense of direction checked, Mr. Day Manager."

"Wow! We've never booked all the rooms before," Sam said. "We should have a celebration!"

"I guess we could," Mom said. "Though we can hope that it gets to be so frequent that we don't even need to take notice."

"I say we celebrate anyhow," David said, breaking the crusts off another piece of toast. "This whole hotel business is a lot of work."

"Almost the exact opposite of a permanent vacation," Alex murmured, yawning, then noticed Kateri's downcast look. "Wait a second," he said. "Kateri, your birthday is on Tuesday, isn't it?"

Kateri stared at her plate, her cheeks red. "It doesn't matter," she said in a stiff monotone. "Business is business. We should definitely celebrate booking all the rooms."

"Let's celebrate that, and your birthday, on Monday," Alex said, going to Kateri and squeezing her shoulder. "How about that, Mom?"

"Sounds like a plan," she smiled.

Kateri looked up at him, suddenly wary. "Oh no. You're about to go and buy me some ridiculously expensive present, aren't you?"

Alex grinned. "How did you know?"

"We're *supposed* to be saving money."

"Not at the expense of treating you, our valuable employee."

"You just look for justifications for buying me presents, don't you?"

He rumpled her hair. "Kateri, you are finally figuring me out."

Mr. O'Donnell was nearly finished sifting through the data, and he proudly showed his progress to Alex and Kateri on Monday evening. Kateri squinted at the green and black data. It still looked like pages and pages of numbers and figures that didn't make much sense to her.

"You're sure you're sifting this the right way?" Alex asked. "How do you know what to look for?"

"Looking for repetitions," his dad said. "Finding structure. Sorting by key fields. Some of the variables are things like 'Yes' and 'No.' The Perl scripts I'm running suggest that more than likely, each record has about thirty fields. And sorting the user logs this way, I seem to get the equivalent of forty users. At least, that's how it makes the most sense." He exhaled. "But of course, it's a lot of trial and error."

The desk phone rang, and Alex went to answer it in his usual professional voice. It was a guest question about the local pizza parlors, and Alex gave a recommendation. "Anything else I can help you with tonight? Have a good night, and thanks for staying with us." He hung up with a sigh. "Dad. Kateri's party's at nine. You'll have to be on call. Is that okay?"

"Fine with me," Mr. O'Donnell said. "Thanks again, Kateri, for choosing to be part of the madness."

Kateri glanced again at the columns of incriminating numbers. "Did I really get a choice?" she murmured.

She hadn't wanted a party: her idea of a birthday was a day off to relax and get things done. Including, maybe, an extra day just to sleep. Still, it wasn't worth complaining about.

But when she walked down the corridor past the gleaming weapons to the O'Donnell living room, to be greeted by boisterous strains of "Happy birthday" and "Stolot" (the Polish birthday song), she couldn't help but be touched. Not only had Mrs. O'Donnell baked a homemade cake—lemon poppy seed with white icing and twenty-two candles—but there was green tea, spring rolls, and rice pudding with coconut and mango.

The nice thing about the O'Donnells was that they were pleased by exotic foods, and even the youngest boys ate them without complaining. Kateri had never met five more non-picky eaters in her life.

"You must have called my mom," she said to Mrs. O'Donnell, taking an artistically arranged flat blue plate with a sliver of cake and a sample of each of the desserts.

Mrs. O'Donnell laughed. "I did. And I had a wonderful conversation with her. She seems like such a fascinating person: all her life experience and all the things she knows how to do!"

"She's definitely that," Kateri agreed. "And this is delicious."

"Present time!" Sam cheered as he handed her one. "This one's from me."

Kateri unwrapped her very own copy of Mangan Ninja 2010. "Gee, thanks!" she said. "Uh—guess I'll have to play it with you sometime."

Sam nodded eagerly. "I'll show you how!" he said happily.

Mrs. O'Donnell gave her a pair of comfortable stylish shoes in black. "Clarks. I've worn them for years," she said. "Thought you might want a break from sneakers sometimes."

"Thanks," Kateri said gratefully.

"And this is from Aunt Mona: I talked to her yesterday and she wanted to send a present." Mrs. O'Donnell handed Kateri a printout of a certificate. "It's a trip to a day spa. I told her you could use one!"

"She's certainly right," Kateri said, and made a mental note to email Aunt Mona and thank her.

David gave her bath salts, and Mr. O'Donnell, who came in from the lobby to hand her a gift bag, gave her a book of Vietnamese folk tales and a gift card. "The gift card is in case you wanted a different book," he said apologetically.

"No! This is very nice," Kateri assured him, flicking through the pages and admiring the illustrations. (She always appreciated books with pictures.) "Thanks!"

"Ready for mine?" Alex said, handing her a large box wrapped in printed foil paper.

"Should I be?" But she ripped open the paper, and lifted the lid. There were two paper fans decorated with birds covering something made of pale purple silk embroidered with beads. She removed the fans, lifted up the cloth and gasped. "Where did you find an ao dài?"

"Where else?—eBay." Alex grinned. "Like it?"

"It's beautiful," Kateri held up the traditional Vietnamese outfit, a long-sleeved silken dress with matching silk pants.

"Try it on. See if it fits," Alex urged.

"Okay." She took the box to the bathroom.

In the little room, she changed into the dress. The silk slid smoothly over her shoulders: it was well made. She finished fastening the countless buttons up the front and looked at herself. The dress had a mandarin collar and a sleek, form-fitting silhouette that broadened into a skirt with side slits at the bottom. Demure and elegant as the ao dài was, she always felt a little uncomfortable in the style. Perhaps because she felt she was nearly the opposite of the poised, graceful archetype of Asian femininity. Her mother and sisters looked gorgeous when wearing an ao dài, but she wasn't sure that she could pull it off. Still, Alex had gotten the right color for her: purple suited her, even if it was the traditional color of the nobility. Trying fruitlessly to tame her waving hair, which would never be the glossy curtain of silken strands that Vietnamese fashion adored, she took a deep breath, and threw open the bathroom door. "Ta da!"

"Yowza," David got to his feet. "You look awesome!"

"Not yowza. Owzye," Sam said, mimicking Kateri's pronunciation of the dress. David smacked him.

"You look simply beautiful." Mrs. O'Donnell said. "That color really works for you."

As for Alex, his eyes were shining, and for once, he didn't speak. He merely walked up to her in his usual chivalrous fashion and bowed.

"Would you dance for us?" Sam said. "You know, that fan dance?"

"Yeah!" David said. "Please, Kateri?"

Kateri looked to Alex to shoot them down, but she could tell that he thought this would be a fantastic idea. "I don't think so," she said. She already felt on display enough as it was. "Well, it fits!" she turned to go back into the bathroom, but Alex quickly grabbed her hand and led her back to the table.

"Mom, this pudding is really excellent," he said, sinking onto a cushion around the coffee table. "I think we should start eating out here, don't you?"

Kateri started to object, but realized there was no way she could gracefully escape wearing this dress for the rest of the evening. *Outmaneuvered again by Alex O'Donnell.* She felt a prickle of resentment.

After the party was over, Kateri hoped to go back and change, but Alex asked her to go for a walk with him. Because there wasn't much space to walk outside, they ended up strolling around the pool. Fortunately no guests were using it. Even though the summer night was hot, the water seemed to provide a respite. The pool lights glowed golden in the blue water, casting iridescent reflections on the concrete.

And the dress was really beautiful. As she fanned herself with one of the paper fans, she watched the reflections from the water shimmer on the pale purple silk trousers and the beaded silk gauze. She had changed into the black shoes Mrs. O'Donnell had given her, which fitted well with the ao dài. Even though she was afraid the dress spotlighted each curve and bulge of her figure, she had to admit it was comfortable: not to mention a nice change from the stiff white cotton uniform she'd been wearing.

Alex paused by the tall iron fence that separated the pool area from the woods beyond. "We really should plant some flowering vines here," he mused. "I guess Mr. Bhatka liked to keep it clear, but I think it would look a little less industrial that way. What do you think?"

"I think you really care about this hotel, Alex," she said.

"I do," he said, and his voice sounded happy. "You know, going to a liberal arts college, I never considered business. But I'm actually really enjoying it. I like the coming and going of the guests, and it's sort of challenging, in a good way, to take something that's already good and make it even better."

Kateri toyed with her hair. "When do you think you can afford to re-carpet the place?"

"What's wrong with the carpet?" He glanced at her. "You don't like the tulips?"

"They freak my eyes out. I'm not sure what sort of demented designer on drugs picked out that pattern. It doesn't exactly say 'rest and relax.' At least not to me."

"Oh, it was the 70s and no one had their heads screwed on straight," said Alex lightly. "I had no idea you hated the carpet so much. I guess I thought it was unique."

"Unique is not good," Kateri said. "If we could switch to something beige or brown, I'd be much happier."

"I'll think about it," Alex said, sounding a bit put off.

"So you talk as though you're going to be here long-term," Kateri said.

"Yes," Alex admitted. "I think I'll finish my college degree online and just make my career here." He looked over at her. "What about you?"

Alex never missed a trick. He was meeting her eyes, his own green eyes dark in the shadows. She swallowed. "I don't know."

"But yet, you've obviously been thinking about the carpet. You can't hate this hotel business as much as you pretend, Kateri."

"Oh, I've always dreamed of washing bathrooms and cleaning kitchens," she said, trying to dampen her sarcasm.

"You know you only do that because you don't like the way the maid service does it," Alex reminded her. "You and your pointless vendetta against the Maids In Time."

"I'm trying to save your family money."

"And we appreciate it," Alex said, leaning over her. "We really appreciate it."

She accepted his kiss, but pulled away. In this silk dress, she felt shy. "Thank you for the birthday party," she said.

"It was a pleasure." He sighed and sat down on a poolside chair.

Kateri lay down in one of the lounge chairs, straightening the skirt of her dress and waiting for him to ask her again about her long-term plans.

But Alex had apparently changed gears. "I hope things aren't too crazy for you with this hotel full of guests tomorrow."

"Let's hope they're not wild partiers," she said. "Did you fix the drapes in that one room and replace that chair?"

"I did," Alex said. "I figured out how to slide the wheels back into the slot on the hanging bar. I also fixed the drapes in 201 and 213 that were sagging."

"What about the scratches on the breakfast tables?"

"There's some scratch repair Mr. Bhatka had in his toolkit. That worked well enough. We'll have to resurface them eventually. Oh, and remind me to tell the family to keep Link out of the reception area. I've been finding cat hair on the carpet, and we haven't had a guest bring pets with them for a week."

"That cat's been sneaking into the hotel whenever she can," Kateri said, shaking her head. "Oh, did you ever paint over those scratches on the wall in room 304?"

Alex nodded. "Two days ago, and I've been airing out the room, so it should be ready for the guests." They had both fallen into their working lists of repairs. "That reminds me. We've got to order more sugar substitute and Irish-coffee creamers. We're almost out."

"Okay. I've already got red square napkins, toilet paper, and A33 cleaner on the list," Kateri said, stifling a yawn. "I'll also have the dry cleaners drop off the jackets. Is there anything else you want me to do?"

"Dance for me, Kateri?" He looked at her longingly.

She closed the paper fan she'd been carrying and shook her head. "No."

"Why not?"

"I'm too self-conscious," she said.

"It's only me out here."

She glanced up at the draped windows. "Plus whatever guests are spying out the windows."

He laughed. "I doubt it. Come on. Dance."

She hesitated. "I'm really not that great of a dancer."

"I don't believe you." He put his hands on his knees. "Come on, can't you do just a short one? For me?"

"Is this part of your playacting at having a trophy Asian girlfriend?"

"Partly. But why do you have to be so sarcastic, Kateri?"

"Alex," she said, shaking her head. "When you come up with these crazy ideas of yours, what do you expect me to do?"

"It would be more fun if you would play along," he said, leaning back in his chair. "You know? Come on, Kateri, you need to have more fun. You're wonderful and competent and organized and put together, but you're going to get ulcers if you can't just relax and lighten up. Don't take things so seriously. Why should I have any agenda? I love you, and I love your country and I love your heritage, so why shouldn't I ask you to dance? Stop analyzing so much."

Everything in her wanted to argue, but she recognized that he was right. "Okay. I'll stop analyzing. But I'm sorry, I just don't feel like dancing right now."

"That's fine." Alex stared at the pool, and she wondered if she had hurt his feelings.

"Thank you for the dress, though," she offered. "It's really lovely."
"You're welcome. I'm glad you like it."

The next morning, Alex caught Link trying to make a break for the lobby. Quickly he snagged the large tortoiseshell cat, who, luckily, was out of exercise, and threw her gently onto the couch. "No roaming for you today, Link. We gots lots of peoples coming."

The cat protested with a meow, and rolled onto the futon, grumbling as Alex closed the door to the apartment. Striding back into the lobby, he caught a whiff of baking cinnamon rolls and sniffed appreciatively. Maybe the guests wouldn't arrive right away, and he could snag one.

Buttoning his red jacket, he checked his image in the bamboo-framed lobby mirror, smoothed his short beard down, and straightened his pony tail.

Dad looked relieved to see him, getting up creakily from the lobby desk. "Nice morning," he said. "The last two rooms are leaving early. They asked me to set their wakeup calls for 7:30 AM."

"The hikers?" Alex said. "Must want to get on the road. Hope they had fun rock-climbing."

"I think they did," Dad said. "Kateri's already up. She started the coffee."

But Alex didn't see any sign of his girlfriend. He helped himself to a cup of black and a bagel from the plastic Lucite display case in the breakfast area. Carrying his breakfast to the desk, he paused to clean a table and dust a windowsill, then settled himself behind the desk. He kept a Liturgy of the Hours book in the drawer, a habit he'd started at Mercy College, and he read a few pages while eating his bagel. Hearing the whoosh of the elevator, he got to his feet, wiping his mouth quickly.

The hikers were packed and ready to go. It was a mom and dad and several teenagers, the latter in various states of waking, ranging from blinking and stumbling to obviously sleepwalking. But they trooped eagerly into the breakfast area, where Kateri was dishing out the cinnamon rolls. "How was everything?" Alex said to the dad.

"Oh, just fine," the dad said, looking out the door at the sunshine. "It *would* be a great morning today, when we're leaving. Shame we can't go on one last hike."

"Yeah, yesterday when we went rock climbing, it rained till sundown," the oldest teen boy complained, coming over with a bun on a paper napkin.

Alex shook his head sympathetically. "Better come back soon and try again!" he said.

"Oh, we will, for sure," the mom said. "We had a great time!"

Alex checked them out, and asked if he could help carry their luggage, but the dad shook his head. "There are enough of us to get it," he said. The teenagers groaned in unison.

"Have a safe trip home, then, and come back and see us!" Alex said, matching his southern accent to theirs.

"Sure will!" The dad waved goodbye, and his muttering teenagers followed him out. Alex replaced the cap on his pen and watched them go, feeling sympathy for the teens' weary expressions. They had probably been up late after a long day of more physical exercise than usual. He knew what it was like to follow energetic parents around on a hiking trip. Of course, that was back before Mom had gotten sick…

Suddenly two of the teens perked up, looking at something as they walked to their car. They began to laugh, and pointed surreptitiously. Soon the whole family was looking and smiling. Curious, Alex watched.

Someone was walking up to the entrance door, but the sunlight obscured his face until he came into the lobby. Alex did a double-take: it was a Martian.

Actually, it was a man in a sports shirt wearing an alien mask. At first, Alex wondered if this were a hold-up, and tensed, but the masked man pulled out a wallet instead of a gun.

"I believe I have a reservation?" the alien said.

Alex sputtered in laughter. "Do you?" he said, flipping open his book. "Everything's booked for the Windham Olaf business conference."

The alien inclined his head. "That's me," he said.

Alex looked at him, blinking. "You're with the conference?"

"We're attending a gaming convention," the alien explained. "We don't all work for Windham Olaf, but we all go to the convention together. I just made the reservation in my company's name."

"Oh!" Suddenly this all made sense. "Cool!" he exclaimed. "I had no idea there was one in the area! I'm a gamer myself."

"Well, it's not exactly in the area. A bunch of us meet here to go down to the convention in Atlanta," the alien said. "More of us should be arriving soon."

Alex returned the man's credit card and spread his hands. "Well, we have the whole place reserved for you, so make yourself at home." He indicated the breakfast area. "Cinnamon rolls just came out of the oven. Help yourself."

"Oh! Thanks. But I'm on a low-carb diet," the Martian said, shouldering his laptop bag and taking his plastic card key.

As he left, Kateri came out of the kitchen, a flabbergasted look on her face. "Who was that?"

Alex indicated the vanished alien. "Apparently our incoming guests are all attendees at a gaming convention. Kind of cool, eh?"

"And I bet they're doing it on company time." Kateri shook her head. "Of course, a hotel run by your family *would* attract a crowd like this."

And a crowd it was. By noon, nearly a dozen guests, most of them wearing character masks, had checked into the hotel. Alex had fun chatting with them about their favorite games, and David and Sam were eagerly helping with bags and making small talk with the oddly-attired guests. One guest had an enormous amount of luggage, and tipped Sam and David handsomely, which only added to their fun.

"Hope these guys come every year!" Sam enthused, pocketing his twenty dollars.

Alex even decided to change the hotel's elevator music to science fiction soundtracks, just for fun. He half-wondered if he should be wearing a mask himself, to add to the holiday enjoyment for the guests.

But surprisingly, there didn't seem to be a lot of mingling going on among the guests once they arrived. Alex fully expected them to use the pool area, the weight room, or even the conference room, which they had booked, but the halls were deserted, except for arriving guests. Maybe they were all tired from their travels? Or they were visiting between rooms? Alex wasn't entirely sure.

The day went on. Alex checked in the next two guests, two men in Spider Man masks, both in business suits. Next came a heavyset woman in a tiger mask, carrying a bulky briefcase and wearing shorts that were too small for her. A half hour later, a Japanese man, monosyllabic, carrying a laptop and several bags, entered, not wearing a mask. At first Alex wasn't sure he was with the same group.

"You here for the gaming convention?"

"Ah, yes. Yes I am," the man said hurriedly. He bent down, took something out of a bag, and put it on. An Adolf Hitler mask.

"Oh, that's better," Alex said. "So, you a gamer too?"

"Actually no," the man said, trying with difficulty to adjust the mask.

"You just coming to hang out with your friends?"

"Yes. It's a lot of fun, the gaming convention," the man said, taking his key and hurriedly going down the hallway.

Another man came in wearing the mask of a samurai. He paused in the doorway and gave a tremendous sneeze.

"Bless you!" Alex said, looking around on the ground. Sure enough, he spotted Link the Cat sniffing at something on the carpet. Quickly he left the desk. "Excuse me," he said, and swiftly ran Link back down the hallway to the apartment. "Stay here!" he said, setting him on the couch. "Mom! Make sure the cat stays in!"

"Sam or David must have let her out!" Mom said from the couch, where she was folding laundry.

Shaking his head, Alex ran back down the hallway to the lobby, and stepped behind the desk again, wiping his hands with antibacterial cleanser. "So sorry about that," he said. "Can I help you?"

"Checking—atch!—for the Windham—Achoo!—Olaf—" the samurai choked, pulling on his mask. "I need a—pet free room."

"Absolutely. Those are on the top floor," Alex said, checking him in. "Say, weren't you here before?"

"Achoo!—No, I don't think so," the man said, sniffing. "Can I have my keys please?"

"Here you go. So sorry. Sam! Get his bags for him!" Alex said, and Sam, who had just come back into the lobby, hurried to comply. Alex stared after the man, whose build looked familiar. *And I could have sworn I recognized his sneeze.*

Kateri was vacuuming the breakfast area, which she had just finished shutting down, but made more coffee after one guest requested it. "Wonder if I should bake another batch of rolls?" she wondered aloud.

"Maybe not a bad idea," he said, scanning over the computer list of reservations. Thirty-nine guests checked in. The hotel was almost full.

He looked up eagerly as the door opened to admit a weary couple with a baby, but it turned out that they didn't have a reservation: they had just stopped in from the highway. Apologetic, Alex recommended the bed and breakfast downtown, or one of the other motels. After the couple left, he figured he might as well turn on the "No Vacancy" sign. Hopefully the last guest with a reservation would know to come in anyhow.

Still no stir from the guests who had already arrived. It was getting towards the dinner hour. Several pizza men and Chinese takeout delivery boys arrived and went to various rooms. But aside from that, not a peep.

"I'm wondering if we should get takeout ourselves," Kateri said, pushing out a cart to stock up the breakfast area for tomorrow morning. "That Chinese food smelled delicious."

"Why not? I'll order now," Alex said, glancing at the clock. "I'm off in twenty minutes." He checked to see if anyone had requested anything on the answering machine: nothing. Unusually non-demanding guests. "So what do you want?"

Kateri said, "Something with lots of vegetables."

Alex made a face as he pulled out his cell phone. "Something with a lot of vegetables. Can you be more specific? There's a menu in the desk drawer there." He waited for his phone to connect, but instead "Looking for service" blinked on the screen. "That's odd."

Not wanting to wait, he dialed the number from the desk phone and ordered General Tsou chicken, moo gai pan, and vegetarian hoisin for Kateri. When he finished, his mom came out, rolling her wheelchair and looking puzzled.

"Hey mom. I just ordered some Chinese for me and Kateri. Did you want anything?"

"No, the boys and your dad and I ate earlier," Mom said. "Something odd just happened. I was using the Internet, and I got booted off. Now I can't get back on."

"Where's Dad? Have him check our connection." Alex opened the door to the office, where his dad was ensconced as usual. "Dad, Mom can't get on the Internet."

Dad switched off the database work and slid to the hotel computer. "She's right. It's down." He clicked on the menu, then after a moment or two, frowned. "It can't find the connection. That's really, really odd."

He kept working on it while Alex and Kateri chatted with Mom and waited for their food. But by the time the Panda Chef order arrived, he still hadn't managed to repair it. Alex and Kateri took their cartons of food into the office and watched him work on it.

Finally Dad pushed himself back from the computer. "Something's wrong with our system," he said. "It's completely down."

Alex whistled. "Do you think it's the hacker?"

"Could be. But that's odd, because I've been monitoring suspicious access patterns, and there haven't been any intrusion attempts." He got up. "I'm going to go check the connection."

Alex followed him down to the utility room in the basement. His dad slid the card through the lock and opened it. Turning on the lights, he went over to the panel, and began to look at the wires. Finally he shook his head. "It looks like we have a hardware problem."

"That stinks. That means the guests can't connect either. Weird that we haven't heard them complaining."

His dad was studying the panel. "I could try to fix this, but I've got to get on duty. I'll send an email to our tech guy and have him come by in the morning."

"Dad," Alex said, as they walked back upstairs. "Um. How are you going to send an email if we can't get on the internet?"

His dad smiled. "I've got another way to connect," he said.

Upstairs in the office, he booted up a program on his laptop. "It's a software ad-on I put together. It can detect any wireless networks being used in the area."

"But we're up on a mountain. How many wireless networks can it find up here?" Kateri asked, eating her broccoli with chopsticks.

"Well, normal wireless adapters just scan for other networks that they can be connected to. This one's going to look for any traffic out there, any broadcasting points in the vicinity. Sometimes you'd be surprised at what you can find." He clicked an icon on his screen.

Alex reached for the duck sauce, and glanced at his dad, who was staring at the screen. "So, are you surprised at what you found?"

His dad blinked. "That's an understatement. I thought I'd get the usual trace of one or two signals near here, but this mountain is crawling with traffic."

"What?" Kateri and Alex both leaned over his laptop.

"There're lots of users using the internet all around us. But not through our network. They have a network of their own." He adjusted his glasses and looked closely at the screen. "And they're all communicating with the same access point. An access point which isn't identifying itself." He watched the stream of lines crawling across his screen. "I'm counting ten signals—no, twelve— fourteen—curious. Wonder how many there actually are?"

"Can you find out?" Alex said, as his dad continued to stare at the screen.

"I'm not sure—wait, call David. Get him over here."

Alex vaulted over the desk chair and hurried out to hunt down David. He found his younger brother at the pool, reading a novel, and beckoned to him. "Dad wants you."

When David came into the office, Mr. O'Donnell said, "Hey, David—do you still have that cantenna you and I made in Scouts last year?"

David was toweling his hair. "Yeah, I actually do. I hid it in the back of my closet so Kateri couldn't downsize it."

Kateri stuck out her tongue at him as he passed, hurrying back to his room. "Okay, so what's a cantenna?" she asked.

"Pretty neat thing. We made it out of a tomato juice can. It extends the reach of a computer's wireless adapter," Mr. O'Donnell clicked on another icon, then stood up and rummaged around in one of his junk drawers until he found a cable. "Alex, grab the video camera tripod from that corner and set it up near here."

By the time Alex had located and set up the tripod, David had returned holding a tin can with a couple of screws sticking out of it and two wire rings around it holding it to a clamp. He mounted it to the top of the tripod with expert precision, so that the can was pointed up at the ceiling.

"Point it south: best signal from down there," Dad said.

Meanwhile, Kateri cleared off a spot on the office counter and sat on it, shaking her head.

Dad had plugged one end of the cable into his laptop, and handed the other end to David, who screwed it into the side of the can.

"You did this in Scouts?" Alex asked.

David shrugged. "Most of us will do anything for an Eagle's badge," he said.

Dad was focused on the screen again, counting. Then he shook his head. "Too many to see. I'll run it through a script filter for a unique count…"

He typed quickly on his keyboard and frowned. "Now this is very, very odd," he said slowly. "It's almost—sinister."

"What?" Alex and Kateri and David crowded around the screen.

The screen said:

```
Unique wireless connections detected: 40
```

# Chapter Thirteen

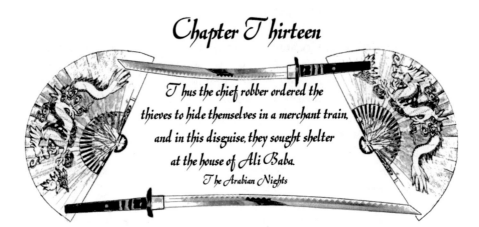

Thus the chief robber ordered the
thieves to hide themselves in a merchant train,
and in this disguise, they sought shelter
at the house of Ali Baba.
*The Arabian Nights*

lex stared at the message from the wireless detection software. "Forty connections detected? What does that mean?" Kateri demanded.

"It means that in this immediate vicinity, there are forty people connected to a wireless signal broadcasting from an unknown access point somewhere in this area," Dad said in a slightly strained tone.

"Where would the signal be coming from?" Kateri asked.

"Hm. Did you see anyone carrying in a parabolic antenna?" Dad asked. "Sort of like a large satellite dish?"

"One the guests did have an awful lot of luggage," David said.

"My guess is that the unknown access point is a satellite connection, and that's what they're all using to connect: a private satellite network they set up in the hotel." Dad glanced out the window. "Or maybe in the woods."

"So forty people using a private satellite network. And the bizarre thing is," Alex said, mentally checking his reservation book. "We only have thirty-nine guests checked in."

This sank in.

"So chances are that our guests," Dad said slowly, moving the mouse over his screen, "are all techies."

"Or cyberthieves." Kateri supplied.

They all continued to gaze at the monitor. Forty unique wireless connections. And thirty-nine guests had arrived in masks. And possibly someone else was in the woods, with a satellite dish, helping them all to communicate.

"The oddest thing," Alex murmured, "is that we can't tell if this is an emergency or not. Yet."

"Maybe you should call that FBI agent, just to see what he says," Kateri suggested.

"Not a bad idea," Dad pulled out his cell phone. "Rats. No service."

Alex immediately checked his again. "Okay, mine's still off too. Dad, someone's running a jammer."

"Use the landline," Kateri said, getting to her feet.

But when Alex picked up the hotel phone, it was dead.

"I'm going to guess that whoever disabled the internet connection cut the phone lines too," Dad said.

"But it wasn't cut when we were down in the basement a few minutes ago," Alex said. The two men looked at each other, and thought the same thing.

Alex ran to the family living quarters and grabbed a bokken from the weapons wall. Kateri followed him. "What are you doing?"

"Going to check the basement for rats."

"You're crazy."

"Stay up here." He shrugged off the red jacket and pushed the blade of the wooden sword through his belt loops, figuring that the chances of his looking like a medievalist fool were diminishing, and hurried to the basement steps.

He opened the door softly, and looked downstairs. The lights were on.

Stealthily, he sidled down the steps. He heard someone moving about below, and, drawing his sword, mentally prepared himself.

When he reached the bottom, he saw that the utility room door was propped open. Inching his way towards it, he could hear someone. When he peered in, he saw a large heavy-set man wearing an albino Wookie mask crouched in front of the main circuit board for the hotel. The hairy head turned when Alex came in, and immediately the man drew a semi-automatic.

Instinctively, Alex brandished his sword, but he was aware as he did so that he had chosen to carry a non-lethal weapon, and that the man had the upper hand.

"Get back against the wall," the man rasped.

Alex obeyed, but didn't relax his two-handed grip on the sword.

The Wookie came closer, fiddling in his pocket. He pulled out a pair of handcuffs as he came through the door into the hallway and advanced on Alex.

"Put down the toy sword," the voice came through the mask. Alex fixed his eyes on the gun. Definitely not a toy. Deadly, gleaming blue steel.

"Come on, move it!" ordered the man, motioning from side to side with the gun, and, staring at the gun, Alex caught a glimpse of a white dot on the side of an angled metal switch. In a second, he realized what that meant: the gun's safety was on.

It would only take a second for the man to click it off and fire, but Alex seized his fraction of an advantage and swiftly swung his sword, simultaneously lunging out of the line of fire.

With a crack, his wooden blade landed on the flat of the man's hand. The man roared in pain and dropped the gun.

Alex reached down for the gun, and in a split second recognized he'd made a mistake as the Wookie launched forward. *Shoot.*

Next thing Alex knew, he was flat on the floor with the big man on top of him, and he had lost both his sword and the chance of grabbing the gun. Snarling, the man punched Alex in the side with his good hand.

Alex twisted around, trying to get out from under the man, but the Wookie pushed his fat stomach right onto Alex's face. Unable to breathe, Alex gasped and tried fruitlessly to free his nose and mouth while the man grabbed at Alex's arms. Realizing he was about to get definitively pinned, Alex decided to squeeze himself further *under* his opponent. With a violent effort, he pushed himself downward, towards the man's feet, evading the man's brawny arms. Yelling, the man tried to regain his hold on Alex, but Alex, wriggling ferociously, popped out from under the man's side and tried to scramble to his feet. But the Wookie grabbed him by the legs and tackled him again, causing Alex to trip and fall, this time on top of the handcuffs.

*This guy might not know how to fight, but he knows how to use his weight.* Alex pushed himself up on his elbows and with a fierce twist, smashed the Wookie in the face with his right elbow, changed direction and grabbed the Wookie's arm to shoulder-roll his opponent over and off him. The Wookie landed flat on his back with a crash, and a relieved Alex jumped to his feet and lunged for the gun—only to be stopped by a wrenching pain in his wrist. Stunned, he glanced down and realized that during the grappling, the Wookie had snapped the handcuff on his left wrist. Now the masked man had Alex chained, and was holding the other cuff in both his meaty hands.

Desperate, Alex tried to snatch at the gun with his free hand, but it was just a few feet too far away. Quickly the Wookie yanked hard on the cuffs, and Alex, thrown off balance by his reach, went down. The big man kicked him in the side, and bent over to pick up the gun himself, but Alex kneed him in the gut. When the man stepped back, gasping, Alex regained his feet. With a roar, the big man swung Alex around into the wall, out of reach of the gun.

Winded, Alex tried unsuccessfully to jerk the cuff out of the man's hand, but the Wookie still wasn't letting go. He tried to pull Alex closer, but Alex swung away, circling him, avoiding the metal support pole in the center of the basement room.

Alex was thinking fast: *if I can get the cuff out of his hand, I could loop it around my own fist, use it as a brass knuckle. That might be enough to give me a slight advantage.* But the Wookie had a good grip on that cuff, and was angling himself to pull Alex into a headlock.

*Let me see if I can use that weight of his against him.* Alex tugged on the cuffs, and the man tugged right back. Hoping to throw him off, Alex pushed his cuffed hand suddenly towards the man, and the man predictably pushed right back at him. Seizing the moment when his opponent was off balance, Alex aimed a quick blow at the nerve cluster of the man's forearm. He struck, hard.

The man let go of the cuffs and fell—but unfortunately Alex had misjudged both his own position and the man's weight: Wookie-man plunged right into him, crushing Alex to the ground for the third time. Stars flared up in his vision as he lay stunned on the floor.

The Wookie creaked to his feet, using Alex's stomach for help. Vaguely Alex became aware that the man was dragging his hands together. The handcuff snapped around Alex's other wrist. Captured, Alex realized he had only one last chance to defeat him. *And I'd better not mess up this time.*

He pulled up his knee and simultaneously grabbed a handful of the furry white Wookie mask with his cuffed hands, yanking it downwards so that the man's forehead made contact with Alex's bent knee. The man howled, and Alex furiously smashed the man's head down on his kneecap again.

With a whimpering groan that sounded strangely in character, the man sank to his knees and wavered.

"No," whispered Alex, but too late—the man collapsed right onto Alex's stomach, a dead weight.

Handcuffed and trapped beneath his fallen opponent, a breathless Alex struggled to get free. He looked up, and saw Kateri standing on the cellar steps, her face white as her uniform.

"May the Force be with you," he managed to say.

She ran to him. "It looks like the Force is *on* you."

Alex stifled a laugh: his ribs hurt too much. "Yeah. I'd be much better if this particular Force was *not* with me. Can you check to see if he has the handcuff keys in his pocket?"

Fortunately Kateri found them after a quick search and unlocked Alex's wrists. Groaning, Alex pushed his fallen assailant off him with Kateri's help. "Cuff his hands together around that metal support pole over there. Thanks."

She started to, but glanced at Alex with a queer expression on her face. "Are you sure you're okay?"

He put a hand to his head and felt a wet mass in his hair. Somewhere along the line, he'd gotten a gash on his head. It wasn't large, but it probably looked bad: head wounds bled a lot. Quickly he pulled his gray polishing cloth out of his pocket and mopped up the wound, glad to have the cloth on hand.

"I'm okay, thank God. But we're not out of this yet. In fact, it's barely started." Shaking his head to clear it, he got to his feet and retrieved his sword, and the gun. The handgun was heavy, and he checked to see if it was loaded. It was.

A chill went down his spine: *The gun was loaded. This guy could have shot me. Why didn't he?*

He stared at the unconscious masked man. "Was he carrying a wallet? Any ID?"

"No. Seems to me that they're pretty concerned about keeping their identities secret," Kateri said, indicating the mask.

"Yeah," Alex said, regarding the Wookie face. Suddenly in a burst of curiosity, he yanked off the hairy mask. Beneath was a bearded, red-haired man who looked vaguely familiar. The man mumbled, but didn't regain consciousness.

"I know who he is," Kateri whispered. "I've been seeing his picture on the FBI website. He's William Radnor Gaston. One of the top wanted cybercriminals in the country." She took a deep breath. "I think we're looking at one of the cyberthieves."

*One* of the cyberthieves, Alex realized. He swallowed, feeling his wound and bruised ribs, and tried again to breathe normally. And the other thirty-nine were upstairs. And his family was trapped on a mountainside, far from help. With no cell phones. And, from the looks of the sliced wires in the panel, no phone lines and no internet.

He scrambled to his feet. "We've got to get the police."

Kateri joined him. "It might be harder than you think. Your dad's been trying to get onto that satellite network, but it's pretty well secured. He's pretty sure they've got to have something set up in the woods. And there are quite a few men just hanging out at strategic places in the parking lot."

Thirty-nine cyberthieves. Surrounding the hotel, hemming them in.

"Right." Alex steadied himself on the metal pole, thinking fast. "Through the woods. It's the only way down. Come on!"

They raced upstairs. "Your mom won't be able to make it down the mountainside," Kateri said breathlessly as they hurried to the living suite.

Alex had already realized that. "We'll send Sam and David. The rest of us will stay here and hold them off."

Back in the living room, all of the male members of the family had taken their individual swords from the weapons wall. Alex quickly told them what had happened and what should happen next.

"I bet they've got a person watching each of the exits. But there's the pool fence." He glanced out through the window at the eight-foot-high iron rail fence that surrounded the back of the hotel. "That might not be guarded. Sam and David, can you make it over the fence, quick?"

"No!" exclaimed his mom, just as Sam and David both said, "Yes." She argued, "Alex, they're too young! And if these people are armed…"

"Mom, the guy downstairs had me under gunpoint, but he didn't try to shoot me: I suspect he—or someone in charge—wanted to take me alive. I admit, it's not much to go on, but since we don't *have* much to go on, let's assume the others will act the same way." He took a deep breath. "I'll create a diversion. I'll go straight out the front door and try to make a break for one of the cars. I bet they'll try and stop me. Maybe they'll capture me, but at least it might let Sam and David get away. They can get into the woods, run down the mountain, and call 911 as soon as their cell phones are clear."

His mom's face crumpled, and she looked down at her shriveled legs. "If only I were healthy," she whispered. "I'd get over that fence myself. But now I'm just a burden…"

"Stop that!" Dad said firmly, squeezing her shoulders. "For better or worse, Kitty. In sickness and in health. And we've made it this far. If we're going to be hunted down and shot—or not shot—I'd rather the boys get out if they can. And I'll go down defending my bride, to the death if necessary."

Mom blinked at him and managed a smile. Dad said, "We'll barricade ourselves in the back room, and I'll keep trying to break into that network and jam their communications. It's encrypted, but I'm going to keep trying."

"I think you two should keep the gun," Alex said, handing him the captured handgun and giving his mother a quick kiss. "Wish me luck."

"The luck of the O'Donnells," his dad said solemnly. "And our prayers."

Alex glanced at Sam and David, who looked soberly back at him. "Okay guys? Remember your training: 'A soldier surrounded by enemies, if he is to cut his way out, needs to combine a strong desire for living with a strange carelessness about dying. He must desire life like water and drink death like wine.'"

Sam pushed his blond hair out of his eyes and nodded, but David just checked his sword blade with a slight incline of his head. Alex took a deep breath, hoping he didn't look as nervous as he felt, and glanced around. "Where's Kateri?" he said suddenly.

"Right here." She appeared in the doorway, holding the white-furred Wookie mask in her hands and wearing a strange look on her face. "Who were you quoting just now?"

"G. K. Chesterton. Why?"

She shook her head and muttered something that was obscured as she slid the Wookie mask over her face.

"What are you doing?" Alex asked as she tucked the strands of her black hair inside the mask and straightened her white uniform.

"Hoping to confuse the enemy," she said, her voice muffled by the mask. "And maybe find out what's going on."

Kateri's heart was racing as she slipped out into the lobby, sweating slightly beneath the white Wookie mask. She was carrying Mr. O'Donnell's cell phone and tried to walk nonchalantly, like a guest in the hotel on vacation.

She crossed to the breakfast area and tried to think of what she could do that would seem normal. Noticing that she'd already prepped the coffee machine for the morning, she flipped it on. Yeah, she'd make some coffee and wait for something to happen. Sam and David, weapons in hand, had already stolen out to the pool area. She hoped that no one was watching for them out there. And Alex was waiting to make his move.

In the lobby, everything looked absurdly neat and deserted, so much so that Kateri felt reality was out of joint. Aside from the handcuffed man in the basement and her mask and throbbing heart, everything might be normal at the Twilight Hills Hotel. The summer evening sun was sinking into the western ridge of the mountains. The floor tiles were gleaming, newly washed by Sam and David. The pavement of the parking lot looked smooth and undisturbed in the fading light.

Alex, his bloody face and rumpled black dress shirt a stark contrast to normality, strode into the lobby and looked around, sword in hand. He had tied the gray cloth around his head like a pirate's bandana. Even though she was pretending not to see him, she noticed he had switched the bokken for the katana: his real, lethal sword, and dimly recalled that he'd said several times that he wouldn't use that sword unless he were prepared to kill someone. Seeing the sword made her realize how dire their position actually was.

Alex put a hand on the door's metal handles. For a moment, he looked out at the still twilight. Then, whistling a tune that sounded vaguely Irish, he pushed open the door and stepped outside.

*A strong desire to live combined with a strange carelessness about dying.*

"Hey! Excuse me!"

Midstride, several yards from his car, Alex paused, sword in hand, and turned. There were five masked figures outside, some of them hanging out by the shrubbery and smoking. But Alex noticed that now they were hurriedly butting out their cigarettes as one man, dressed in a Freddy Kruger mask and gloves, came forward swiftly towards Alex. Sword at the ready, Alex eyed the man's gloves and wondered if there was a chance the embedded knives were real weapons. But they looked like rubber ones.

"Yes? Can I help you?" Alex said courteously.

The man halted a safe distance from Alex's blade. "Nice sword," he said.

"Yeah, thanks," Alex said. "I've just got to run out. Anything you need?"

"Actually, there is," said another man wearing a Joker mask, stepping forward. He was a tall, thin man, wearing cargo pants and a tight black shirt that revealed his biceps. Deftly, he reached into his pocket and pulled out two slim metal cylinders linked by a silver chain. "We need you to stay right where you are. Sorry, you can't go anywhere." He swung the cylinders in a tight circle, and flipped one back over his shoulders.

Alex took a deep breath and bellowed his signature battle cry that was Sam and David's signal. "SAC-RA COR!"

As he guessed, several people who had apparently been standing in the woods came running towards him. They halted as the Joker advanced on Alex. The dark green hair of his mask sticking out in every direction, the Joker flipped the nunchucks forward and twirled them with an expert hand. They looked heavy, and dangerous and even Alex's katana seemed frighteningly slender by comparison.

Kateri, her eyes fixed on the men surrounding Alex, heard someone else coming out into the lobby and turned with a start. Two more masked figures holding cell phones were approaching.

One was a blue-faced alien with long white hair, and the other was some sort of superhero Kateri couldn't place.

"Has it started already?" the alien asked in what was clearly a woman's voice. The superhero, probably a man, shrugged. Kateri made an incoherent movement with her shoulders.

The alien girl picked at her mask. "Can't wait till I lose this. The whole gaming charade is so lame."

The superhero gave a hollow laugh. "I've never actually even played a video game. Spend all my time on mainframes. Had to nip this thing from eBay."

The alien chuckled. "Yeah, database reconfig is my thing, not timewasting." She turned to Kateri. "But I have to say, I like your 'Planet of the Apes' look."

"Thanks," Kateri said, straightening her white cotton uniform.

"Do you know what we're supposed to be doing? I've been waiting for instructions from Admin."

"Admin wants everyone to remain in their hotel rooms until further instructions are given," Kateri said in her most authoritative voice.

"Really?" The superhero said, holding up his phone. "That's not what I read."

Kateri lifted her chin beneath the mask and decided to keep bluffing. "Remember why we're here, and who we're after. Someone's been jamming communications. Sending out incorrect updates. Admin told me to stay here as the fail-safe."

"Oh," the man said, sounding surprised. "Do you know Admin?"

Again, Kateri gave a noncommittal shrug. "I have instructions to tell everyone to remain in their rooms until the signal is given."

"Oh!" said the alien and the superhero together. They both began sidling out of the lobby. "We'll just go back and wait then," said the alien.

"What should we wait for? What's the fail-safe signal?" the superhero asked.

Kateri tried not to hesitate. "I'll be going from door to door with further instructions."

"Right then." Both the masked figures hurried from the room and Kateri turned away from them, trying not to breathe too hard. She gave a fleeting glance towards Alex, then hurried into the hotel office as fast as she could.

*Nunchaku.* As the Joker came forward, Alex gripped his katana with both hands and held it out in front of him at the ready, his mind racing through martial arts theory. He'd fooled around with flail weapons, but had never encountered them in a serious fight. *What do I know about nunchaku? First strike and defensive weapons, used to block and trap. And technically, flexible weapons trump bladed weapons.*

*…Okay. Guess I don't know much.*

*Guess I'll have to find out what he knows first.*

He locked his eyes on the center of his opponent's body as the Joker circled slowly around him. Alex tried to back himself in a corner by the cars, and determined to swing the instant the man made any move.

*I've got a 28" blade with maybe a three-foot reach. He's got a reach of about two feet with those clubs. So theoretically, I should be able to get him before he gets me.*

The Joker whirled his clubs with such force that his fellow attackers took a step or two back. Alex managed to keep his blade steady as the Joker flipped back the club over his shoulder and advanced again.

Seeing an opening, Alex raised the blade to strike when suddenly the Joker lunged forward, whipping the nunchaku at Alex's wrists with smashing force. In surprised agony, Alex dropped his sword, but, desperate not to be disarmed again, he snatched and caught the wooden handle before it hit the pavement, dropping and rolling to barely escape being hit on the back. Alex swung up to his feet, gripping his sword even tighter, breathing hard, his hands flaming with pain.

*Are my fingers broken?* He couldn't tell. For a fleeting instant, he dropped his eyes to his fingers. The Joker noticed and laughed beneath his mask.

"Did I give you a finger fracture?" the masked man taunted. "If I were you, I'd put that sword down. And then I won't hurt you too bad."

Alex took a deep breath. Kateri was depending on him. His whole family was depending on him. Every moment he could delay the cyberthieves in their attack on his family gave Sam and David more time to get to the police.

*Okay. Got to make sure I swing wide: don't let him get that close to me again.* Alex swung. The Joker leapt back, snapping the nunchaku into a shield and blocked his blow. Then he struck back again, but Alex easily avoided it, now that he knew to keep his wrists away from the twirling flails. He thrust again, and the Joker swung.

*Crack!*

His blade thrown back by the power of the blow, Alex swung around and regained the ready position, only to stare in horror at the end of his sword. Six inches of the blade had snapped off. The advantage of his reach was almost gone.

*This is not good. Not good at all.* And the Joker was advancing, the rubber mask leering as he snapped his chucks into a shield again. When Alex swung, the Joker raised his arms, wrapped the flails, and neatly caught the blade in its iron grip. The sword blade was trapped.

Metal squealed against metal as the Joker and Alex closed, Alex fighting to twist his blade free from the chains. The Joker laughed. Alex drove a side kick into the man's leg, and then followed with another into his ribs, pulling the sword violently in the opposite direction. The blade swung free, yanking the nunchaku out of the Joker's hands. As Alex swung his sword around to regain his balance, the jagged tip raked the Joker's pants, slicing the fabric and digging into the skin.

*If my blade had been longer, I'd have sliced his artery, and he'd be in trouble.* Alex met his opponent's gaze, and saw the same thought in the Joker's now-fearful eyes.

The Joker retreated to the protection of the others, clutching his bleeding thigh. Taking advantage of the distraction, Alex ran through a gap in his attackers.

"Stop or I'll shoot!" someone shouted, but Alex didn't stop. He tried to make a break for the driveway, but two figures with guns, Jar Jar Binks followed by a ninja, emerged from the woods and blocked him. Alex skidded and turned towards the hotel, slamming through the glass doors into the lobby. Amazingly, no one fired.

In the office, Kateri was ransacking the contents of the desk, trying fruitlessly to search through Mr. O'Donnell's computer detritus. *Where is it? Where is it?*

In agony, she stared at the humming computer screen, wishing that she'd extended her cleaning activities to Mr. O'Donnell's jungle of an office.

Suddenly, she blinked. The cursor was moving on the screen. On its own.

Slowly, Kateri took the mouse and opened a text box. She typed:

CKTC?

There was a pause, then the cursor clicked on the box and typed:

Kitty's Kat frend?

She typed,

Where is the emergency locking key?

In a second the answer came back:

Purple keycard=Top upper drawer

Gasping in thankfulness, she dug through the mess of junk in the right hand drawer and at last she spotted it: the purple plastic card.

Grabbing it, she typed frantically.

Going to lock some doors.

She hurried out of the office just in time to see Alex disappearing into the hotel kitchen, followed by several masked men. More men were hurrying across the lobby, and some of them were waving guns.

Her heart in her mouth, Kateri ran for the doors, pulled them closed and slid the emergency keycard through the slot, locking them.

Then she rushed down the hallway to the guest rooms, ignoring the banging and shaking on the doors behind her.

# Chapter Fourteen

*Having discovered the presence of the thieves, the quick-witted servant girl decided to trap the robbers in their hiding places before their chief could alert them.*
The Arabian Nights

ausing to catch her breath, Kateri faced the hallway of first-floor guestrooms. There was one masked figure in the hallway, but when he saw her, he nodded, pointed to his phone. Kateri nodded back at him, and the man went back into his room and shut the door.

Kateri wondered how long it would be before the word got out about her bluff. She also wondered when the cyberthieves would get mad enough to shoot. Well, she didn't have time to find out.

She pulled out the purple keycard that had the ability to trigger both the inside and outside locks and slid it silently into the first door until the light turned red and she heard a click. *Locked.* Swiftly, she crossed the hallway to the next room number. *Locked.* Back to the left side. *Locked.*

In the same manner, she locked the first ten doors. Probably many of them were empty: their occupants were outside or chasing after Alex. But maybe keeping them out of their rooms would be just as useful as trapping them inside.

Running through the lobby, Alex had made a decision. He was winded, and would eventually lose energy, although right now adrenalin was still pumping through his veins. He was drawing the cyberthieves after him, and away from Sam, David, and his parents. So he'd have to continue to run, and lead the thieves as far away from his family as possible—even if it meant a chase to a dead end.

He dashed into the hotel kitchen, hearing his attackers coming fast behind him in a stampede.

The kitchen was small and cramped, with an island taking up most of the space. He dashed around the counter, sheathing his sword, and grabbed a handful of knives. By the time the first three cyberthieves—a gorilla, a Storm Trooper, and Zorro—had gotten inside the kitchen, he had leapt onto the stove and was ready to fight.

With a banshee yell, he hurled the knives at his attackers, who shouted and ducked under the countertops. Thanks to Kateri's organization, there were plenty of weapons within reach. He threw spoons and ladles, hurled silverware and plates. The masked men couldn't get close to him but barreled around the room, taking refuge behind the island. He waited until as many of them had crowded into the room as possible, hurling artillery all the while. When he ran out of silverware, he seized the bowls of cinnamon roll dough and dumped them on the heads of the first two who charged him, leaving them sticky and bewildered.

He knew he couldn't keep it up forever. Just when he guessed that they were massing themselves for an attack, he leapt from the stove to the island countertop and out the kitchen door, where the fragrant smell of fresh coffee greeted him. Quickly he grabbed both pots off the machine and tossed the boiling hot regular and decaf onto the gorilla and Zorro. The masks protected their faces, but they yelped when the hot coffee hit their arms and clothing. After hurling the pots, which smashed like bombs, Alex turned and plunged through the lobby.

He caught a glimpse of a crowd of men outside, huddled around the doors, apparently working on the locks. There was a shout as he sprinted by, hurtling down the hallway to the stairs. He could hear feet pounding behind him, and Alex yanked the stairwell door open just in time to hear a gunshot. It missed him, but shattered the window just behind him.

Somehow, being shot at brought the first sweat of real fear into him. He knew the line had been crossed, and the hackers were ready to kill.

*Hope Sam and David are getting down the mountain,* were his only fleeting thoughts as he pounded up the stairs. As he passed the second floor, he heard them coming behind him, an ominous rumbling. And Kateri? Where was she?

When Kateri reached the second floor, she reached the first guest room door just as it opened. The Martian put his head out. "Is it time?"

Kateri shook her Wookie-masked head. "Not yet," she said. "Everyone's to continue to stay in their rooms."

The Martian put his head to one side. "But Admin just said…"

Kateri shrugged. "It's on the latest message. Did you check?"

"No—let me see." The Martian turned away from the door, and Kateri, seizing her chance, pulled the door shut and locked it swiftly. Now she dashed from door to door double-time, jamming her keycard into each door slot until the light turned red: *locked.* She crossed the hallway. *Locked.* Back to the left side. *Locked.*

Behind her, handles were jiggling. Soon hammering began as the people trapped inside the rooms began pounding on the doors. Would they climb down the balconies? If some of them were as fat as the cyberthief in the basement, maybe not…

Next door: *locked. Locked. Locked.* All second floor rooms, locked. She took a deep breath, struggling to stay on her feet.

One more floor left to go.

Barely able to breathe, Alex hurled himself up the steps. He didn't dare go onto the other floors, for fear of disturbing more cyberthieves. There was only one place left for him to go.

The roof.

He reached the door, pulled out his master key, and opened it, pushing the door open and feeling the evening breeze hitting his hot face. He looked behind him, and saw the first of the cyberthieves reaching the landing below. With a wink, Alex locked the heavy metal door and pulled it shut behind him.

He hurried around the side, wincing as the gun went off again and again and again, reverberating on the steel. *Maybe they'll use up all their bullets that way,* he thought.

Recollecting himself, he dropped to his hands and knees and crawled to the edge of the roof, peering over the three-foot high ledge into the parking lot. It was darker now, but he could still see figures down below. Three? As far as he could tell, they were standing around and talking on cell phones. He couldn't tell if they had gotten the front door open yet. He crept to the other side of the roof and checked the side entrances. One figure stationed there. On the other side, the trees covered the service entrance, but he was willing to guess there was another guard there. Plus the two men he had seen come of out of the woods. There was no trace of anyone in the pool yard, and no one seemed to be searching the woods, so perhaps Sam and David had broken through. But how long would it take them to get down the mountain?

He took a deep breath and counted in his head. Seven outside … one handcuffed in the basement. That left thirty-two cyberthieves at large. He stared down at the blue square of the pool and then turned and walked towards the center of the roof, trying to think of how to handle all of them. He knew he couldn't do it.

There was another gunshot, and he spun around, reflexively drawing his broken sword.

Five masked men straggled onto the roof, still masked but looking a bit winded. One of them, sporting a bulldog mask, held the gun. The Joker gave a loud, trademarked cackle, "Now the fun begins at last."

They were all on the roof now, and ranged themselves in a half circle. Alex was silent, sword still at the ready, back to the roof wall and the setting sun.

"Ready to give up and come quietly?" the Joker taunted. "Or do I have to use a knife?"

Alex waited, and took a deep breath. What he needed now was to be calm, absolutely calm. As was habitual, he began an invocation to the Blessed Mother.

The bulldog took a step closer. He began to gesture, making short jabs with the gun. "Drop the weapon, or I shoot."

Alex concentrated on keeping his sword absolutely still, despite his sweating palms. Another deep breath.

"Are you deaf? I said, drop the sword, punk!"

Completely focused, Alex closed his eyes for a brief second and felt the warmth of peace spread through him. With another deep breath, he opened his eyes and gauged the distance between himself, the bulldog-masked man, and the edge of the roof.

"Drop it!"

Without a word, Alex turned. In a few steps, he sprinted to the edge of the roof, and leapt.

"SA-CRA COR!" he shouted as he cleared the roof ledge and fell, trying to point his toes downward and holding the sword tightly in his hands over his head.

There was nothing but the rush of silence and wind around him.

*Foosh!*

The water closed over him swiftly and he gasped and bent his knees as he hit the bottom of the swimming pool's deep end: hard, but not hard enough to crush any bones. He sprang upwards, his sword point piercing the surface of the water as he came up, gasping and feeling more than a bit disoriented. But the sound of gunfire quickly cleared his brain. He grabbed the ledge, grappled for a moment, then hurtled himself out of the pool, running for the living quarters as the second gunshot ricocheted off the concrete. *Thank God they aren't great shots.*

Pounding on the door to the living quarters, he was fumbling for his keycard when Dad finally scrambled out of the bedroom to open the door, and Alex spilled into the living room, slopping water everywhere.

"Where were you?" Dad asked.

Alex just gestured upwards with his head, winded.

"Okay," his dad said, after locking the door. "I don't think I'll tell your mother what you just did. She'll have a heart attack back there."

Alex attempted a smile, as he bent over, hands on his knees. "Where's Kateri?"

"She said she was going to try to lock doors," Dad said, frowning, still brandishing the gun at the pool door. "I hoped she was with you."

On the third floor, the hallway was deserted, aside from the sweating, panting Kateri. She paused for a moment to adjust her furry mask, purple card in hand, trying to strategize. Just in case anyone came up the steps after her, it might be best to start with the rooms furthest from the stairwell. Trying to be as silent as she could, she sprinted down the hallway and slid the purple card into the lock for door 310. *Locked.*

Next one: *locked.* Next one: *locked.*

Seven more doors. 307: *Locked.* 306 across the hall: *Locked.* 305: *Locked.* 304: *locked.* 303: she fumbled, dropped the card, grabbed it with damp hands, tried again: *locked.* 302 started to open: she snatched the handle, pulled it shut, *locked.* 301…

Door 301 was opening. By the time she had locked 302, there was a masked figure standing in the doorway of 301, watching her.

Kateri tried not to let her voice tremble as she said, "The instructions from Admin are for everyone to stay in their rooms until he gives the signal."

The figure, which was stout and wearing a rubber pig's mask, snickered as it pulled out a gun. "That's funny," said a high-pitched woman's voice. "Because my instructions from Admin say that I'm supposed to search for an albino Wookie, and put it out of the way." She dug the barrel of her gun into Kateri's side. "And I think I just found her."

Kateri swallowed, and thrust the purple card into her pocket, then glanced over at the gun. It was small and silver, and the muzzle felt very cold. Kateri was sure it was real, and that this lady knew how to use it.

Her captor pulled the mask off of Kateri's face. "What's your name, chino girl?"

"Wanda Ling," Kateri said quickly.

The woman snorted. "I don't think so, Kateri Kovach. We've done our research, even if you did take us by surprise for a bit there." She dug in her pocket and then tossed something at Kateri's feet. "Pick up that rope," the woman directed in a voice that was too sweet. The pig's face smiled, but the little eyes peering through the mask were cold.

Kateri bent down and found herself holding a small coil of thin white nylon rope.

"Tie it around your wrist, chino girl, and make it good and tight."

The gun twisted into Kateri's ribs, and, gulping, Kateri wrapped one end of the rope around her own wrist and knotted it.

"That's it," the woman said, and before Kateri had realized what happened, the woman yanked the rope out of her hand and quickly looped it around and around Kateri's shoulders, until Kateri's arms were squeezed tightly against her sides and her wrist was twisted up painfully behind her back. Dizzily she staggered, the carpet pattern swimming before her eyes.

"Get down on the ground," the woman directed, shoving the gun downwards, and Kateri toppled onto the carpet, while the woman tied her wrists together. When the woman released her grip, Kateri rolled face down on the ground, completely helpless.

The woman chuckled. "Lie still, chino girl." She settled her bulk on Kateri's back and began to tie Kateri's legs and ankles with the rope, with the same jabbing, painful motions until Kateri was sure she'd lost all feeling in her lower body. Crushed into the carpet, trying to catch her breath, Kateri twisted her head to one side and saw the empty corridor of locked doors. Her efforts to stop the cyberthieves had almost succeeded. But 'almost' was not enough. Not enough to save herself. She hoped Alex was still alive and fighting.

Her one wrist was close to her pocket. With feeble fingers, she grabbed at the edge of the purple card and managed to ease it out of her pocket.

She could hear people hammering on doors and shouts, but the fat lady didn't seem to care. Finished with Kateri, she hobbled to her feet, grabbed her captive by the ankles, and dragged her into room 301, burning Kateri's cheeks on the carpet as she did so. But the woman didn't notice the purple card lying behind them on the ground, camouflaged by the rest of the outrageous colors of the carpet.

The door locked behind them with a heavy *thunk*.

There was no way out. Kateri knew she was trapped, and more in danger than she'd ever been in her life.

Setting down her gun on the plastic-covered bedside table, the woman heaved Kateri up onto the bed, which had been stripped and covered with a plastic sheet. Twisting onto her side, Kateri got her first glimpse of the room.

Room 301 had been turned into a costume shop. There were plastic bags, and molding compound, paints, wigs, and makeup spread out on the beds and tables, which were all covered in plastic, making it look like some kind of laboratory. Kateri noticed a row of handcuffs laid out on the window sill.

A laptop stood open on one table, and the woman wearing the pig's mask sat down and typed rapidly on the keyboard.

Lying on the plastic-covered bed in her cotton scrubs, her sides and wrists aching from the tight ropes, Kateri felt like a white rat trapped in a lab. She shifted, trying to find a more comfortable position, but there wasn't one.

"You're one of the forty cyberthieves, aren't you?" she said at last, trying to steady her voice.

The pig chuckled. "Wouldn't you like to know?" she mocked. "Let's say I'm one of the more talented ones. I'm very useful when it comes to operations like this one. Mostly because I've got a little more spine."

"What are you doing?" Kateri asked, as the woman continued typing.

"Telling Admin that I got you. He'll be pleased. At least one of us hasn't screwed up yet."

She paused. "Huh. Admin's not answering, but that's his problem. No time to waste. I'm getting started on you." She stood up and grabbed a large camera from the bedside table, and stood over Kateri. Regarding her for a minute, she abruptly smoothed back Kateri's disheveled hair. Then she held up the camera. The massive flash blinded Kateri. By the time the balls of light in front of her eyes subsided, the woman had laid aside the camera and was snapping on rubber gloves. Next, she unrolled a sheet of what looked like thick plastic wrap and clicked on a hair dryer. She ran the hair dryer over the plastic dexterously.

"What's that for?" Kateri asked, feeling a surge of dread.

"That's for me to know and you to find out," the woman said, clearly focused on her work.

Then she approached Kateri, holding the warmed plastic. "Better take a deep breath, chino girl. I don't care if you suffocate."

Kateri barely had a chance to take a breath before the plastic was pressed over her face. For a few minutes she writhed, gasping while the woman pushed the soft plastic over her nose and mouth and eyes, molding it into place.

"Hold still and you can still breathe," the woman's voice came through the nightmare of Kateri's panic.

Finally the mask was gone, and Kateri lay on the bed heaving and trying to breathe despite the unyielding ropes around her ribs, while the woman busied herself with the molded plastic.

"What are you doing?" Kateri managed to ask at last, trying to master the tears that still crowded her eyes.

"Making you," the woman said, and held up the plastic. "I think it's a pretty good likeness, don't you?"

Kateri saw her own image looking back at her. She could tell the face was distorted with pain, but it was close enough.

The woman put down the rapidly-hardening mask and picked up a spray can of rubber foam. With quick and careful strokes, she sprayed rubber compound onto the mask and turned it over for Kateri to see.

"Like it? So do I. Mostly because that means I'm done with you now," the woman said, her eyes gleaming through the pig mask. She set the mask down on the other bed and picked up the gun. She approached Kateri. "Say goodbye to living, chino girl."

And Alex's sword hilt came down on the small of the woman's back.

The female cyberthief fell like a stone, and Alex stood over her, his long black hair and black shirt wet and dripping, breathing hard, his broken sword blade pointing at the woman's neck. Kateri could see her shoulders shaking with fear.

"Sorry I couldn't get here sooner," he said to Kateri. "Couldn't find you. Dad said you were locking doors. Saw the card outside the door. Just a guess."

"There's handcuffs on the windowsill," was the only thing Kateri could say.

Nodding, Alex snatched up the woman's gun, grabbed a pair of handcuffs, and kneeling, handcuffed Kateri's assailant. The cuffs almost didn't fit on the woman's fat wrists, but Alex seemed to have no problem forcing them on, despite the woman's grunts.

Kateri had twisted her way into a sitting position, trying to regain her composure as Alex dragged the twisting, cursing woman backwards. He shoved her into the bathroom and shut the door. Then he turned back to Kateri, and his fierce expression softened. He leaned over her, pushing back her hair and kissing her tear-stained cheeks. "Mother Mary, I'm so glad you're still alive."

"I'm sorry I got caught," she whispered.

"Are you kidding? After saving us all by locking those doors? No, I'm the one who should be apologizing for getting you into this mess in the first place. Here, lie down and let me get at those ropes."

Obeying, she lay down again and tried to relax while Alex, using his sword with careful skill, sliced the ropes off of her sides and legs. Gratefully, Kateri sat up and held out her wrists, which were each still tied with a cuff of white cord. Cutting those cords were a bit trickier, but Alex, being Alex, managed it. She still couldn't figure out how the same hands that could fight so ferociously could be so gentle.

"Thanks," she said weakly when she was finally free, and leaned her head against his chest, feeling the world swimming around her. He held her, stroking her hair, and part of her realized that she was in serious danger of actually fainting in Alex's arms. But Rose was right: it wasn't such a bad prospect…

"Is your mom okay?" Kateri finally managed to ask.

Alex nodded. "At least she was a few minutes ago. We'd better get back downstairs." He glanced around, saw the mask of Kateri's face, and the other wigs and costumes and stiffened, but he didn't say anything. Suddenly he cocked his head.

"You hear that?" he said to Kateri. "The sound of government intervention. Every once in a while, it's a really beautiful thing!"

Listening hard, Kateri recognized the sound of sirens in the distance, coming closer. Alex was right: it was beautiful. She leaned into his arms again, her heart rate finally beginning to slow down to normal.

# Chapter Fifteen

*The family of Ali Baba praised
the servant girl for her quick thinking and
bravery, which had saved them from the thieves.*
*The Arabian Nights*

ood work!" Agent Furlow seemed bemused as he came into the lobby to witness thirty-nine prisoners being booked by the police. The FBI had arrived an hour after the police had driven up with Sam and David triumphantly leading the way. When Agent Randolph arrived forty-five minutes later, he didn't even pause to give any sort of compliment, just headed right for the police chief and reminded him loudly of jurisdiction requirements.

Nursing his own wounds, Alex was surprised to find out how little most of the cyberthieves had actually tried to fight. When they had discovered that they were locked into their hotel rooms, many of them had just given up. Only one or two of them had even tried to climb out of the window into the parking lot, and those that had were easily picked up by police. One hacker had remained at his computer the entire time, playing solitaire, even when the police had come in.

"Guess they weren't up to fighting," Alex said to his dad in a low voice.

"Well," Dad patted his own stomach. "They're mostly techies. Computer work doesn't always help you stay in shape."

He glanced down at Kateri and sobered. "I'm sorry you had to go through this, Kat." Kateri was trying to clean the cuts on her wrists, while Alex stood by with the bandages. "We owe you a lot. I can't begin to think of how much."

"I'm glad it turned out okay," was all she said. Alex squeezed her shoulder and carefully smoothed back her hair from her cheeks, which were still pale.

Dad turned away, a somber expression on his face. He moved to stand next to Mom, who, her arms around Sam and David, sat watching the proceedings from her wheelchair.

"So you got the police," Alex said to his brothers.

"Yeah," David said. "There was only one guy with a walkie talkie in the woods on our side, and he ran to the parking lot when you started fighting. We snuck past him easily, and got down to the highway. Then I checked my cell phone, found that it worked, and called 911."

"I wanted to go back and help you guys, but David wouldn't let me," Sam complained.

"I felt better knowing that you were out of the way," Mom said, squeezing him. "You did just as you were told, and that was the right thing to do."

"I'm just glad you guys are okay," Sam said, and reached over to hug Kateri too, who looked startled, but then joined the hug.

It was way into the morning by the time any of the O'Donnells were able to turn in. Feeling like every bone in his body had been bruised, Alex checked to make sure the "No Vacancy" sign was still on and stumbled off to bed for some much desired-sleep.

The next morning, he awoke, nearly paralyzed by his stiff muscles, and, calling Dad into the bedroom, decreed they should keep the hotel closed for the next day, and everyone seemed to agree. Besides, the only guests they had were the forensics team, who continued to work all hours of the day and night as they argued over how much of the hotel would need to be kept off limits for taking evidence.

"I actually feel sorry for the guys," Alex confided to Kateri when he had hobbled out of bed to watch her put the fifteenth pot of coffee on to boil in the breakfast area. "Thirty-nine arrests at once! That's got to be some kind of record, at least for this town."

"Thirty-nine," Kateri said, disinfecting an already clean table. Alex knew she was frustrated that she couldn't get in and clean any of the rooms until evidence-taking was completed. "Wasn't there supposed to be forty?"

"Yeah. Dad's been wondering about that too. There were forty passwords on the website, even though there were only thirty-nine personal data logs listed. But Dad's fairly sure that whoever administered that site never logged his personal info. I guess it all depends on whether or not one of the thirty-nine cyberthieves also served as administrator, or whether the administrator was a separate guy."

"Didn't your dad count forty wireless connections just before the fight started? So didn't that mean that there were forty people?"

"There were only thirty-nine guests checked into the hotel," Alex pointed out, massaging his knees.

"So who was the fortieth user? Someone offsite?"

"There were forty reservations," Alex said to himself. "But maybe that was just to fill up the hotel so there wouldn't be any witnesses. Or maybe the last guy just stayed in the woods running the network from that portable satellite dish that they found in the woods."

"So if there was a fortieth hacker, he—or she—got away." Kateri said.

"Right. Not exactly a pleasant prospect," Alex admitted. "But hey, maybe the last cyberthief will have learned his lesson, and will take the remaining money and just go away to start a new enterprise somewhere else."

He glanced at Kateri, and could tell she was thinking the same thing he was. *Yeah, right.*

Right now the thirty-nine suspects were being held in jail without bond as accessories before the fact for attempted murder. Several of them had previously been indicted for cybercrime, and it seemed it would be a matter of time before the entire story came out.

As usual, the FBI was fairly tight-lipped about the investigation. Agent Randolph, his blond hair bristling, wouldn't even say that the suspects were cyberthieves, and had only conceded that they might be when Sam had pointed out that one of them, William Radnor Gaston was on the FBI's Most Wanted List for cybercrime.

But before the FBI finished up their investigation, Kateri managed to corner the more amiable Agent Furlow and got him to give her a few more details.

"Look, you have to tell me what you think that lady who held me at gunpoint and tied me up was doing," Kateri said, setting a cinnamon roll on a plate in front of him at a table in the breakfast area. "She was making a mask of my face. What was—can you tell me what that was all about?"

Agent Furlow accepted the cup of tea she handed him gratefully. "Well, I suppose I can tell you that. Apparently, the plan was that you and the O'Donnells were going to disappear."

"Disappear? How?" Kateri asked, sitting down across from him.

"Well, your bodies never would have been found," the agent paused to bite into a bun, chew and swallow. "These are really good, by the way."

"Uh, thanks," Kateri said, feeling queasy. "And the mask she was making of my face was for—?"

"Life masks, or in this case, death masks," Agent Furlow said, sipping his tea. "They would have made masks from the faces of each of you, masks that would each be worn by one of the cyberthieves. So that witnesses could say they saw you all packing up your belongings, leaving, and disappearing without a trace."

"And you and the police would have guessed that we took the money and ran," Kateri guessed.

"Yes. It would have made a federal investigation very difficult. You'd be presumed to be overseas someplace."

"Right." Kateri closed her eyes, imagining her remains being buried in a landfill, and shivered. "My parents never would have believed that story."

"No?"

Kateri shook her head. "Not in a million years. They know my principles. They'd have thought the O'Donnells kidnapped me before they'd ever believe I went on the lam." She blew out her breath. "Thank God and His Mother that it didn't happen."

"I'll say," the agent took another bite of the cinnamon bun. "Very narrow escape. But hopefully, you're safe now."

"You don't think there's a fortieth cyberthief out there?" Kateri couldn't help asking.

Agent Furlow looked at her in surprise. "What makes you say that?"

"Well, there were forty usernames on the Mystery Website. And forty reservations were made at the hotel."

"Of course," he said, and straightened. "Like I said, there still might be one more out there. You'd better remain on your guard." He glanced quickly around. "Don't tell the chief I missed that one. They might cut my budget."

She smiled. "My lips are sealed."

Now his blue eyes grew serious. "So there were forty reservations."

"And forty people using the internet the night of the attack," she reminded him.

"How's that?"

She told him about how Mr. O'Donnell had detected forty users on the satellite network, and thought to herself, *surely one of the O'Donnells must have told this to the police? Maybe Agent Randolph hadn't told his partner everything?* It just showed how many things could fall between the cracks in a complicated investigation like this one.

Now Agent Furlow sank into his chair, thoughtful. "This could be significant," he said to himself. He looked at her for a moment, seeming to debate. "How well do you know—?" he started to ask, and then stopped.

"What? What were you going to ask?"

"Nothing. It's not important. But how long have you been working for the O'Donnells? When did they hire you?"

Kateri chuckled. "Well, it's not just an employment relationship. I'm dating their son."

"Oh, that's right. So you're living here with their son?"

Kateri's cheeks flushed. "No, no," she said quickly. "I'm living *at* the hotel, and I'm dating Alex, but I'm not living *with* him. We don't do that sort of thing. Principles again."

"Oh! I'm so sorry. These days, you just assume…" the man shook his head. "I'm sorry. So you're dating the son, and working for the family."

"Yes. I just met the family this summer, actually."

"When you started dating the son."

"No, I knew him from college."

"But you just met his family now."

"Yes."

He cocked his head. "This might be a delicate question, but you strike me as a religious person. Am I right?"

"Yes, that's true. I'm Catholic."

"I respect that. There are some good Catholics on my staff. And the O'Donnells are Catholic too, right?"

"Yes."

"But you only just met the family."

"Yes."

"Interesting." He finished his tea. "Well, Kateri, there are two things you can do for me. Get me that recipe for your cinnamon rolls," he winked, "and let me know if you see anything else suspicious around here. Anything. Don't hesitate to call." He handed her his card, then his expression grew serious. "After all, the consequences could be severe if we've let one of this gang slip through our net. As in, severe for you."

"Thanks," Kateri said, automatically grabbing his cup and plate and napkin to clear his place as he rose. But her hands were already sweating.

As Kateri could have predicted, the news of the arrest of the thirty-nine suspects, among them several of the most prominent cyberthieves in the nation got around quickly, and it made the O'Donnell family—and the Twilight Hills Hotel—famous.

After the last forensics team had left, and the surly maids had come in to do their job, the hotel reopened—and quickly filled up. As day manager, Alex spent a lot of job time telling the story of how the O'Donnells had managed to hold thirty-nine suspected criminals at bay until the police arrived, and Sam and David were glad to step in when he got tired.

It required a bit of sleight-of-hand to tell the story without mentioning the Mystery Money or Uncle Cass's death, but somehow they managed to do it. Kateri marveled at how the O'Donnells could deflect any questions by phrasing the story so that no one even thought to wonder what the O'Donnells themselves might have done to make themselves a target to a band of thirty-nine internet thieves.

And although Kateri didn't say much to anyone, she remained on her guard.

Even though the unfinished business with the last cyberthief hung over his head, Alex was almost too busy to think about it. There was seldom a break in the routine. He and his dad worked one shift after another like clockwork: checking guests in, checking them out, monitoring the computer network (his dad had taken the opportunity to upgrade the entire security system yet again), taking stock of supplies, attending to crises ranging from the usual guests who had locked their keycards in their room to a broken sofa bed in the honeymoon suite to the couple who had a marital spat in the lobby.

None of these seemed quite as nerve-racking as they might have been, since now his standard for stress was having ten armed cyberthieves rushing him in the lobby. *That* was the ultimate bad day.

The good part of the entire situation was that the hotel was booming. They were even starting to put a significant amount of money in the bank, thanks to Mom's careful budgeting, and she said she was thinking that they might not need to depend as heavily on the ever-in-danger-of-vanishing Mystery Money. That was cause for rejoicing.

So things were looking up for the family. Sam and David enjoyed their local status as heroes, and more than once Alex had found David lolling by the pool recounting the story to wide-eyed teenaged female guests when he should have been working.

The only bad part of the boom was Kateri. Alex barely saw her, and every time he did, she was scrubbing something, stripping a bed, pushing a cart, mopping a floor, reorganizing, disinfecting, or trudging toward her hotel room in a sleepy, surly daze.

This he did not like. His vision for having Kateri work the hotel had involved a picture of her doing light office work, making coffee, and lounging about the office keeping him company. A receptionist/assistant manager, not a workhorse and general servant. But she was determined to pull her weight, as she put it, and he couldn't figure out how to tell her that her generosity was unnecessary and unwanted.

"Hey, want to go out tonight?" He cornered her as she came out of a guest room with a pile of dirty sheets and towels.

"Please move," she said, but he didn't. Taking the sheets out of her arms, he tossed them into the laundry cart.

"Kat, you're only doing the work of four women instead of five today. You must be tired."

"Think so?" she pushed back a long straggle of hair that was falling out of her ponytail. Her white uniform looked rumpled and a bit dingy. "We can't go out tonight, Alex. The washing service is delivering towels."

"Oh, come on. That's at seven. We can go out at nine, after I get off work. We can catch a movie. Come on, you need to get out."

"What I need is more sleep," she said.

He looked down the hall. "How many rooms are you cleaning today?"

"Thirteen."

"You said you would call the maid service on days where there were more than ten."

"I can do the three extra rooms. It's not a big deal."

He made a decision. "No, you can't."

She glared at him. "What do you mean, I can't?"

"I won't let you."

Putting her hands on her hips, she said, "How are you going to stop me?"

For an answer, he picked Kateri up and threw her into the laundry cart. She landed head-first into the pile of fluffy white sheets and yelped.

"Alex!" She scrambled to get out, but he grabbed the cart and sprinted down the hallway.

"Laundry coming through!" he called.

"Alex! Let me out! Alex!!!"

Ignoring the guests who looked askance at his mad dash down the hall, Alex threw open the door to Kateri's room, pushed the cart inside, then shut the door and locked it with the purple key. "And stay in there until your day off is over!" he intoned through the keyhole. "Get some rest!"

Ignoring her shouts, he strode to the phone and dialed the maid service. While it rang, he addressed the guests who were standing or sitting around the lobby, staring at him. "Here at the Twilight Hills Hotel, we always strive to give you our best. Sometimes our staff gets a little carried away in our enthusiasm to help you, but know that we always mean well." He nodded to Kateri's door, which shook from her pounding on the other side. "We don't even like to take a day off."

Most of the guests laughed, and he nodded and returned to the phone.

After he had arranged for the Maids In Time to come, he called Kateri on her cell phone.

She was furious. "How dare you! I have never been so embarrassed! How dare you imprison me like this, after what happened...Only trying to do my job..."

"Kateri. I am not letting you out until you've taken a shower and a nap, and changed into non-work clothes."

"I should just climb out the window... if you ever ... I will flay..."

"Sleep well, darling." He hung up on her. Part of him was enjoying her fury, but part of him hoped that he wasn't pushing her too far.

He was somewhat reassured when the pounding stopped and he heard the faint whoosh of water from the pipes leading to her room.

His cell phone rang just as the Maids arrived. He waved at them and picked up. "Alex O'Donnell speaking."

"Alex. This is Agent Furlow from the FBI. We've had a bit of a breakthrough in our investigation."

"That's great! I mean, that's good, isn't it?"

"Yes, from our end at least. I'd like to discuss it with your family. When would be a good time for me to come by? I know you're running a hotel there, and I want to find a time when I can speak to all of you at once."

"Hmm, that might be tricky," Alex flipped open his reservation book but was greeted by a blank column. "Tell you what: Wednesday tends to be our slow day. Why don't you come by tonight? Dinnertime? We'll feed you."

"That's really kind of you. Actually, since I'll be coming down from DC, what about this? I can come and spend the night at your hotel. If you have a room, that is."

"Absolutely. We'd be glad to have you. We'll have the hotel to ourselves tonight anyhow: everyone's checking out. So yeah, come and stay. It'll be on the house."

"No, no, I insist: let the government pay for it," Agent Furlow laughed.

"Our tax dollars at work," Alex quipped. "However you want to work it is fine. We'll look forward to seeing you and Agent Randolph."

"Oh, it'll just be me this time. Carter's taking a personal day."

"Oh. No problem. See you then." Alex deleted the second reservation he had automatically made.

When he got off the phone, he listened at Kateri's door. The water had stopped, and there was silence. Either she had climbed out the window, or she was sleeping. Quietly, he unlocked her door and returned to the desk.

By lunchtime, he had checked out the last guest. Well after one o'clock, he looked up to find Kateri glowering down at him. But she had showered and was dressed in a pale blue peasant blouse and cropped jeans.

"Ah. Don't you feel so much better?" he asked.

"Let's talk."

He made way for her to sit down as she came around the desk, pulled out a chair, and sat down next to him.

"I don't think I like working for you," she stated.

"I don't think I like the way you're working for me, either," he responded equitably.

She ignored him. "Alex, I just think this whole idea was a mistake."

"What was a mistake?"

"Working for the hotel. You. Me. Us. I just don't see it's going to work. We just frustrate each other."

"Kateri, I think you're overreacting here. You need some time off. I was just trying to get you to see that."

"But you—Alex O'Donnell, what do you expect me to do when you do something like dump me into a laundry cart and lock me in my room?"

Alex pulled the lid off of his pen, put it back on again, and then pulled it off before he answered. "You could laugh," he offered.

"Laugh?"

"Yes, laugh! Kateri, do you have any idea how many things I do just to get you to laugh? And you just insist on taking me so seriously! I don't want to offend you. I don't want to get a rise out of you. Most of the times, all I want you to do is... laugh at me."

She stared at him. "Laugh. At you." Her question hung in the air.

"Yes." He threw his pen in the trash can. "Just a simple request. Quit analyzing me. I might look complicated, Kat, but my needs are very simple."

"Simple." Kateri blew out her breath.

"I'm easier than you think."

"So—that would solve all our problems?"

"Maybe forty percent of them." He stood up. "So what about that movie tonight? Let Sam and David do the sheets, or towels, or whatever."

"I'll think about it."

"Okay, scoot." The phone was ringing. "I've got to focus on work here."

*Angels can fly because they can take themselves lightly.* With a groan, Kateri shook her head as she sat down at the computer and took a handful of pistachios out of the bag by her bed. Having missed lunch, she was ravenously hungry. And she had to respond to her parents' email. Explaining the entire Attack of the Cyberthieves to her parents had been one heck of a job. They now seemed to think that she had fallen into another dimension where she was living in some sort of video game. *Not that I don't feel like that too,* she thought to herself.

*So what's up with you and Alex?* her mom had written. *How long are you going to stay there?*

As Kateri munched and stared at the bootup screen of her computer ("Loading your personal settings") she felt the last of the morning's anger dying away. *Alex is right,* she realized. *I have been working too hard. And why?*

*Have you been trying to evade something?* Her inner self prodded. *Have you been using work as an excuse to not deal with Alex?*

Yes. But what was it that she was trying to evade? That she wanted to break up with Alex, or because she didn't want to admit that she wanted to marry him?

She wasn't the only one who'd been evading the issue.

Taking another handful of pistachios, she glanced at the clock. Two thirty. Four and a half hours before Alex got off work. She could talk to him then.

Her computer was taking a long time to boot up. A *really* long time. Since she was growing paranoid about anything that had to do with computers, she pushed the 'control panel' button. *Show hidden files.* Just as Mr. O'Donnell had demonstrated, she began to look for suspicious icons. According to her notes, she should have 173 files in this folder.

There were 174.

Something had been installed. She located the extra file. It had an "x" icon.

When she clicked it, praying it wasn't a virus, something opened up into a window. A desktop. Someone else's desktop. On the background of the desktop was a huge anime cat in a red jacket holding a samurai sword.

She recognized it. Mr. O'Donnell's desktop. She saw the mouse flicking around, and guessed that Alex's dad had woken up from his sleep and was clicking around as usual.

*Why would this be on my computer?*

Somehow, the answer came to her. *So someone could reach Mr. O'Donnell's computer from my laptop.*

But who would want to do that? Who could possibly be using her computer to control Mr. O'Donnell's computer?

*Mr. O'Donnell could.*

Bits of information began to rain down through Kateri's consciousness as she stared at the computer-within-a-computer. Mr. O'Donnell had been a hacker. He knew how to get onto other people's computers. He knew how to steal databases. He knew how to get into cyberthieves' banks…

He could steal money from cyberthieves, and then set up a scheme to trap all the rest of the cyberthieves, so that he went free, while they sat in jail.

*He could be the fortieth hacker.*

Her hands shaking, Kateri closed her laptop, not wanting to see what so clearly fit together. She tried to conjure up Mr. O'Donnell before her eyes: Alan O'Donnell. Father. Husband. Catholic. Provider. Kitty's husband. Alex's dad. She thought she knew him, but he spent so much time behind that computer, how much had she really gotten to know him? Somehow, the man that she thought she knew wasn't holding together. The virtual reality of the computer had superseded all that.

All she could think was: *there's such a thing as an anonymous witness, isn't there? I can call the FBI. They can find out the truth. Right?* The O'Donnells never needed to know.

*If Mr. O'Donnell could use my computer to fool his entire family, then I can use my cell phone to fool them.*

She pulled out the card Agent Furlow had given her and dialed the number. "Agent Furlow?"

"Speaking." She recognized the agent's friendly voice.

"It's Kateri. Kateri Kovach. From the Twilight Hills Hotel."

"Yes, Kateri. I'm on my way over there right now."

"Uh, I have some information. Or a question. I wanted to give it anonymously. I mean, ask a question anonymously."

"You can do that. Shoot."

Her throat constricted as she tried to speak quietly. "I was wondering—remember our conversation the other day?"

"I do."

"Do you think it's possible—you think that maybe—Mr. O'Donnell could be the fortieth hacker?"

There was silence.

Kateri waited.

"What makes you think that?"

Kateri felt wretched, deceived, and treacherous. "I found some of his software on my computer. It looks like he's been using it to do things to his own computer. Like, maybe look like he was hacking into his own computer to fool us. I don't know, all I know is that it's his software."

After a silence, Agent Furlow said, "Does he know you—found this?"

"No." She fought to speak. "This isn't a surprise to you, is it?"

"I don't know what I'm allowed to tell you, but—well, it's not completely a surprise. Our conversation was helpful to me."

"Great." She quivered down onto the bed. "What should I do?"

"Well, I'm on my way over there now. I'd already arranged with Alex to see you all at dinner tonight. Just hang tight. I'll be there soon."

"I will. Goodbye then," she said weakly, and hung up the phone.

# Chapter Sixteen

*Yet the servant girl worried about the
chief robber, who had fled from the house,
knowing he would return.*
The Arabian Nights

*H*er world was spinning around her, and she set her head down on the pillow. It seemed a moment later that a knock at her door made her jump.

"Hey, Kateri! It's me!"

It was Alex, vaulting over the laundry cart, which was still parked in her room, and looking pretty happy. "Hey. I'm off early."

She struggled to sit up. He was still swimming in her vision. She hadn't thought at all about Alex. How it would affect her relationship. With him. *Did he know?*

"Dad said he needed to do some more work on the front desk computer, so he told me to go find you. He'll cover the desk for me now, and I'll do a few hours after we get back from the movie." He sat down on the bed next to her. "So—what about this? I'll take you up north to this winery, and we'll get some dinner. We might even be able to do some hiking first, if we want to check out the national forest out there. Then we'll go catch that movie you wanted to see. So we're emancipated from the Twilight Hills for a few hours at least. What do you say, hey?"

He was so focused on his plans that he apparently hadn't caught onto her mood. *Did he know about his dad? Could he know? And Kitty? Did she know? What about Sam and David?* The prospect of being collectively deceived by the entire O'Donnell family was too much for Kateri to handle, and her mind rejected it.

*No, they can't know. I know Alex. I know Mrs. O'Donnell. They couldn't, wouldn't trick me like this.*

So they must be deceived too. *It's so easy for a father to hide his true colors from his family.* Shaking, she got to her feet.

"Kateri. You're not listening to a word I'm saying."

"Alex, I'm leaving."

"What?"

The words had spilled from her mouth without thinking. Now she tried to brace herself. "I'm sorry. I've just got to leave. I'm sorry."

He was open-mouthed, agog. "Kateri. What has gotten into you?"

She couldn't explain. It was too painful. She didn't want to see the look on his face. "Alex. Please. Just let me go."

"Now wait a second," he blocked her way, took her by the shoulders. "What happened? Tell me."

She tried to raise the barrier of inscrutable detachment that she had practiced for years. "Nothing's wrong. I just need to go home. I need to see my parents. Get some perspective."

"Kateri, hold on. Stop. What are you upset about?"

She pushed his hands away woodenly. "I'm not upset."

"I'm sorry I threw you in the laundry cart."

"It's not that. It's nothing you've done."

He shook his head. "I don't believe it. Come on, tell me!"

"No, it's nothing you've done." She held her face in her hands and he quickly put his arms around her. "It's just that you were raised to be loyal, that's all!"

He stiffened. "Loyal? What do you mean?"

She knelt down to grab her suitcase out from under the bed. "It doesn't matter. Please, just let me go."

"Kateri!"

His voice sounded so plaintive that she broke down, sat on the bed, and cried. His arms were around her, and she could tell, even as she sobbed, how utterly confused and bewildered he was. *He doesn't know*, she realized. *He doesn't. His dad's deceived him too.* This only made her cry harder. With ferocity she pulled herself away from him, wiped her eyes, and grabbed her suitcase.

Alex kept talking. "Look, I'm sorry, Kat. It's probably my fault. All this summer, I've been dodging you. I haven't let you talk about our relationship. If that's what you want to do now, that's fine." He seemed to draw himself up, as if saying, *hit me. Hit me where it hurts.*

She paused, and looked at him, on the verge of saying something. The words almost flew out of her again. *I don't want to break up with you.* She could picture the exhilaration and exasperation on his face if she were to say that. But she didn't say it.

An evil voice said, *break up with him. You've been wanting to do it all summer anyhow. Distance yourself from him. It'll stop you from being hurt. Save your own skin.*

But she couldn't do that either.

The only thing she could do was pack her suitcase, while Alex watched, in an agony of frustration, unable to stop her, unable to get her to say anything else.

"Can you drive me to the bus station?" she said at last. She was casting about for some way to get there without involving him, but couldn't figure out how to do it.

"You really want to leave, don't you?"

She didn't *want* to leave. She *had* to. It was a completely different thing. But she couldn't explain.

*I never should have come here. I never should have gotten mixed up with this crazy family and their computers and their hotel. I should have stayed far away from all of this, been sensible, gotten a regular job, stayed in Jersey.*

"Kateri. Please tell me *something.*"

She looked at him, and her lips began to shake. "I'm sorry," she said at last.

Alex turned away from her, went to the wall, and, looking down, pressed his hands against it, as though he were trying to push it over.

"Okay," he said at last. "I'll drive you to the station. Just give me a little bit to pull myself together, okay?"

"Okay."

"I'll let you finish in here."

He edged around the laundry cart and walked out of the door.

In the empty lobby, Alex blinked hard in the bright sunlight streaming in from the door. His dad was not at the desk. Big surprise. The lure of the office computer must have proved too much for him. *What's he always doing on there anyhow?*

He heard voices and glanced around to see that the maids were coming downstairs, loads of sheets and towels in their hands.

"We're all done now, Mr. Alex," the one older Hispanic woman said, looking a bit bothered. She indicated the sheets. "We will bring them to the basement before we go."

"We could not find the laundry cart!" one of them called out as they passed him.

"Oh. Yeah. Sorry." He rubbed his eyes. They walked away from him, chattering in Spanish. He paced up to the desk, looking for something to do. Where was Dad?

*That's okay. Kateri and I can just leave. I can drive her to the bus station, and then stay out. Maybe go to a bar or something. No one has to know that she left until tomorrow.*

The shame of it hit him then, of having to tell his parents that Kateri was gone. She was done with him, done with his family.

He rubbed his face as a car pulled into the empty lot. A dark green car, slightly familiar. The door opened, and Agent Furlow got out.

Alex met him at the door, anxious for something to do. "Hey. How was the traffic?"

"Much better out here," the agent said, lugging a duffle bag and his briefcase.

"Let me get that for you," Alex said.

"I'm fine. Where do you want to put me?"

Alex got behind the desk and hit the bar on his computer. "Well, let's see. Everything from 101 through 310 is empty. You've got the pick of the house. What's your birthday? Your favorite lottery number?"

"Wow. That's a toughie. How about you give me something on the top floor and far away from everything? I'm a light sleeper."

"310 is yours. Can I have someone bring up the bags for you?"

"Don't bother. I've got it." Agent Furlow took his key, thanked Alex, and disappeared into the elevator.

No sooner had the doors shut than she walked out into the lobby, trailing her three bags behind her, looking more than a little furtive. So Kateri was embarrassed about leaving too.

"You ready?"

She nodded, silently. Her cheeks and eyes were still red.

Shaking his head in frustration, he grabbed the bags. "I wish you would tell me—" he started to say, when suddenly the office door opened.

"Hey, Alex!"

It was his dad. Alex hastily dropped the bags behind the desk. "Yeah?"

"Oh, sorry I'm not out there. Just something on the computer…"

"Yeah, yeah." Alex said. "Hey. Kateri and I are leaving."

"I'll be right out. Mind if I finish this up first? It will only take me a moment."

Alex waved his hand. "Sure." As his dad shut the office door, Alex turned to Kateri to roll his eyes, but saw her looking at the closed door with a mixture of fear and anger that startled him.

"Let's go." She turned abruptly for the door.

"In a minute, Kat. He said he'd be right out."

"Alex, you notice how he always says that? But look at how much time he's on that computer? Hours and hours and hours!  It's about time you started noticing!"

He wished she would lower her voice. "Kateri. What are you trying to say?"

Instead of answering, she stomped around the floor in frustration, waving her hands. "Computers! They're a curse! They blind you to what's going on around you! You just get so wrapped up in that little world that you don't notice anything! Not even things that are right in front of you!"

She paused right in front of him, looking up, her black eyes glowering at him.

"Kat, you are really, really frustrating. Can I tell you that?"

"Sure. Likewise." She grabbed her bags.

He tried to delay her one last time. "Look, are you sure you want to go now? Agent Furlow is here. He said he wanted to meet with the whole family over dinner. I presume he meant you, too."

"I don't want to see him. Just tell me what he says. Later."

She crossed to the door and put her hands on the bar to push it open.

At that moment, the phone rang. The guest phone.

Their eyes met. "I'll get it," Alex said automatically.

"You're stalling, Alex."

He glared at her as he picked it up. "Maybe I am. Hello?"

"Hi. I'm having some problems with the television in my room. Could you come take a look at it?"

There was only one guest in the entire hotel. Alex knew what room he was in. "Not a problem, sir. Not a problem at all. I'll be up to room 310 in a moment."

Kateri glowered at him. "Alex O'Donnell. This is just another excuse."

He was mad. Pulling out the van key, he tossed it at her. "Go ahead. You can leave. Drive yourself to the station if you're so anxious to go. I'll pick up the van later on."

He couldn't say goodbye as she walked out the door. Stalking out of the lobby to the elevator, he wondered how much of their conversation Dad had overheard. But the office door remained shut.

Leaning against the side of the elevator as the doors closed, he tried to calm himself down. *Wasted, wasted,* he thought to himself. All the time he'd spent with Kateri. *Wasted.* He'd thought that if he just kept her from leaving long enough, she'd change her mind. But now it was all over. A gaping hole blown through his life.

He rubbed his eyes again. Time enough to get emotional later on. Yeah, he had time. Years, maybe.

Feeling weary, useless, and stupid. A dumb fat kid holding a wooden sword. Feeling like a fool for playing at being a warrior. He knocked lightly on the door to Room 310.

"Sorry to keep you waiting," he said, when the agent opened the door.

"Not a problem." Agent Furlow walked back into the room, and Alex followed him.

"So—what's wrong with the television?"

The agent had taken off his suit jacket. He ran his hand through his dark hair, rumpling it. "I can't get all the cable channels to work." He threw himself on the bed and leaned back against the pillows.

"Hmph," Alex said, going up to the television and clicking the remote. "Which channels?"

"66, 210, 340…"

"The adult channels? Sorry, sir. We have those blocked."

Furlow stared at him. "Why's that?"

Alex bowed slightly. "We're a family company here, sir. We don't support pornography. I'm sorry if it inconveniences you."

"Oh. Well, I'm pretty inconvenienced," Agent Furlow said, pulling off his tie. He looked unusually miffed. "You're sure you can't unblock a channel or two just for me? Come on, what's a single guy supposed to do in a hotel room this far away from civilization?"

Alex shrugged, figuring that a sarcastic reply wouldn't be kosher. "That's our policy, sir."

"Well, if that's your policy, and it inconveniences me, will the staff be able to provide some alternate entertainment?" He grinned. "What about that Kateri girl?"

It was like something Uncle Cass would have said. Alex remained calm. "Sorry to not be able to help you out." He attempted a smile. "We'll see you downstairs for dinner." *We're going to have to eat with this guy? That's going to be an ordeal.*

"I'll be down." The agent leaned back on the bed and smiled broadly, reaching under his pillow.

Alex had already turned to go, and as he did, a thought flashed through his mind: *never turn your back on a known enemy.*

But it was already too late.

# Chapter Seventeen

*The disguised robber spoke most courteously to the family, who bade him dine with them, yet the servant girl recognized his features*
*The Arabian Nights*

There was throbbing pain. A headache. The blood was pulsing in his skull, disorienting him. Alex moved his head, and immediately wished he hadn't as the world swirled around him. He vomited into a sea of white.

Coughing, he lifted his head and the world shifted around him. He had been leaning, head down, over the side of a hard white fiberglass surface. Despite his headache, he shook his head and tried to focus. To one side was a familiar silver faucet and dial spigot. He was hanging over the side of one of the bathtubs in the Twilight Hills Hotel. Room 310's bathtub, to be exact.

With difficulty, he sank backwards onto his knees and realized that someone had taken off his jacket and handcuffed his wrists tightly behind him. His head was still pounding, and he felt a stinging burn on his neck. That was where the agent must have stunned him.

"You up, Alex?"

His enemy. Pulling uselessly at the metal clamping his arms, Alex slowly looked up at the smiling face of the man who had pretended to be his family's friend and ally through this whole predicament. A carefully played masquerade, while all the time waiting to make his move.

Agent Furlow leaned against the door jamb of the bathroom, still toying with the Taser gun. "You recovered pretty quick. Think you're all done in there? I hope so, for your sake."

Alex tried to position himself, to kick, to fight, but realized he was still too limp and dizzy to do anything but kneel there, panting and powerless.

"I don't know what those thirty-nine idiots were thinking," Furlow said, stepping forward and flicking on the water to clean out the tub. "I don't know why I bothered to organize that whole operation for them. I told them to let Admin handle the whole thing, but no, they were too paranoid. Couldn't trust me. Had to see for themselves that it was done. So they all turned out, and got themselves caught. Which is a shame, because it really was a one-man job."

He put a hand under Alex's arm, twisted it, and hauled him to his knees. With easy practice, he maneuvered his captive into the bedroom and deposited him in one of the room's boxy chairs. Then he reached into his duffle bag and pulled out a handful of what looked like red bungee cords with silver locks on the ends. He snapped an extra-long one between his lean and muscular arms, testing its strength, then pulled it around Alex's shoulders and wrapped it around the rungs of the chair back, clicking it shut.

"A one-man job," Furlow repeated, and leaned over to look at Alex, a smile darting onto his face. "So long as you do things in the right order. Number one: start out by neutralizing the dangerous son."

Alex winced as the taut rubber cord pressed his arms and back against the chair. He couldn't help a bitter smile of his own as the agent yanked a second one around his lower back. *Guess I'm only dangerous so long as my luck holds. And mine ran out. Less than an hour ago.*

Whistling, the agent wrapped and clamped Alex's still-numbed feet to the legs of the chair with the red cords. When his prisoner was bound hand and foot, Agent Furlow sat down heavily on the bed, tossing his Taser into his duffle bag. Trying not to let the man see his fear, Alex swallowed as unobtrusively as he could and attempted to meet the man's eyes.

"But having to do this over a second time isn't all bad. There was one flaw in the original plan I didn't know about," Agent Furlow mused. "Religion. I had no idea you and your girlfriend were so moralistic. Kateri said her parents would never believe she'd skip town with a million dollars. I believe she's right. But she seemed to indicate that your family had the reputation of being a little more— well, let's just say 'sticky fingered.' After all, you all did cop that million dollars and kept it secret. So I thought, it'll make more sense to her parents and the courts if the O'Donnells vanish with over a million dollars, and the only stiff the feds find is—hers."

He grinned, apparently enjoying Alex's expression. Alex was trying not to react, but he wasn't as good at the stoic thing as Kateri was: he was sure that Furlow could easily see straight through the impassive glare to his anguish. It didn't help that rubber cords were contracting around his muscles, squeezing him in the stomach and the legs, making breathing painful and movement impossible.

The man went on, still watching Alex's reaction. "It helps that I have her on the record as saying that she believed your dad was the fortieth hacker—and the software I bugged onto her laptop will confirm that. I'll have to make sure that laptop turns up in a landfill somewhere. Near where they'll find the pieces of her body."

Alex turned his face away to the wall.

Something beeped on the laptop computer lying on the room's desk. With a grunt, the agent sat up, moved to the desk, and flipped open the computer. Swiftly his fingers flew over the keyboard. Alex recognized the site on the man's computer: the Twilight Hills Hotel security system. *He's hacked our server already. Wonder if dad's picked him up? Probably not. This guy's had a lot of practice hacking us.* Alex flexed his useless fingers again.

His eyes flickering in Alex's direction, the agent turned his computer screen away from Alex's sight. For a few minutes, he tapped and clicked, then shut the computer, and slid it into the briefcase. Alex caught a glimpse of some of the contents of the case and flinched. His captor noticed.

"Want to see my toolkit?" Agent Furlow displayed the handcuffs, knives, and razors inside the case. "Got a long night of interrogation ahead of me." His blue eyes hardened. "And I can promise you this: I'm not going to kill you all until I find the location of every copy of our site logs, every scrap of data he stole. You and your dad are going to lead me to every single hard drive, server storage, and remote account where you might have hidden something, or your crippled mom and Chinese girlfriend are going to have a really miserable time of it before they die. You got that, Alex?"

He checked the gun in his side pocket, closed his briefcase and stretched. "I'll start with your kid brothers. Just to give you and your dad a sample of what I can do. I'm pretty ticked at your dad. It took a lot of trouble to make sure the data he turned over to the FBI vanished down the bureaucratic black hole. Now the O'Donnell family's about to enter that same black hole." He took out a roll of tape from his duffle bag and peeled off a piece. "Well, Alex? Got anything you want to tell me to make my job easier?"

Feeling nothing but the steady pulsing pain around his forehead, Alex stared at the carpet. He had nothing left inside him: he was a gutless, hollow man, with nothing to give.

"Still stubborn?" Agent Furlow shrugged. "All I can say is, be ready to talk, and talk fast, when I return. When it comes to torture, I'm a very impatient man. I'm afraid I tend to overdo it." He grabbed Alex's chin and smeared the tape across his mouth, then patted him on the head. "Sit tight. I'll be back soon. And I won't be alone."

He went into the bathroom and turned off the water, then came back. "Oh yeah." He forced his way into Alex's back pocket and pulled out his wallet. With two fingers, he extracted the master keycard. "Almost forgot that handy thing," he remarked, dropping the wallet on the bed. It flopped open as the door closed behind the agent, the keylock snapping shut.

Alex gazed the creased photo of Kateri in his wallet, sitting nestled over a worn holy card of St. Patrick. It was her college graduation photo. She'd never looked so lovely. He couldn't keep looking at her, and looked up at the ceiling instead.

Outmaneuvered. Trapped. Leaving his family to a grisly death. He didn't want to think: he couldn't escape the pictures crowding into his head.

Only one thing that Agent Furlow hadn't counted on: Kateri leaving him. Squeezing his shoulders against the rubber ropes, Alex prayed. *I hope she really left. I hope she's driving as fast as she can. Away from me.*

Kateri sat in the parking lot, engine running. Finally, she threw the van back into park with a groan. *I'll wait for Alex,* she thought dismally as she turned off the engine. *I owe him that much.*

Why? Why was it that she couldn't leave Alex O'Donnell, even now?

The van was hot. Even with the windows down, it was hot. At last, the heat did what anger and guilt and virtue could not: Kateri yanked the key out of the ignition, and went back to the hotel.

She pulled the glass doors open, stepped inside, and stood in the empty lobby, feeling the rush of air conditioning gratefully. No sign of Alex. She leaned against the glass door, glanced outside. Her bags and purse were still in the van. And she had meant to call her parents. She leaned into the glass door to push it open.

It wouldn't budge.

Quickly she checked the lock. It was jammed shut. Mr. O'Donnell's stupid security system malfunctioning again.

Or…. was it an accident?

Feeling queasy, she walked up to the office and knocked on the door. Mr. O'Donnell swung around with a guilty start.

"Oh! Kateri, I'm sorry. I really will be right out there."

His ears were red, Kateri noticed. Licking her lips, she said, "The doors won't open, Mr. O'Donnell."

"I know. The security system's gone haywire for some reason. I can't get anything to open. I've been almost frantic, trying to get it fixed. At least we don't have any guests here."

She managed a smile. "But we do. Agent Furlow. The FBI. He wants to meet with the family."

"Does he? Oh." He still looked red-faced. Embarrassed. Guilty.

"Hello!"

Both of them looked up, to see the agent in question beaming at them. She was struck again by his blue eyes and handsome smile.

"Mr. O'Donnell. Kateri. I think we have a dinner date."

"Yes…" Kateri said, her eyes drawn back to Mr. O'Donnell. "I think that Mrs. O'Donnell is expecting you."

"We'll be right there," Mr. O'Donnell said to the agent. "You know your way in, right? Just through that door and down the hall. Please, let yourself in."

"I will, thanks," the agent said with a wave, and walked off, whistling.

*At least someone's in a good mood.* Kateri nearly followed him, but Mr. O'Donnell caught at her arm.

"Listen, Kateri…"

Kateri almost yelled for Agent Furlow to wait for her, but something in Mr. O'Donnell's eyes made her stop. Something that reminded her of Alex. "What?"

"I heard what you said. To Alex." He pushed up his glasses. "Look, you're right. I do spend too much time on the computer. Way too much. I just—it's a way for me to escape. Real life. I know it's wrong. It's time for me to change. You helped me recognize that. I think our whole family has learned a lot from you. You being with Alex." He hesitated. "It sounded like you two were having a bad fight. I don't mean to interfere, but I hope you can make it up with Alex. I think—I think you two are good for each other."

She didn't know what to say, her eyes locked onto his. His eyes were a lot like Alex's—there was something in them. Something irritating, and irresistible. She paused.

"Okay," she said. Even if he were a thief, he was still Alex's father. She half-smiled. "I promise I won't do anything rash."

"Thanks," he said, and got up. "Thanks again for being part of the madness."

"You're welcome," she said, and followed him out of the office.

This would have been the perfect cue for Alex to show up, but the lobby was deserted. Troubled, she looked around. Maybe he had gone to his bedroom? As Mr. O'Donnell held the door open for her, Kateri entered the suite and hurried down the dark hallway to the living room.

The sound of pleasant conversation and the smell of good food greeted her. Mrs. O'Donnell had left her wheelchair and was sitting on a low cushion in front of the coffee table, talking with Agent Furlow, who was squatting on the futon. Sam and David were bringing out platters of food from the kitchen to set on the table. Kateri could smell fish sauce and vegetables and fried rice. Her mouth watered, despite her fear.

"We decided to eat Vietnamese tonight again," Mrs. O'Donnell said brightly to Kateri. "Where's Alex?"

Kateri glanced in the boys' bedroom. It was empty. "I thought he might be down here—" she started to say, but the agent waved a hand.

"My bad. Alex ran out to the store to get something for me," he said lightly. "He said not to hold dinner for him. He'll be back soon. I have to tell you, I'm really impressed by your service here."

Kateri turned to the hallway, and the agent added, "Kateri. He said you should wait here for him."

"Oh. Okay."

She hadn't seen Alex leave the building, but of course, he could have gone out the side door to his own car and driven away after she'd gone back into the lobby. She could see Alex doing that, trying to avoid her. After all, he'd been avoiding the question of their relationship all summer.

The agent and Mrs. O'Donnell continued talking about Northern Virginia and favorite stores. Kateri stood in the doorway, feeling strangely ill at ease. The food was on the table; Sam and David were arguing over who got to sit on which cushion. Only Mr. O'Donnell looked a bit perturbed. Their eyes met, and Kateri felt her unease heighten.  He thinks that something's wrong too…

"Uh, I'm going to get something from my room," she said, running down the hallway. "Be right back."

"We'll wait for you, dear!" Mrs. O'Donnell called.

In the lobby, Kateri plastered herself to the windows and craned her neck around, trying to see if Alex's battered red car was still in its corner spot. But she couldn't tell. The van was still parked in front. She tried the lobby door: still jammed.

Unconsciously she reached for the lobby phone, and thought, *I bet there's no dial tone.* She was right. Something told her that if she had had her cellphone, it wouldn't be working either.

*Something is not right.* Really *not right.*

Thinking that she had heard steps in the passage, she opened the door to the living quarters, hoping against hope to see Alex's strong, confident form sauntering down the hallway. But it was empty.

From the living room came the sound of laughter, and glassware. Mr. O'Donnell was pouring out drinks. She listened for Alex's repartee, any words of greeting. No. He was not there.

But something else caught her eye: the weapons wall. It was bare. Every sword and weapon was gone from the hooks embedded in the Oriental curtain. Only the two fans adorned each corner.

Now she was certain something was wrong.

But what could she do? Without Alex?

She returned to her hotel room, pacing madly about the space she had recently torn her belongings out of. In her haste to leave the O'Donnells, she had forgotten her picture of the Sacred Heart taped to the wall, and her rosary, which still hung from the hotel wall lamp. Abstractedly she touched its beads, and searched the room again for some sort of answer.

She wandered towards the door, and glancing through the open bathroom door, realized she had completely forgotten to pack that room. Makeup, beauty products, and jewelry were scattered around. Plus something purple shimmering in the corner: her ao dài was hanging from the towel rack. She had been trying to steam the wrinkles out of the silk. Alex's gift to her.

Alex. The main reason why the cyberthieves had not destroyed the O'Donnells last time.

*And now Alex was not here.*

Coincidence?

*Alex has just run out to the store for me…he said he'd be back. Not to hold dinner for him… Kateri, he asked you to wait here for him.*

Suddenly deep, terrible certainty washed over her. It was a lie. Alex would not have told her to wait for him: Alex had told her she could leave. He didn't expect her to be waiting for him. He thought she was gone. If he hadn't returned, there was certainly another reason.

*Was he dead? Already? Was it already too late?*

She grabbed the ao dài. She wasn't strong, or trained, or even very clever. But she had one thing she could do. Something Alex had wanted her to do. She could do it now.

Quickly she unbuttoned the collar and pulled the dress from the hanger. She didn't have much time.

# Chapter Eighteen

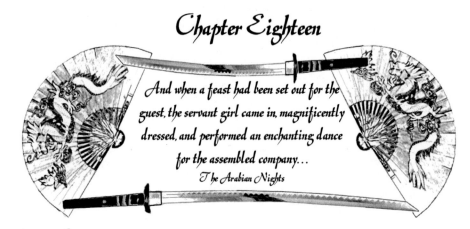

*And when a feast had been set out for the
guest, the servant girl came in, magnificently
dressed, and performed an enchanting dance
for the assembled company...*

*The Arabian Nights*

Wrenching himself back and forth, Alex tossed and turned in the chair, straining this way and that, trying to find some give. Sweat poured out of him, he was exhausted, but he couldn't give up. He couldn't.

The chair toppled and fell forward, his head smashing on the base of the nearby table. His eyes spun around, and he struggled to remain conscious, breathing through his nose. He couldn't throw up again with his mouth gagged, or he'd suffocate.

Feeling all resolve draining from him, he slumped, his forehead against the carpet, and tried hard to focus, to find that center of trust in God that had always seen him through the worst battles before. But the tangled images in his imagination cut into that center, jabbed knives into his chest as he tried again and again to calm his breathing and his heart rate.

It was hopeless. He knew it. A meaningless battle against despair.

There was nothing he could do.

Timidly, Kateri stepped towards the dining room, holding one fan close to her face, the other fan cocked alluringly across her stomach. No one saw her yet.

Tears crept up into her eyes and she pushed them down. For a moment, she wavered. *What am I doing? I'm no siren of the South East.*

*Speak for yourself.* Alex's voice. Alex's hand, touching her cheek gently. *You're so very beautiful.*

She felt her earrings trembling on her earlobes, and swallowed. Throwing a quick glance over her shoulder, catching the golden glimmer of an earring in her peripheral vision, she prayed to find that comforting masculine figure, sword in hand, watching her back—but no. She had demanded to leave, and he had let her go.

And now he was gone.

*I call myself pro-life, but I didn't mind hurting him,* she thought bitterly. *And then leaving him, with no explanation. I wasn't kind or fair, not to him or to those he loved.*

Yes, the very least she could do was defend the family she had mocked him for being loyal to.

The movement of her head had drawn Sam's eye, and now he stared at her, his jaw dropped. "Yowza."

"Ao dài," David said, blinking. "Uh… Kateri? Is that you?"

Delicately, Kateri nodded her head, her hair heavy in its topknot, which she'd skewered with half a dozen bobby pins and a pencil. With small steps that her mother would have been proud of, she inched forward, making a graceful curtsy with the fans.

She could not have produced a more shocked audience. Mr. and Mrs. O'Donnell stared, the young boys were statues, and Agent Furlow gave a long, low whistle.

"I would like to dance for you," Kateri said. "In honor of our guest."

"The fan dance?" Sam asked, as though he couldn't believe it.

"The fan dance."

"Awesome!"

"David," Kateri inclined her head towards him. "I need some music."

David scrambled to the stereo system. "Uh—anything in particular?"

"Something appropriate."

"Put on the sound track to *Kung Fu Panda*," Sam suggested. Kateri winced, but she knew it would have to do.

She waited for the music, and then gracefully swept forward, curling the fans. Unbidden, the dance came into her memory: she could almost hear her mother's clapping hands and high-pitched commands. *One step, two steps to the right, fan raised high. One step, two steps to the left, fan down. One step to the right, fan up, one step to the left, fan down. Turn around and curl the fans, and bow. Step again…*

David pumped up the music, and Kateri leapt to and fro with the music, sweeping around the table, around the guests, the folds of the ao dài trailing beautifully behind her. She was a butterfly, an angel, a silken gossamer siren, flitting right—flitting left. She had to get close… Back to the steps, the curling, the high and the low. Hop step right—and clap the fan—hop step left—and clap the fan. Nod and smile, lift the fan, smile, smile.

Agent Furlow was rubbing his nose, sliding his hand into his pocket where she knew he kept his gun. She fluttered in front of him, lowered her lashes, looked up at him with wide eyes. He gawked at her, withdrew his hand. She turned around, looked at him again, a wisp of a look, turned around, one more time—turn around, look at him and—the music was almost done—she turned around, flipped the fan and furled it, braced herself unconsciously, and leaned into his personal space. As though bowing over him, as though to hover on him with a butterfly's kiss, she unfurled the fan with its hidden blades.

She set its metal razor edge at the base of his throat and held it. The music sank into silence.

"Remain still," she said steadily. "Or you, sir, are dead."

There were jagged intakes of breath all around the room. Agent Furlow's blue eyes looked at her. He started to smile, and she pressed inward. He felt the sharp metal against his thorax and gasped. He swallowed, and remained still, his blue eyes twitching as they stared into hers. No one moved.

Mr. O'Donnell finally recovered his voice. "What are you doing, Kateri?" He sounded as though he were trying to talk her down from a ledge.

"Catching the last cyberthief," Kateri said. "David and Sam, disarm and immobilize him, will you?"

She knew they only had seconds before the agent reacted. But Sam and David didn't disappoint. They moved instantly to either side of the man and grabbed his arms, David tossing the gun to his dad. Mr. O'Donnell caught it, trained it on the agent, and cocked it.

"Make sure he doesn't have another gun," Sam urged. "That one was too obvious."

Mr. O'Donnell said dubiously, "You'd better be right about this, Kateri: I believe there's some kind of law against threatening a federal agent."

"There sure is," Agent Furlow said huskily, barely moving his lips.

"I'm willing to take the risk," Kateri said. And she blinked, still holding the fan to the man's throat. "First," she said steadily, trying to control her voice. "He has to tell us where Alex really is."

David handed his father the man's wallet with his ID on the front. "Check to make sure he's really a federal agent, Dad."

His dad shrugged. "I've no doubt of that," he said, opening the wallet. Suddenly he started and picked up a golden charm that had tumbled out of it. "But are you also a ninja?"

Agent Furlow didn't say a thing, but his face darkened.

"You were the one I followed," Mr. O'Donnell said, holding up the charm, of a tiny ninja with nunchucks. "You're the one who asked me to join the forty cyberthieves." He swallowed, and his voice grew stronger. "And I said no."

"Your choice," the agent said contemptuously. "Your fatal error."

There was a gasp from David. "Look!" He had pulled something familiar from the man's pocket: the red keycard that was the master key.

"Alex's," Mrs. O'Donnell said.

The tears were flowing out of Kateri's eyes now. "Give that to me," she said. "Mr. O'Donnell, don't let him move an inch, or I swear I'll kill him. Everyone stay here."

And she tore out of the apartment.

As she raced up one flight of stairs after another, swinging around the banisters so fast that she barreled into walls and tripped over her silk trousers.

*If he's dead—I want to be the first one to find him. It's my fault. Please, God, no—*

The topknot flopped into her face, and she pulled it out as she ripped through the last door and raced to the room at the end of the corridor, room 310, Agent Furlow's room.

But even as she skidded to a stop, she heard the noise and knew someone was alive in that room. She grabbed the door handle and heard a tremendous crash, and breaking glass. In a terror, she slid the card to unlock the door, and threw the handle and the door open.

What greeted her eyes was a room that had been hit by a hurricane. The drapes were ripped, the covers off the bed, the mattress crazily leaning off the bed, furniture overturned, the television set shattered on the floor. And in the middle of it lay the hurricane, wrenching itself over to face his foe: a wild-eyed Alex, gagged and bound hand and foot to the remains of what had been a chair.

Kateri felt herself sliding down the open door as the silk gave way beneath her, and she staggered to her feet. She hurried over to him, knelt down, and carefully pulled the tape off of his mouth. "Alex. They're okay. We're all okay. We caught him."

With a gasp of relief, Alex sank back against the ruined frame of the chair. "Thank God," he said feebly. "I almost died here, trying to get to you."

"It sure looks like it," she said, surveying the wreckage, blinking. The devastated room bore testimony to Alex's frenzied attempts to come to the rescue of his family. "I'm so sorry I left you."

"Don't worry about it," he said gratefully. "I'm just glad you came back." He twisted himself to his knees. "Want to pull that cord off of my leg? Thanks." Staggering to his feet, he lifted the remains of the chair on his arms and crashed them down on the bottom of the overturned table. The chair shattered, and he shrugged out of the pieces. "That helps."

"Let me get your hands," she urged, getting to her feet.

"Can't. They're cuffed. Furlow has the keys. Wait a second."

He jackknifed himself in two, straining hard, and managed to pull his chained wrists over his seat and up to the back of his knees. For a moment he wriggled like a cat trying to get through a small hole, but in another moment he was back on his feet, his shackled wrists in front of him. "Much better."

"We'd better tell your parents that you're alive. I think your mom is about to have a heart attack—this time for sure," Kateri said, grabbing him by the arms, but he twisted his wrists up and managed to grab hers.

"Wait a moment," he said, breathing hard. "I just need to know one thing. When you wouldn't talk to me before, was it because you couldn't tell me that you wanted to break up with me?" His green eyes bored into hers.

She couldn't speak, but shook her head.

He cocked his head and looked at her carefully. "You *didn't* want to break up with me?"

"No," she managed to say through the tears that were spilling down her cheeks. "In fact, quite the opposite."

He sank to his knees. "Oh thank God. Kateri, you don't know how humiliated I feel right now. This is not at all how I was planning to propose to you. My plans involved something more like a surprise trip to the city, an exclusive restaurant and a ring with a rather large ruby. But if you can accept me now—I know it'll be for real. And that's what I really want from you. That's what I've always wanted from you but never dared to hear: the truth. Kateri Maria Kovach, can you—could you—would you—marry me?"

"Alex O'Donnell," she whispered, pushing back the hair that was straggling over his forehead, knowing that she was ready, at last, to leap off that cliff her mother had talked about. "I will."

With a gigantic spring he jumped to his feet and threw his chained hands around her, pulling her to him and kissing her with less than his usual restraint. Caught now, for good, she laughed at him, and spun around with him crazily in the rubble and shards of the ruined hotel room.

Alex was happy. His family was alive. His enemy was in the hands of the local police, who were delighted that another high-profile criminal had been nabbed in their precinct. (He suspected they were enjoying lording it over the FBI as well, but he couldn't be sure.) And Kateri had agreed to marry him. Even if he was still sore and bruised again from his recent kidnapping, he didn't have much to complain of.

"It doesn't get better than this, does it?" he said, ruffling the fur of Link the cat, who was sitting on his chest while he lay on the futon. She purred in agreement.

He watched as Kateri, who was still wearing the silk dress he had gotten her, crossed the room spontaneously and hugged his dad. It occurred to him that he'd never seen them show any affection towards one another: most of the time, she'd held Dad at arm's length.

"Mr. O'Donnell, I'm sorry I doubted you," Kateri said.

He grinned. "Welcome to the family."

"Thanks," she said, leaning her head on his shoulder. "I think I'll stay."

David and Sam had jimmied open the closet, where Agent Furlow had locked up all the family's weapons, and now the boys were restoring the swords and throwing stars to their places. But Alex noticed that they had moved the fans from the corners to the place of honor in the center.

From her wheelchair, Alex's mom was busy in the kitchen, reheating the food from the feast that everyone had been too excited to eat. "We'd better check it for poison," Sam had opined. But David had already eaten some of the casserole, and when he didn't fall over frothing at the mouth for real (he did it a few times for effect), they agreed to eat it if Mom would microwave it again.

His father emerged from the bedroom with a curious pile of slabs: he set them down on the floor, and Alex finally recognized them as laptops. His laptop, his dad's, his mom's, his brothers', even Kateri's.

"I say we put these away for a while," he said. "You kids can use the hotel computer for schoolwork if you need to, but I say we put away the recreational computers. What do you think? A family pact? We can get to know our future sister-and-daughter-in-law, go hiking, maybe camping—get to know the real world for a little bit. What do you say?"

"I'm game," said Mom and Kateri together. They looked at each other and smiled. Alex knew they would always be friends and allies. Sam looked put out, but David only yawned.

"Oh Dad, I barely have time for computer any more. I'm too busy running this hotel."

Dad grinned. "I'll take that as a yes. At least I'm going cold turkey for the year."

"Just one year?" Alex asked.

He winked. "Until the wedding, son." He opened one laptop. "Just shutting them all down for now."

Sam gave a huge sigh and collapsed next to Alex on the futon. "The best part," he said to Alex, "was watching Kateri dance. And you missed it!"

"I bet it was spectacular," Alex said, "And I missed it!"

"It was the most beautiful fan dance I've ever seen," Mom said, and added to Kateri, "Your mother would have been proud."

"I'd love to see it," Alex said, casting a yearning glance at Kateri. She smiled at him.

Her dark eyes were sparking. "Alex, the entire time I danced, I was doing it for you."

"Really?" He waited for the punch line.

"Really." She knelt down and kissed him, then nestled against him. "It was all for you."

"Wow." He took that in. Kateri Kovach, fan dancing for him. Pretty cool. "Would you do it again sometime?"

"Absolutely. Minus the razors."

He stroked his beard thoughtfully. "But if it would help me shave…"

She laughed at him. "You're insufferable."

He grinned broadly. "And you're learning."

"Yeah, I'm a quick study. Once I see there's something in it for me." She put her arms around him. "You're by far the best trophy I've ever won for a Fan Dance performance. And no matter what happens, I love you, Alex O'Donnell."

"Aww." When they finished kissing, he leaned against her and closed his eyes, smiling. Night was falling in Virginia. As the last computer whirred into silence, he could hear the crickets' song outside rising like a chorus of celebration.

*And so with great rejoicing the son of Ali Baba was married to the brave servant girl. And they all lived long together in great wealth and with boundless generosity. And who is to say which is the greatest treasure?*

The End.

# A Little Bit About This Book

The Arabian Nights tale of "Ali Baba and the Forty Thieves" is a wonderful story that deserves to be read on its own, and if you haven't done so (or haven't for many years!), please treat yourself by picking up a quality translation of this truly excellent adventure. My story is more of an homage to the tale rather than a replacement for it.

Curiously, the origin of this tale is under dispute: though it appeared in a 1704 translation of a 14th-century manuscript of Arabic tales, some scholars think it was simply created for the book by the French translator, a man infatuated with Arab culture. Others think the translator's Maronite Christian scribe might have supplied the story from an oral tradition otherwise unknown to scholars.

So, is the story "Ali Baba and the Forty Thieves" a truly Arabian story, or just one with Arabian aspirations or pretensions?

It was intriguing to discover that I'd chosen a folk tale that might be only a 'pseudo-folk tale' as the base for my story, which occasionally muses on the conflict between real versus virtual culture!

For a long time I've wondered whether the Internet culture of virtual reality could ever become truly authentic. And what should our attitude towards it be? Should we be purists, and insist on only dealing with the real: real people, true culture, pure solid reality? Or should we make compromises with the endless mélange of images, virtual realms, and pretended identities that comprises modern online society? Kateri wants to be a "reality-only" girl, but even she finds the Asian wanna-be Alex attractive. And I suspect that even those in most sympathy with Kateri's ideals also find something about the Internet that woos us.

So what's the answer? Endless compromise? Or is there a chance we can find parameters and balance? I hope that this light-hearted story will spur more serious reflection for some readers when the tale is done. At any rate, Alex's story was a nice change of pace from the weightier themes of the Fairy Tale Novels I've written thus far.

And since it was my first attempt at anything remotely resembling a technological thriller, I'm once more indebted to the generosity of many intelligent people who lent their expertise to this novel. Among them, I must particularly thank Spike Bowman, formerly of the FBI, who gave me background on law enforcement procedures regarding cybercrime; Dr. Sean O'Mara, a longtime friend who just happened to develop a specialty in the medical treatment for biohazard exposure; and especially Jerome

Heckenkamp, who shared with me his detailed and intricate knowledge of web servers and computer hacking.

Many other people volunteered or contributed their computer knowledge as well, particularly my husband Andrew Schmiedicke and my friends Dan Pesta and Andrew Hague, who helped me sketch out the lines of the computer plot and critiqued what I got wrong. Similarly, my brother David (doctor) and sister-in-law Maura (nurse) and Dr. Frank helped point me in the right direction regarding medical issues, and my brother Paul and friends Michael Russell and Joe Babineau did the same for me with financial fraud and cybercrime.

And I couldn't have created all the elaborate fight scenes in this book without the expertise of my reliable "violence experts," Ben Hatke and Andrew O'Neill, who came to my house for not one, but two sessions where we staged the fights, including the one with handcuffs I simply could not visualize without help: that scene nearly had me crawling under my desk to whimper in frustration.

Mr. and Mrs. Dipaka and Nimisha Patel, owners and managers of the Relax Inn of Front Royal, Virginia, were kind enough to spend hours sharing with me the ins and outs of running an independent hotel. And Larry Bickford, consumer sales agent for the Kaba Corporation, gave me the lowdown on how hotel keylock systems actually work and helped me brainstorm about how Mr. O'Donnell would put his system together. Madalena LoaNguyen responded to my shout-out on Facebook and graciously agreed to read over and critique the sections on Vietnamese-American culture. Sean Dailey, editor of *Gilbert!* Magazine, gave me a prod in the right direction for the Chesterton themes.

Having acknowledged the contributions of all those above, I want to claim any factual or procedural errors in this book as my own, as many times I extrapolated from information that was provided to me for the purposes of the plot.

Other friends who listened in and helped me with their feedback and ideas include Helen Babineau (who listened to me vent), Elizabeth Hausladen (who helped babysit my kids and who insisted Fish and Rose make a cameo in the book), and Matthew Bowman (who gave advice in several areas and also put me in touch with his father for the FBI sections), as well as my own children, who are finally old enough to have opinions on my writing, a wonderful development! (I'm grateful they still enjoy reading it!)

Michelle Buckman, Kathy Pesta, Anna Hatke, and Jean Vencil all helped me with proofreading, as well as several of my siblings who read the books and gave me feedback. I want to thank my husband Andrew and the incomparable Elizabeth Yank for doing the final proof.

Special thanks to Craig Spiering, my inveterate photographer friend for his wonderful photos, and to Michael Clark and Angela Swagler for serving as cover models. Plus kudos to Andy O'Neill for the loan of his sword and fighting fans, and to Katherine, who won the Fairy Tale Novel Forum contest by tracking down a real ao dài for me on eBay!

Also particular thanks also go to Tariq and his son Zain for allowing us to shoot the photos at their lovely showroom of Oriental rugs on Main Street in Front Royal, Virginia. (Their rugs appear on both the front and back of the book.)

The decorative fonts for this book were all created by Dave Nalle's Scriptorium, and I'm particularly grateful for their Arabian Nights package, which provided both type and inspiration.

My husband Andrew continues to be the most valuable and valued reader and editor of my work. I relished the many mornings last summer when I woke up early and typed out paragraph after paragraph just so that he could enjoy reading it when he came up to my workroom at 7 AM with a cup of hot tea and breakfast on a tray for me. One of the greatest joys of my life continues to be sharing my writing with him.

This time around, my children not only enjoyed hearing me read them the book, but they also put up with many days of frantic editing, and helped by cleaning house, making dinner, watching siblings, and just being good and not making (too much) trouble. I hope they feel the effort was worth it! Thank you Caleb, Rose, Marygrace, Thomas, Joan, and Polly!

And as always, thanks to my son Joshua, for your prayers.

Regina Doman
Shirefeld, Virginia
May 2010

## About the Author

Regina Doman lives near Front Royal, Virginia with her husband and their six children.

More information about her Fairy Tale Novel series can be found at www.fairytalenovels.com. Regina always welcomes email, feedback, and questions from readers.

www.FairyTaleNovels.com

Breinigsville, PA USA
04 October 2010
246592BV00005B/6/P